PA... ... ...
spent his infancy at Wandsworth Prison, which his father
governed, then grew up in Winchester. He now lives on a farm near Land's End. As well as writing and reviewing fiction, he has published a biography of Armistead Maupin, a short history of the Dorchester Hotel and chapters on Mozart's piano and mechanical music for H.C. Robbin Landon's *The Mozart Compendium*. His most recent novel is *The Whole Day Through*. His new collection of short stories, *Gentleman's Relish*, is published this year.

Visit the website: www.galewarning.org

From the reviews of *The Cat Sanctuary*:

'A powerful and moving novel in which the darkness is often lightened by the author's deft touches of comedy'
                                    Independent on Sunday

'*The Cat Sanctuary* is a book with claws. It has a soft surface . . . a story set in sloping Cornish countryside, touching on love, families and forgiveness, delivered in a gentle, straightforward prose – but from time to time it catches you unawares. Scratch the surface, suggests Gale, and you draw blood'   *The Times*

'Splendidly realised Cornish moorland setting, wellies, ruts, dripping sheep . . . Gale's specialist forte being pathos into bathos, tears of desolation leaking into the gravy, but he writes about the difficult emotions with delica... ... ...ocious charm' *Guardian*

D0413865

'Gale's novels always catch one a little short with their flaky situations and obliquely deranged behaviour. It is only later – when the slippery charm has conveyed its resilience to every day brutalities never far away – that his books reveal their grace and beauty'   *Observer*

'Sophisticated in its conception and stylish in its execution, it is easily his best novel to date'   *Gay Times*

'A dark tale of loss, sex and mistrust . . . A sensitive, thoughtful novel with a conclusion that is both unsettling and consistent'   *Time Out*

By the same author

The Aerodynamics of Pork
Kansas in August
Ease
Facing the Tank
Little Bits of Baby
Caesar's Wife
The Facts of Life
Dangerous Pleasures
Tree Surgery for Beginners
Rough Music
A Sweet Obscurity
Friendly Fire
Notes from an Exhibition
The Whole Day Through
Gentleman's Relish

PATRICK GALE

The Cat Sanctuary

FOURTH ESTATE • *London*

Fourth Estate
An imprint of HarperCollins*Publishers*
77–85 Fulham Palace Road
Hammersmith
London W6 8JB

www.4thestate.co.uk
Visit our authors' blog at www.fifthestate.co.uk
Love this book? www.bookarmy.com

This Fourth Estate edition published 2009
3

First published by Chatto & Windus in 1990

Copyright © Patrick Gale 1990, 2009

PS Section copyright © Rose Gaete 2009, except 'The Writing of *The Cat Sanctuary*'
by Patrick Gale © Patrick Gale 2009

PS™ is a trademark of HarperCollins*Publishers* Ltd

Patrick Gale asserts the moral right
to be identified as the author of this work

A catalogue record for this book is available from the British Library

ISBN 978-0-00-730768-5

Set in Monotype Apollo by Palimpsest Book Production Limited,
Grangemouth, Stirlingshire

Printed and bound in Great Britain by Clays Ltd, St Ives plc

Mixed Sources
Product group from well-managed
forests and other controlled sources
www.fsc.org Cert no. SW-COC-1806
© 1996 Forest Stewardship Council

FSC is a non-profit international organisation established to promote the
responsible management of the world's forests. Products carrying the FSC
label are independently certified to assure consumers that they come
from forests that are managed to meet the social, economic and
ecological needs of present and future generations.

Find out more about HarperCollins and the environment at
www.harpercollins.co.uk/green

This novel is entirely a work of fiction. The names, characters and incidents
portrayed in it are the work of the author's imagination. Any resemblance to
actual persons, living or dead, events or localities is entirely coincidental.

All rights reserved. No part of this publication may be reproduced,
stored in a retrieval system, or transmitted, in any form or by any means,
electronic, mechanical, photocopying, recording or otherwise,
without the prior permission of the publishers.

This book is sold subject to the condition that it shall not, by way of trade
or otherwise, be lent, re-sold, hired out or otherwise circulated without the
publisher's prior consent in any form of binding or cover other than that
in which it is published and without a similar condition including
this condition being imposed on the subsequent purchaser.

for Patrick Pender

His Integrity of Heart
And distinguish'd Abilities
(*never prostituted to base purposes*)
Render'd Him at once,
The Ornament of Society
And the Delight of all who knew him.

Memorial in Church of
St Mary Magdalene, Launceston

'Quand il me dit, "Viens!"
J'suis comme un chien.'

Mon Homme

One

Deborah was waving Julian off to work when he was murdered. At any other time it would have embarrassed her deeply to make such a display – she usually took a leisurely breakfast in bed with yesterday's newspaper – but the Foreign Secretary and his wife were staying. They were visiting Seneca for four, long days.

'You really must make more of an effort,' Julian had insisted. 'Get them to think of us as a team. I know you hate being little wifey but She's the power behind more thrones than his and if we can make the right impression on Her it could just get us out of this dump. It was all thanks to Her that the Maxwells were brought back from Zimbabwe last year.'

So Deborah had played a lot of bridge, had kept quiet about her desultory work for the poverty action group and had affected a tireless fascination with Lady Coltrane's narrow-minded reminiscences of pre-War Kenya. Last night, she had thrown a party, after closely supervising the assembly of ten, broad trays of exquisite canapés (left to their own devices the kitchen staff did nameless things with tinned mackerel and sliced bread) and now, in full view of their breakfasting guests, she was waving Julian off to work.

The car was intended to ferry the Foreign Secretary to a meeting with some local government officers, but he had overslept after drinking too much the night before, so it was hastily decided that Julian should take the first car while the chauffeur made a second one ready.

'Bye darling,' Julian said, kissing her cheek.

'Bye,' she said back. 'Don't forget those medical people are coming for lunch a bit early because of Bill and Diana's helicopter jaunt.'

He kissed her other cheek, winked to show his approval and left her, sun-dappled, on the porch. She watched the chauffeur close the door for him and walk out of sight. At the breakfast table, Diana Coltrane laughed immoderately at something someone had just said. The engine started, Deborah waved, Julian smiled and the car had barely begun to pull away when it exploded.

The noise sounded nothing like the full-throated roar of explosions in films, but that may have been because Deborah was standing close enough to have her hearing temporarily scrambled. The rush of air threw her backwards onto the hall rug. For several hideously drawn-out seconds she lay there, quite deaf, watching pieces of Julian and the consulate car slap down onto the drive and surrounding flowerbeds. Then she realised that her mouth and eyes were filling with blood so she lay back, shutting them. As yet she felt no pain. There was only the irritating ringing in her ears. Hands, rough with panic, touched her, arranged her legs and slid a cushion beneath her head. A cold, damp towel dabbed at her face. She tried to open her eyes again but they filled with blood as swiftly as it was wiped away. Behind the ringing, she made out the thin, old-fashioned ding-a-ling of the town ambulance ('A gift from the people of Bradford shortly before Independence,' she felt she should tell her guests). From nearby came the similarly reduced phut of gunfire.

'That'll be the chauffeur,' she thought. 'But no. If Coltrane hadn't drunk so much, the chauffeur would have died with . . . Or perhaps not. Perhaps he was prepared to die for the cause or whatever and couldn't believe his luck when Julian said not to . . . No? Then . . .'

Someone laid fingers on her lips and she realised she had been thinking aloud.

'Hush dear,' cooed Diana Coltrane half a mile away. 'Here's Doctor. Hold still now.'

Now she felt pain; sharp stabs as tweezers teased things out of her skin.

'Julian!' she shouted and tried to push everyone away. 'Julian!' Hands held her down and she felt a pinprick in her arm. 'Daddy! Stop them!' she pleaded. 'I have a thing about knives and needles,' she told them. 'Anything sharp makes me faint. Ask anyone. Ask Cook. Ask Judith.' The drug worked fast. The ringing in her ears was swiftly exchanged for cotton wool. 'Judith!' she called faintly and passed out.

TWO

Judith was working. When she had lived alone, which felt so long ago, she had always worked in bed. She had found that, with her mind focused on her writing, her body became utterly still, a prey to marauding draughts. Working in bed with a quilt about her bony shoulders had seemed the obvious solution. Now that her bachelor pad in Clapham had been almost entirely abandoned for the connubial farmhouse in Cornwall, now that her days and nights were shared, this practice had been abandoned as an unjust intrusion of labour into the realm of love. Her jealously guarded savings were accordingly broken into for the conversion of the hayloft of the old stone-built barn. The latter still housed a chestnut mare, hay bales, a sit-up-and-beg lawn-mower and Judith's senile but faithful Morris 1000. However a handrail had been attached to make the stone steps which ran up the outside wall at one end rather less perilous in damp weather and the overhead space they led to had been transformed into Judith's white-painted domain, sleeker and better-heated than any room in the main house. A capacious chaise longue and exquisite patchwork quilt had been tracked down for her in local sales and she found that, with a few adjustments, her old sickroom trolley was still ideal for supporting her word processor at a comfortable height over her travel-blanketed knees.

The windows they had let into the entire length of the

sloping ceiling would normally have given her a view of sweeping moorland spotted with rain-hewn granite lumps and, closer to, a gathering of wind-bent trees. A flock of bedraggled sheep usually sheltered beside one of several ancient dry-stone walls, green with moss and navelwort, which had defined a field before tumbling once too often. Today there was no view. The nearest villages, Treneglos to one side and Martyrstow to the other, were set high above the rest of Cornwall, and the house was a further steep climb above them so, when local weather forecasts contained, as they had today, the dread word 'overcast', she wound up the blinds to find a shifting blanket of cloud inches from her nose. The thin winter sunlight lent this moisture wall an eerie luminosity, as headlamps did mist. Marooned, laden with sodden fleece, sheep bleated out their melancholic code, lost to the world and lost to each other. They were quite invisible from where Judith sat but she could distinguish a few long-horned, half-wild cattle and the occasional utterly wild pony as dark shadows looming in and out of the shifting grey.

She turned back to her word processor and read yet again the little she had managed to write that morning.

'Edgar sat at the kitchen table for an hour after his mother had taken her hot milk back to bed. He sat listening to the familiar midnight tickings and creaks of his childhood home; cooling radiators, contracting woodwork, subtly settling masonry and the sporadic sigh and rattle of wind in the soot-caked chimney above the range. As if it were the most natural thing in the world, his eyes had come to rest, then lingered, on the cutlery drawer. His head felt pleasantly empty of thoughts.'

Judith picked through the words with a critical frown, tapping on the screen's edge with a sharpened pencil she kept uselessly to hand out of superstition.

As was so often the case in her writing, a setting proffered by her imagination as a wholly original confection was transforming, as she etched in its details, into somewhere she knew and so could believe in. Brisk and no-nonsense as a nurse, her imagination was plundering long-abandoned storerooms in her memory. She had sat at Edgar's kitchen table. She knew every knot on its surface, was familiar with the jam jar covers, candles and tea cosies in its drawers, could recall the exact feel of a nailhead protruding from one of its legs which her infant fingers had nervously worried beneath the tablecloth through countless teatimes. She could catch in an instant the precise sensation of its soap-scrubbed deal on her cheek. If she concentrated she could conjure up a compound memory: the greasy feel of a Latin textbook beneath her hand indivisible from the smell of the pencil she was chewing and the weak, warning tone in which her mother said, 'Ten more minutes and Daddy'll be home. I want those books out of sight, your hair brushed and for heaven's sake get that ink off your hands before he sees it!'

She touched one of her hands on the knuckles of the other and felt again the furious scrubbing of a pumice stone on skin already raw from cold.

In a sudden flurry of keys, as though she were trying to take herself by surprise, she added,

'Edgar rose at last, tugged open the drawer and picked out the long, large-toothed knife they used for sawing frozen meat.'

Startled, she deleted the sentence almost as soon as she had typed in its full stop. Then she typed it back in, biting her lip as she looked in vain for some crucial alteration that might suggest itself. She pushed the sickroom trolley aside and paced to the farthest window which she swung wide open, taking a blast of cold dampness full in her face.

The situation bore all the unfamiliar hallmarks of a creative crisis. The twelve novels that had brought her critical recognition, two niggardly but prestigious prizes and this hayloft had done so in spite of, and quite possibly because of, the failure of their central characters to take any direct action before they absolutely had to. There was no shortage of action around them. People stole their wives or drowned their husbands, fortunes were made and lost, adolescents attempted suicide and children were trapped in hotel fires. On one memorable occasion, which resulted in a prolonged correspondence with several none-too-gentlemanly farmers, Judith had even connived at the devouring of an inoffensive baby by an outraged sow. It took four to five hundred pages of impulsive gestures and inhuman brutality on the part of author and supporting cast, however, to goad Judith's heroes or heroines out of their philosophical deliberations and into the arena of conflict. Whilst her grasp of psychological truths and eye for fresh dilemma had saved her work from becoming formulaic, its structural pattern was yet predictable enough to provide a source of security to her loyal readers and an easy target for critics, baited by the impotence her success had visited upon them. And now she found herself barely five chapters into a new, still untitled work, and the hero, a moderately well-adjusted solicitor (an idealisation, she began to suspect, of how Judith liked to remember herself in her early twenties), was arming himself against his mother with a lethal weapon.

Judith closed the window again, switched off the word processor because it was giving her a headache and reached for her notebook. She wrapped herself back in her quilt and blanket then turned to the pages where she had mapped out the terrible, often amusing chain of events to which Edgar was only meant to respond with direct action in the novel's last chapters. She looked for a way of talking him back from the dangerous step he was taking, all too aware that the pursuit was as feeble as a policewoman's attempt to sound understanding when talking to a would-be suicide through a loud-hailer.

Judith met her reflected gaze in the word processor screen. When she first won a prize, a Sunday magazine had sent a famous, titled photographer to bring back her likeness. He had cleverly pictured her reflected in a screen full of the recently published text. A signed print of the photograph hung on the wall behind her now. It showed her anxious, oval face, framed by her glossy but irredeemably brown hair and seemingly marked by stripes of green-glowing prose as with war paint. Understanding what the photographer had been at and conniving with him she had moved the position of the text on the screen so that the pronouncement, 'I hate you. More than words can say' ran cleanly across her forehead. An unkind friend of her mother's, remarking on her wise childhood habit of sitting quietly out of harm's way, had dubbed her Puss-in-the-Corner. The nickname was duly borne to school by her disloyal sister where it became Pussy, Katkins and, for moments of rank spite, Mewdith. She had long since removed herself from spite and disloyalty but she still liked to sit quietly and unremarked in corners. Her brown hair had been shot through with a streak of dramatic grey since the photographer's visit but something vaguely feline remained about her face; in the largeness of her eyes and the delicacy of her otherwise unremarkable nose.

She scratched her nose to break the spell, sighed and lay back with her eyes closed, letting the notebook fall to her lap. This was only happening because Joanna, her fount of sanity, her rock of strength, had expressed a sudden desire to take a trip on her own. Briefly, because the luxury was perilous, she allowed herself the sensation of red hair tumbling thickly at her touch, of breast-warmed cashmere brushing her lips. In all her career she had only once found her creativity blocked and that was seven years ago, when she let Joanna slip away for a whole month of long-begged solitude in London.

She opened her eyes. She never wore watches – something about her made them stop or even go backwards – so with the house buried in cloud she had no way of telling the time. Snatching at an excuse to escape from this contemplation of her failure, she decided that it must be nearly time to feed the cats. She rose, turned out the light and wrapped herself in Joanna's mackintosh which she had successfully demanded as ransom. Even with the cuffs rolled up it all but swamped her, a stern if comforting reminder that not all slight, brown, wood nymphs were lucky enough to count Juno as even an absent admirer. She dug for the keys in its pockets, locked the door behind her, then climbed up into Joanna's Land Rover. She scrabbled in the damp clutter that strewed the shelf above the dashboard and found a piece of clotted cream fudge she had given up for lost. Chewing, she started the engine and drove across the cattle grid and onto the lane to Martyrstow. The fog lamps caught the Satanic eyes of sheep and before long, as she edged into the cloud, were the only sign of her presence on the vast expanse of moor.

Three

Joanna had never suffered from the heat. After Cornwall, Seneca had been a surprise, certainly. Cornish heat – intense by English standards – was softened by Atlantic breezes, but Senecan breezes had nothing to cool them. The half-finished Hotel Continental had air conditioning and, were it not for the views it afforded of a blue-domed mosque and a camel market, might have been any Hotel Continental in Europe. The blast of heat that enveloped her when she stepped out onto the street had nothing European about it, however, and she revelled in it. She had headed straight for the teeming commercial area on her first morning there and bought several floaty, ethnic dresses. She enjoyed the way the hot air swirled through them as she walked. She had long since dressed beyond or outside fashion, having reached an age when she doubted the wisdom of any violent external change, but there was still a pleasing holiday piquancy to swanning around in clothes nobody would be seen dead in at home.

Her original plan had been to take a fortnight to pursue selfish, solitary pleasure, simply to prove herself still capable of it, but photographers take cameras on vacation with them like everyone else. For months she had been photographing little but restful phenomena of her Cornish surroundings such as tree bark, hedgerows, ferns and dry-stone walls, so the exuberance and colour of even a strongly Muslim community had been more temptation than her high-principled, American respect for leisure could withstand. Forced to admit at last that her work was her chief pleasure, Joanna had ignored the blandishments of swimming pool and camel ride to track down interesting subjects.

Almost at once she had latched on to the local children, most of whom seemed to be set to work. She had taken pictures of street vendors at first (each of whom expected to be paid for the favour), then of a cruelly deformed little boy who had become a carpenter, courtesy of his dextrous feet.

'Children?' she had asked him. 'Do you know any other children who work?'

And he had led her to his sisters, neither of whom could have been much more than eight, who spent their days risking their fingers at large American sewing machines producing dresses like the ones Joanna had already bought. She had photographed latter-day Davids driving their herds of scrawny sheep and even miniature Delilahs dancing in tissue-stuffed bikinis in the back room of a bar. There was a new newspaper colour supplement back home which printed a photographic feature every week; she would have no trouble selling its editor these. One of the girls slipped a bikini strap off her shoulder for the camera and giggled. Her companion tugged it firmly up again and slapped her hard on the face, muttering what Joanna took for some twisted pious reprimand.

Joanna would hunt photographs for hours at a time, returning to the surreal comforts of the Hotel Continental only when she ran out of film. She would hold her dress in her hands as she took a shower, washing it out with the same water, astonished at the amount of grime which body and cloth could accumulate in a few hours. Then she would hang up the dress to dry in the draught from the air conditioner, loose her long red hair from its scarf and lie naked on her bed, breathless from the cold water and enjoying the tingle of her skin as it recovered from the sun. For all her relish of heat, she was terrified of skin cancers and never ventured out when the sun was at its height. Like most redheads she could never decide if her pale skin was her blessing or her curse. She had resigned herself long ago to its inability to tan further than a delicate honey brown and would never roast it the way Judith would at the first sign of a heatwave. Joanna spread her every reachable surface with protective creams and never left the hotel by day without a cotton scarf and wide straw hat which also served to restrain the uncomfortable tumbling of her hair.

This morning she found that she had exhausted her stock of film. The films on sale in the foyer were way past their sell-by date and those elsewhere would probably have been cooked to uselessness in the heat. Slightly at a loss, she wandered out to the hotel swimming pool and swam several languid lengths. But then she grew irritated by all the attention the waiters were paying to her (tall redheads of any age being a national rarity) and took herself out for an early lunch. Never one to venture further once she had found what she liked, she had patronised the same restaurant every day. It was a faintly old-fashioned establishment built around a pretty courtyard with a well and small palms growing in gaudily painted petrol cans. At night it buzzed with what she took for the local equivalent of an 'artistic' crowd. At lunchtime it was altogether better behaved with an umistakably Belgian atmosphere. She took a table in the opposite corner from a grand old woman who rose slightly and bowed to her as though they did this every day. She ordered a bottle of mineral water and some grilled fish.

'And could you bring me a newspaper?' she asked. 'I don't care if it's a bit old.'

They brought her a dish of highly spiced olives and said that the newspaper was on its way.

'Thank you.'

She took out a postcard. As promised she had sent one every day.

'Darling,' she wrote. 'Two days to go and I've no more

film. Yes, I feel your disapproval and I shall make good use of my time by going on a camel ride to the ruins or visiting a mosque. Or perhaps I should spend this afternoon rooting out a Really Special Present for my Pusskin? Mmm? Like the sound of that, do we?'

The newspaper arrived. A five-day-old copy of *Le Monde*. She tipped the waiter for it and set aside the postcard. Serious French journalism always seemed to be written in an elevated form of the language that bore little relation to the slapdash, strictly verbal idiom she had picked up over the years. She skimmed the front page and was about to flip to the second when she found a small item about an assassination attempt that had backfired. Frowning, she folded the paper smaller to bring the piece in question into closer focus. She read it through a second time. She asked for the bill as soon as her meal arrived. She ate half of the fish then abruptly lost her appetite.

'Dear Judith,' she continued the postcard hastily. 'I do miss you. All love. Ever. J.'

There was a post office across the way from the restaurant. She would leave the card there, then she would have to find a taxi. For all her rovings, her knowledge of the town's geography was scant.

Four

Deborah was sitting up in bed. She had finally eaten some lunch. For the first two days she had lost all appetite, then, when she threatened to regain it, had tried to starve herself. Eating seemed gross to her; unjust. Today, knowing her weakness for them, someone had come in while she slept to leave her a small bowl of British crisps. Salt and vinegar flavour. Not stopping to marvel at the incongruity of such a delicacy in a godless land, she lifted the bowl off the bedside table. She had eaten her way down to the last crumb before she remembered her fast. The salt, remorseless, did its work and, when the nurse next came smiling in, Deborah confessed to being ravenous. Now she lay back against the bank of pillows trying to ignore the streak of blood on her empty plate (she had ordered steak) and feeling slightly queasy. Shamefaced, she lifted her tray onto the floor where Julian's photograph could not see it. From the loudspeakers above a mosque several streets away a muezzin wailed his call to prayer like an impassioned mosquito.

It seemed she had dreamt of Julian every time she closed her eyes; of Julian or the emotions his abrupt removal aroused. Most often he was in the room but out of sight, pacing up and down behind her. She knew she was to blame in some way and throughout the dream she sat there, not daring to turn, reciting a circular apology along the lines of:

'Oh darling, yes, I do know, it's all my fault. If I hadn't

given him so much to drink you'd still be here. Believe me, Julian, I'd change places with you if I could. Perhaps if you were to ask someone they could arrange it for us. You're always so good with people. Diana Coltrane noticed it. Yes, she said so. You're so awfully clever and I'm so very stupid and, well, you know how it is. You were always telling me to grow up. I could never live up to you and oh darling, yes, I do know, it's all my fault . . .'

At other times she dreamed he was on the telephone to her but had just lapsed into a resentful silence. She had always dreaded his silences. Often as not they would fall because she was in the right and, quite properly, had tried to justify herself. Defeated in argument, he would draw a terrible veil of wordlessness over the proceedings, under cover of which, by a chemistry of will, he became the injured party and she the aggressor. In this dream, she would feel that alteration happening and break the silence by muttering wild endearments into the receiver; crazed, would-be erotic obscenities of the kind that made him wrinkle his fine nose in distaste, as though to say, 'If this display is for my benefit, I'm sure we both have more worthwhile things to do.'

She was still too uncomfortable to have much chance of a full night's sleep, but already she missed his presence in her bed. They had – they had had – a regular, even extravagant sex life, albeit strictly on Julian's terms. What she missed, however, was his simple bodily warmth. His body temperature always rose as he fell asleep. Even after evenings where he had been bad-tempered or she had been shrill (as he called it) he would crawl into her arms and expect her to hold him until he slept. He never apologised – not with words – but she took this frequent act of almost babyish humility to represent remorse. As he nodded off, lying heavily against her, his body warmed hers – which was inevitably cool – and she came to prefer this embrace to the more athletic demands he made of her. They had no child (dear God they had no child!) so having him hide himself in her unconditional embrace seemed a kind of motherhood. She liked — she had liked — the feel of his sleeping breath against her breasts.

At first the nurse had tried to prevent her looking in a mirror.

'Not yet, dear,' she had said. 'Wait until you're feeling a little stronger.'

But her solicitude had wound up Deborah's mild curiosity into near-hysteria and made it imperative that she see herself. There was little irreparable damage, although she looked quite appalling. Not only had the bomb sprayed her with chips of windscreen, but it had flung at her most of the hall window (whose glass had not been designed to shatter safely). Miraculously her eyes and jugular had emerged unscathed. The jagged fragments of hall window had sliced into her forehead, her left breast and both her thighs. The bandages had now come off these wounds to reveal brown needlework of a neatness she could never have achieved. Her cheeks, neck and the tender undersides of her arms were peppered with little scabs. She could not remember having had time to raise her arms for protection; evidently the gesture was instinctive in even the most unlikely circumstances. Dr Neidpath (a handsome man who had always reminded her of her father, but whom Julian had declared 'too smooth by half and probably Jewish') had assured her that, with the sad exception of her breast, there would be no scars. Sunbathing was out of the question for a while, it seemed. The good doctor told her that, contrary to popular belief, wounds healed best when kept out of the sun because sunrays encouraged the formation of shiny scar tissue. Whether or not this was true, Deborah knew she would be needing no encouragement to linger in shadows and darkened rooms.

'Eaten it all up? That's what I like to see. Not even a little bit for Lady Manners. Good girl! You try to get some rest now.'

The nurse took away the tray, leaving Julian's photograph to wrinkle its nose at his widow's unmannerly greed.

Whenever she knew the nurse to be thoroughly occupied

elsewhere Deborah loosened one shoulder of her nightdress and took out her damaged breast. It felt more comfortable without the fabric pressing on the stitches and, in any case, she liked to examine it. She laid it bare now, knowing the nurse always enjoyed some time chatting in the kitchen. The glass seemed to have cut clean through her nipple. The tidy stitching ran vertically, bisecting the honey brown circle. The teat appeared to have been amputated. She was disturbed to find herself so unmoved by this, feeling that the tiny mutilation needed a mourning of some kind. All she sensed was anxiety that, if she ever produced milk, it would have no means of escape and might build up and curdle with her too embarrassed to tell anybody. At each secret examination she had resolved to ask Dr Neidpath about this, but whenever she saw him again her thin resolve had evaporated beneath his smile.

Sensible shoes sounded on the stairs. Deborah tidied her breast away. She shut her eyes and lay back. The nurse paused in the doorway then said,

'Oh,' abruptly and began to turn away.

'What is it, nurse?' Deborah asked.

'You're sleeping. I'll tell her to come back.'

'Who?'

'You've a visitor.'

'Who is it?'

'A Miss Ventura. She says she's come from your sister.'

'My sister's in England.'

'Well the lady says she's come from her. She seems very nice. American.'

'American?'

'Shall I tell her to come back later?'

'No. Send her up.'

Deborah scrabbled in the drawer of her bedside table for her hairbrush. She tugged it through her hair several times on each side, more from force of habit than from any fond belief that it could improve her appearance. The visitor appeared on the landing and knocked twice on the open door.

Even allowing for her hat she looked nearly six foot tall but, rather than seeming stretched or bony, the rest of her body was built entirely in proportion to her height. She was massive without carrying an ounce of surplus fat. Likewise her mouth, her eyes, even her startling pinkish red hair (when she released it from her hat) were all designed on a scale slightly larger than life. A press agent would have called her Junoesque. She wore the loose ethnic clothes which, in a Westerner, Julian had always said, betokened fashionable socialism. This combined with her size to make Deborah nervous. She did her bed-bound best to draw herself up.

'Good afternoon?'

The woman jumped slightly.

'Oh! Sorry I was staring wasn't I? It's just that, for an awful moment, you looked so like Judith.'

'I hope she doesn't look like this.'

'No. At least,' the woman laughed, 'she didn't when I last saw her. I'm saying all the wrong things as usual. Hi.'

'Hello.'

'We haven't met before, have we?'

'No.' Deborah gestured to a chair by the wall. 'Do sit down.'

'Thanks.' She sat on the bed. Deborah drew in her feet to make more room. Miss Ventura caught sight of the photograph and seemed briefly transfixed. 'I'm so very sorry,' she murmured. 'About your husband.' And then she started to cry.

'Don't,' Deborah asked her. 'Don't cry. Please.'

But her visitor was beyond recall, her red mane tumbling across her face as she searched for, then shook out a large ethnic handkerchief. Rather than use it to wipe her nose she wiped it across her forehead then wrung it distractedly in her fingers, letting tears splash freely on her thinly shielded bosom. Briefly Deborah envied her her tears – they were so plumply generous. Her own recent weeping was her first since childhood (until now she had taken pride in an uneventful life) and it had been quite dry, inducing a pain like acute sinusitis. This strange woman's inexplicable grief was infectious as laughter however and Deborah soon found herself shedding tears as satisfactory as her visitor's. Clawing up a fistful of tissues, she held them to her face then dropped them and lay back, careless, against the pillows to wail her heart out. She wept richly, not for Julian who, however unfairly, was far beyond pity, but entirely for herself.

'I'm so alone,' she cried, incomprehensibly. 'What shall I do? I'm valueless, meaningless. I have been discarded.'

The nurse came running but Deborah shooed her away impatiently and let herself be lifted off on another tearful wave. After a few minutes more her eyes went dry and her sinuses began to hurt again. So she stopped.

'Run out of tears,' she mumbled, and blew her nose. Her visitor had already tidied herself up and bore no signs of her grief except that, if possible, her eyes seemed even larger and wetter. She brought Deborah a cold, damp flannel from the sink.

'Thanks,' Deborah sniffed, wiping her eyes.

'All cried out,' the woman said. 'You'll be able to start again in twenty minutes or so.'

'No thanks.'

'It's good for you.'

'It hurts and the effects are far from flattering. What did you say you were called?'

'Joanna Ventura.'

'Are you American?'

'My grandfather was Sicilian. My real name's Verdura which is like being called Miss Spring Greens. I changed it by deed poll before I moved to England.'

'Oh.'

'I'm sorry for crying all over you like that.'

'Not at all.'

'I cry easy. Always have.'

'I never could,' Deborah admitted.

'Your national failing. Judith finds it hard too.'

'She cried at *Bambi* once. She was much older than me. I remember being shocked. Have you been her friend long?'

'Eight years.'

Their communal weeping had eased the strain on Deborah. She found herself talking freely. Then she remembered their odd social situation.

'Sorry,' she said. 'But why are you here? Nurse mentioned Judith. Is she all right?'

'Fine. I saw a paper, you see. *Le Monde*. It was several days old or I'd have come round quicker.'

'But I don't quite see.'

Joanna Ventura took her hand and peered urgently at her.

'Deborah, come away,' she said. 'Come and stay with us.'

'Us?'

'Judith and me.'

'You live together?'

'Yes. Didn't she ever . . . ?'

'In Clapham?'

'No. She's still got the Clapham flat but we spend all our time in my place out west, on the moor. Five miles from the Atlantic. You'd love it.'

'Ah yes. I think our mother mentioned something. But I . . .'

Joanna pressed her hand.

'You needn't come for long. Just till you decide what to do. You've no one else.'

'What makes you say that?'

'Well, have you?'

'I might have.' Joanna raised an eyebrow. 'Not really,' Deborah conceded.

'It's miles from anywhere. You needn't see anyone or do anything if you don't want to. Do you like cats?'

'Not much.'

'Oh.' Joanna looked slightly crestfallen. Deborah sharply withdrew her hand.

'Look this is nonsense. I don't even know you or anything. Besides, I'm ill.'

'What's wrong with you?'

'I'm in pain and I'm . . . I'm badly scarred. The sun's bad for scars. Dr Neidpath said so and besides, Judith and I haven't spoken in years. We don't get on.'

'Well, whose fault is that?'

'Not mine,' Deborah answered quickly. 'I think you'd better go.'

Joanna stood.

'Sorry. I'm tiring you.' She reached into her pocket for a terrible colour postcard of a half-finished modern hotel in the centre of town. The Continental. 'Here's where I'm staying. I'm off tomorrow evening. Call me, huh?'

'Can you find your own way out?'

Joanna Ventura smiled infuriatingly from the doorway.

'You two are so different but, Christ, you're horribly similar. Ring me, OK?'

She paused at the landing looking-glass to arrange her hair back inside her hat, then walked downstairs, waving over her shoulder in a gesture Deborah instantly recognised as coming from the end of some film. Liza Minnelli in *Cabaret*.

Deborah set Julian's photograph back at its former angle – that woman had shifted it with her inquisitive fingers. Her coarse fingers. She threw some pillows onto the floor then sank back, cross and exhausted. It was the funeral tomorrow. Julian's mother was arriving late tonight. Deborah battened down, like so many complaining coolies beneath a hatch, upsurging thoughts of her sister. She calmed herself by picturing a long, refreshing succession of hats.

Five

Soon after she had moved down to Joanna's Cornish farm-house, Judith killed a man's cat. Her mother, who had not quite died then, had run her to earth by means of some judiciously unscrupulous detective work. She had promptly rung her up, announcing that she was still not quite dead and asking when she could expect an invitation to stay in her daughter's unnatural love-nest. They had successfully not communicated for two or three months; change of address cards had been sent out only very selectively. Judith was furious at the way she had been tracked down but her mother had guilt on her side and so their argument had been bloodier than their usual half-courteous skirmishes. Her mother had delivered a blast of calculated cruelty against her latest novel. Stung into spite, Judith had then confirmed that she loathed the woman who had helped make her childhood a misery and her adolescence a torture and added that the last thing on her list of emotional priorities was coming home for Christmas.

'Well as it's going to be my last,' her mother retorted before hanging up on her, 'I might as well tell you that I shan't be wanting any self-centred lesbian bitches at my funeral.'

Shaking with rage, unable to explain to Joanna, Judith had jumped into her old Morris and driven several miles to the pub at St Breward. There she hid in a corner of the bar behind a loud crowd of farm workers, and downed several whisky macs. Shaking still, but less from anger than a dim sense of triumph, she was driving home when a cat ran out of a cottage garden and under her wheels. There had been a revolting lurch. She knew without looking that it was dead. The owner was a withdrawn old man she had seen in the market once or twice selling cut-price bed linen. He insisted on picking the cat's remains up himself. He furled them gently in what was plainly the old jersey from its basket and carried the sad parcel into his garden.

'I'll bury her later,' he said, waiting for Judith to stop hovering at his side.

'I feel awful,' she said, certain he could smell the whisky on her breath.

'Good.'

'You must let me . . . Here . . . Can't I . . . ?' She had fumbled for her wallet and was holding out some money.

'I won't be buying a replacement for her,' he said quietly. 'She's left some young ones behind.' Feeling worse than ever, she put her money away again. 'Send it to the Pet Protection League,' he told her. 'It'll do more good there.'

So she had driven tearfully and very slowly home and had sent off a large cheque the following morning. She had enclosed a letter of explanation but had not been expecting a reply. She was surprised then to receive a letter welcoming her 'decision to join the League', still more so to receive another, in crabbed blue-grey handwriting, the following week.

'Dear Judith Lamb,' she read,

'You don't know me because I never pay visits now but I notice that we live only two miles apart. I was given your address by the League, which I gather you have recently joined. For twenty years now I've been running a cat sanctuary here but my rheumatism and generally seedy state of preservation have made it impossible for me to do so without help. My most recent assistant has just married a Bristol veterinarian so, of course, she cannot continue

23

to work here. I wonder if you might oblige? It would be interesting to see you in any case. Call in any time, day or night. I'm never out and I rarely sleep.

Yours,

Esther Gammel.'

Esther lived in what used to be the village's rectory when there was a congregation large enough to merit a rector to itself. Now, as in most of Cornwall, the Jehovah's Witnesses and Methodism held sway and the remaining worshippers in the older faith spent their Sunday mornings in pursuit of the mobile priest and organist who shared a Mini to spread their labours impartially across five parishes.

Though the house was built on generous proportions by the local standard, Esther confined the diminished operations of her life to one lovely room on the first floor. Every other room in the house either had its windows darkened with plant life or gave onto the noise and smells of the cat sanctuary at the back. Her severely arthritic pointer, Bunting, lived up there with her, though he would occasionally venture out into the rhododendron jungle at the front. A side door remained ajar in all weathers for his benefit. The milkman, log merchant and local stores delivered all Esther's needs. Apart from bread, cheese and apples, the only food of theirs she trusted came in tins; baked and other beans, tuna, sardines, sponge puddings and creamed rice. This evening Judith had made a detour, plunging down precipitous lanes through the mist to the harbour in the little fishing village of St Jacob's. There she bought Esther a bag of prawns and a jar of mayonnaise, knowing the combination to be a favourite dietary supplement of hers.

The cat food was all paid for by Esther and delivered direct from the manufacturers. She had found a firm which produced catering size cans of imperfect pilchards for schools and the Third World. Crates of these, sacks of cat biscuits and cartons of long life milk were stacked in what had once been an elegant conservatory but was now a glass cavern in a hillock of ivy and Virginia creeper. After two weeks of bruising her fingers, opening fifteen or more tins at a time with an old hand-powered tin opener, Judith had bought the cats an absurdly efficient electric one. She bought it as she walked away from the crematorium where, in defiance, she had attended her mother's last chance to be the centre of attention. This impulse buy was the confirmation of what she had already come to feel as her duty to the sanctuary. The funeral had been the last time she saw Deborah, her younger sister, and her fatuous husband.

She walked around the side of the house, grimacing as the unkempt shrubbery tossed drizzledrops down her neck, and let herself into the conservatory where she set the prawns and mayonnaise out of harm's way. Then she went about her daily routine. First the food dishes had to be collected. As many of the cats were wild ones this had to be performed in leather gauntlets (left over, Esther claimed, from the days when she and a friend dabbled in falconry) often using a garden rake to retrieve the dish from the perilous far side of an enclosure where a cat had pushed it. The dishes had two compartments. Judith had to wash them, then fill one half with a mixture of sardine and biscuit, the other half with long life milk.

As she served up this unvarying meal, she would check on each animal's welfare, greeting the more friendly by petting them, eyeing the others with respectful reserve. There were only twelve enclosures. As sharing was therefore inevitable, so were terrible fights. Although new arrivals were housed according to temperament to give them more of a sporting chance, the mildest stray could turn savage. Although fights to the death were rare, Esther insisted on having chronic aggressors put down. This would involve Judith in the grim and extremely difficult task of holding the condemned still with her gauntleted hands while the vet did her work. In time all but the wildest cats were daunted by the closeness of their confinement, lost their territorial instincts and would save their ferocity for the hands that fed them. Having checked on them all and found no wounds in need of attention or obvious signs of illness, Judith took the prawns and mayonnaise through to the kitchen. She picked a blue and white plate from off the dresser, washed away its thick coating of dust and arranged her offering prettily. She washed a bowl too. With nowhere to throw the prawn shells, Esther was apt to leave them in a soon forgotten pile to rot.

Esther was sitting at her dressing table arranging her long silver hair; a habit of which she never seemed to tire. She smiled up at Judith in the mirror.

'Ah,' she said, seeing the prawns and turning round, silver hairbrush poised theatrically for action. 'You've come to feed the oldest cat of all.'

'Indeed I have. Prawns and mayonnaise. Where shall I put them?'

'Right here.' Esther patted the dressing table. 'How scrummy! I've been trying to eat something for hours but the phone keeps ringing. I've had Prue wanting advice on choosing a new mare. Then Clare rang, who you don't know, and an old schoolfriend, Nora, and Mrs Hatch and, well, the whole bunch really.'

'I can't think why they don't drive over to see you if they've so much to say.'

'Oh well I won't let them. Encouragement's the last thing they need. They'd never go! At least on the phone they have a bill to think of.'

Since Esther's electing to become so immobile, her friends and acquaintances scattered across the land had come to treat her as a telephonic oracle, there to be consulted or complained to both within and beyond office hours. Apart from the convenience of her unflagging availability, she had few qualifications for the job, being eccentric, impractical and highly opinionated.

'Join me?' she indicated the prawns.

'No thanks. I'll eat later.'

'Suit yourself. What's been happening in the world?'

'Don't ask me.'

'Don't you ever get a paper?'

'No. I never get round to reading them. Joanna gets one when she's here and she watches the television compulsively of course.'

'Of course.'

'So I rely on her to tell me things.'

'Very wise. News can be so draining first-hand. I gave it up long ago. If the world showed signs of ending, Nora would be certain to ring and tell me; she'd want to know what to wear. I am intimately acquainted with her wardrobe, you know. Intimately.'

Perhaps Esther was a useful sounding-board, Judith reflected, and the simple action of airing their indecisions helped her callers make up their own minds. She sat heavily on the end of Esther's bed and twined her fingers around the candy-twists of the bedstead.

'Well how . . .' Esther began, hastily finishing a mouthful. 'How's the great novelist today?'

'Diminished.'

'You do understand, don't you, why I haven't read any of your stuff? You see I've never found fiction easy to concentrate on. Unless it's very factual-historical, that is.'

'No. Honestly. I do see.'

'And anyway, I think it probably does you good to be valued by someone for something besides your work.'

'Of course. With you, I'm the Cat Assistant.'

'And very capable too. The Trefew girl was on the 'phone only yesterday to say how well those wild ones of yours have settled into their barn. Three rats already, she said.'

'Good. I never thought they'd stay there. It's so windy.'

'She said you spent a good hour watching them. She was most impressed. But you were saying. What's the problem with the work-in-progress?'

'I'm getting bogged down. I don't seem to be able to control my material.'

'When does L'Americana get back?'

Judith glanced up sharply but found Esther studiously sucking the eggs off a prawn. The eccentric Miss Gammell was more perceptive than she let on.

A combination of genetic chance and malignant history had seen to it that the community scattered across the fields of Martyrstow and Treneglos was almost entirely female – a circle of widows, sisters and daughters. Judith and Joanna's ménage had blended seamlessly into such surroundings. Neither had sought to risk the ease of its outward show with any public acknowledgements of its intimate importance. As far as their neighbours were concerned, they were a photographer with more space than she could use and a very private novelist who could use the extra space. The nearest bookshop was twenty miles away and Judith had always written under a pseudonym, so her privacy seemed assured.

'Oh. Not long now,' Judith told her. 'She gets back tomorrow. She'll stay a night in London then drive down.'

'Where's she been again? I know you told me once.'

'Seneca.'

'Never heard of it.'

'It was renamed after Independence. You probably knew it as something else.'

Esther held out a prawn peeled and heavily coated in mayonnaise. There were not many left.

'Are you sure I can't tempt you?'

'Quite sure.'

Esther popped the offering into her mouth.

'I'll save the rest for later,' she said. 'I might need the sustenance if Nora calls again. She's taking on several local farmers about badger baiting. Apparently she knows they're involved in it and there's a nursing female she's watching which they'll be after next. If she can't persuade the local constabulary to help, she'll keep them off herself with her father's twelve-bore. She's all of eighty-six.'

Esther yawned and pulled her elegant sky blue cardigan closer about her. The electric fire was plugged in but making as little difference as ever to the cold draughts that whistled up from Bunting's jammed-open escape route. His stiff leg stuck out behind him, Bunting was dozing heavily at Esther's feet. Nearer to the fire than either woman, his threadbare coat absorbed most of its heat. Judith stood.

'I'd better leave you in peace.'

'No, no. Stay a little.' Esther waved her back down. 'We can ignore the phone if it rings again. Did I ever tell you, said she à *propos* of nothing whatever, about my forbidden aunt?'

'No you didn't.'

'How strange of me. It should have been the first story to come into my head on meeting you. I call her the forbidden aunt because she was always a forbidden subject *en famille*, which of course lent her far more glamour than she deserved. On the face of it she wasn't much of a black sheep. She played the piano well, read botany with some success at Oxford and even worked at Kew for a while. At first she married a nice, rather dull young man who, conveniently enough, was taken from her by the war. Then she met this woman; a very handsome widow. (Have you noticed how women of average looks but independent position are invariably called "handsome"?) She met this widow and she set up house with her. Just like that. Her family could have turned a blind eye – the war threw a lot of single women together – but then her father started receiving letters from someone in the handsome widow's parish. Her late husband had been the rector you see, and the letter asked did my great uncle realise that his daughter and the late rector's wife had been carrying on most lasciviously even before their husbands had died.'

'How awful!' Judith exclaimed. 'The letter, I mean. Not the women. What did he do?'

'Naturally he challenged his daughter. He was an MP; had

a position to maintain. She faced up to him, denying nothing; so he disowned her. Stupid man.'

'What about the handsome widow?'

'She owned the rectory, which her husband had bought and left to her in his will, and my aunt and she had a few savings. Apparently the same "well-wishing" parishioner had tried to alert the Church of England too, to have her widow's pension cut off but they thought love between women inconceivable at the best of times, much less on church property . . .'

'. . . and on a church subsidy.'

'Exactly. So they lived off her widow's mite and their carefully invested savings and the proceeds of a nursery garden. And they kept a cow and hens so they were all but self-sufficient. It could have gone on forever.'

'Oh no! What happened to them?'

Esther reached out for another prawn but thought better of it and rubbed Bunting with her foot instead.

'The handsome widow had a fling with a man,' she sighed. 'Not as handsome as her, but he was rich and I think she was tired of scrimping and saving.'

'But how awful!' Judith found herself deeply moved. She thought for a moment what would happen if one of her previous male lovers came to claim her back from Joanna and was proud and glad to know that she would laugh in his face. She looked up at Esther who was examining her nails as she talked.

'She would have come back,' Esther said. 'I know she would. She was only restless, not unhappy, but my aunt had got proud from all her suffering. She preferred self-sacrifice to humility.' She turned round and snatched a prawn after all. 'Stupid bitch!' she snapped to herself. 'Sorry dear, but just thinking of it makes me hopping mad. To go through so much, to stick her neck out so far and then to throw it all away for simple pride.' She dunked the prawn in mayonnaise and ate it, quickly peeling and dipping another. She ate the second then stood and walked to the window, licking her fingers. The sun-bleached curtains were moving faintly in the draught. 'Filthy clouds,' she muttered. 'I suppose the Americana's place is buried in them.'

'It is rather, yes.'

'I never asked you how the cats were.'

'OK. Fine.' Judith stood and pulled on Joanna's mackintosh again. 'The tabby one on the end's still a bit jumpy.'

'So would you be if someone left you tied up in a plastic bag. How about Old Grey?'

'Old and grey. He didn't eat much of his food yesterday. I gave him some fresh stuff but he didn't show much interest.'

'Comes to us all in the end.' Esther patted her shoulder. 'Sorry, dear. I've kept you too long.'

'Nonsense. It was lovely to talk. Now, do you need anything for tomorrow?'

'Not a sausage. Battleship Haines does her delivery in the afternoon. Now go on back to the bloody novel. Ye shall overcome.'

'No fear,' Judith chuckled. 'A long quiet evening with someone else's, I think.'

Dusk had fallen on the hillside as she drove up to the house. The cloud bank seemed thicker than ever. She had forgotten to leave a light on so had to grope her way to the kitchen door. The house felt warm but she still had the chill of Esther's room about her. She shuddered and threw more logs into the stove, loosening its little disc slightly to let more air into the grate. As she hurried round the house drawing curtains against the encroaching night and leaving lights on for company, she remembered that Joanna would be back in London tomorrow. Although Judith still had two nights alone to get through, it was comforting to think of her London flat welcoming her lover with its enveloping comforts.

After supper she grew impatient with the new novel she had begun to read. Her mind circling afresh about the problem

of her own half-written text out in the hayloft, she took one of
the psychological thrillers that lined the walls of Joanna's den.
She then drew her legs up on the sofa beside her and prepared
to enter unfamiliar territory.

Six

Deborah had sent out her nurse for a thick black veil which she intended to wear over a small black hat. She did so despite her mother-in-law's insistence that it looked 'theatrical and, anyway, think of Jackie Kennedy'. It was typical of Julian's mother to find a comparison that would make Deborah feel small, even as it glorified her son. Deborah sniped back at her, saying that she thought it tasteless to have worn a bloodstained coat for the sake of publicity. She remembered that Jackie Kennedy had later appeared in full mourning, with a veil, but by then Wendy had changed tack and was talking about 'silly vanity'.

'Silly vanity?' Deborah could scarcely believe her ears. 'Silly vanity? Has it occurred to you that I might feel like crying?'

Shocked into apology, Wendy had then burst into tears; as much a mistress of the upper hand as her son had been its master. She had produced a small bottle of duty free whisky from her handbag and had spent the rest of the evening at Deborah's bedside, hungry for details of Julian's last months, however trivial, which she exchanged for encyclopaedic and not altogether endearing tales of Julian's childhood and adolescence. At last, once the nurse, visibly shocked at the rapid downing of alcohol, wheeled in their lamb chops and rice pudding, Wendy had spoken of the future.

'Of course you'll be coming to live with us for a while. No question of that.'

'With you? In Gloucestershire?'

'But of course. Where else can you go? You'll scarcely want to stay on here. We would lend you the London flat – we go there so rarely nowadays – but I think we should be keeping a proper eye on you for a while. You can have the room over the garage – it's really a sort of staff flat but it would give you more peace and quiet than the main house, what with Gilbert's noise.'

'He always struck me as being so quiet.'

'He's getting terribly deaf. He will not talk at anything less than a bellow and he keeps the telly tuned to the most Godawful sports programmes and things on dry fly fishing, all with the volume on high.'

'Well. I had thought of . . .'

'Sorry. Have you made other arrangements?'

'No.'

'That's settled then.'

'But.'

'Now I've bought you a ticket so we can fly back together as soon as everything's over tomorrow morning. Do you have much packing to do?'

'Not really.'

'Presumably all your furniture and things can be sent on later. So it couldn't be easier.'

'I shall want to wait for Julian's ashes, though,' said Deborah firmly. 'I'm not leaving until I've got those with me.' Wendy dissolved into fresh tears at her bedside. Deborah watched them spatter the congealing gravy on her mother-in-law's plate.

'Here Wendy,' she murmured, desolate at the thought of having to move anywhere just yet, least of all to Wendy and Gilbert's joylessly hearty realm. 'Don't cry. Eat your supper.' Wendy cried on, emitting slow, exhausted clucks of grief and adding to the little heap of crumpled, mascara-streaked paper handkerchiefs at her feet. Turning briefly to her own tray, Deborah progressed as far as sawing away the thick ridge of fat from her chop and stirring the blob of jam into her rice pudding, but found that the combination of neat whisky and Wendy's sickly scent had left her slightly nauseous. She gently wrestled Julian's photograph from his weeping mother's grasp then slid with it beneath the covers.

She drifted through her last morning in Seneca like one fever-weakened and up too soon. As though to compensate for her weaknesses exposed the previous evening, Wendy was all capability and action. Forming an uneasy alliance with the nurse, she set about folding and packing away her daughter-in-law's recent life into the formidable array of luggage that Deborah had scarcely seen since receiving it as Wendy's wedding present. Sapped of will and finding herself in the way, Deborah took a long, dizzying bath, slid into her black cocktail frock ('Quite unsuitable,' Wendy pronounced, 'but I suppose it will have to do if it's really all you've got.') then sat on the stool by her dressing table playing with the veil on her hat.

'You don't want this any more, do you Deborah?' Wendy would ask from time to time, already stuffing whatever it was into one of two large boxes on which she had marked 'Charity' and 'Rubbish'.

'No,' Deborah would answer vaguely. She knew she would regret this, that in a week or so she would be irritated at the loss of some letter or consumed with a morbid wish for some garment of Julian's, but she was powerless; a limp, shed skin of her former self. (And her former self had scarcely been assertive.) Beneath her passivity, however, there also lurked a sly gratitude that her mother-in-law was so readily setting herself up as someone to blame in the months ahead.

The English Church in Seneca dated from the early Edwardian era and, were it not for the dusty avenue of squat palms leading to the door, would not have looked out of place in a leafy suburb of London. Presumably this had been the architect's intention; a piece of foreign soil which, even after Independence, would forever bring to mind the hum of competitive lawn-mowing and the mournful plunk of domestic badminton.

They rode there side by side in a consular car, Wendy's large, dry hand pressing on Deborah's smaller, rather damp one. The Foreign Secretary and his wife had interrupted their tour to return to Seneca for the occasion and there was a small clutch of press photographers at the graveyard's edge. Evidently Wendy was unable to choose between wide-eyed excitement at Sir Bill's presence and motherly disdain. Eventually she opted for the latter.

'The very least they could do for him,' she sniffed. 'After he saved Sir Bill's life.'

Deborah ignored the Coltranes, the press and the full turn-out of the slender consular staff. Secure in her veil and new widow's unapproachability, she walked up the aisle behind the coffin, leaning on Wendy's arm. The pall-bearers, elegant black locals, were of varying heights so Julian's last entry into church was at a slightly drunken angle. It was absurdly wasteful, she reflected, that the consulate had bothered with an adult coffin at all. The little of her husband that had proved salvageable, could have fitted snugly into one built for a child. She could have carried him up the aisle like a baby. She remembered watching an IRA funeral with him, on television, where a grieving mother had done just that, clasping to her tightly buttoned breast a coffin little bigger than a shoebox.

'There is no worse than this,' she thought. 'To have to share him even now.'

Julian had never been hers entirely. When they first met, she was forever surrounded by flatmates whose connivance was only bought by a total confidence on affairs of the heart. Every other precious weekend of their courtship, it seemed, had been spent in the grudging bosom of his family. And then, after marriage, she had been obliged to share him with diplomats, consuls and their army of long-suffering wives and secretaries. There had been a brief spell of real matrimony, in a flat that had not been provided and furnished by his employers. It was in Battersea, in a stuffy block on the park. And even there the weighty service charges had forced them to take in a lodger. And now he was off; the way he used to leave for work − in a rush and preferably in company so that her farewells were cowed and muted. She had disgraced herself at her father's funeral. At her mother's request, the coffin was left in view until the crematorium had emptied. As they filed out, she had fallen, weeping, onto the coffin and kissed the polished wood. She would not do that here. Julian would not have liked it. A painful knot formed in her throat.

'Deep breath,' she told herself to stifle the sob. 'Deep breath. That's it. In out. In out. Shake it all about. I must, I must, improve my bust. Julian? Julian?'

Seneca's English chaplain arrived and controlled her grieving thoughts with his bland delivery and catchphrase solemnity. Studiously looking in any direction but hers, he spent the opening minutes of his address paying lip service to the impossibility of finding any words of comfort in the face of an accidentally murdered loved one. Then, with an inevitability that churchgoers might find reassuring but which insulted Deborah deeply, he dared to smile like a game-show host and speak of Christ's consolation. As his bleating voice rose and fell, regardless of what he was saying, she tried to feel her husband curled in her arms and imagined she was stopping his ears to spare his dignity.

At last, Julian's pathetic remains were borne out to the crematorium and she could stand for the dismissal. The chaplain walked to dole out his condolent greetings in the morning glare. Wendy stood aside to let Deborah be the first to follow. Her face was a dry mask. She made a gesture with her handkerchief.

'What? My veil?' Deborah asked, her voice reduced to a croak from too many swallowed tears.

'No. Your cheeks. Just a quick wipe.'

Deborah dabbed at her cheeks and found them awash. She

wiped them swiftly dry and the brine stung her little cuts. Wendy gave a brief, tight smile of approval and stood further back. Deborah had a vision of the house in Gloucestershire, its emerald lawn, its irreproachable, bugless roses, the rails everywhere to prop up Julian's alcoholic father. She would have to drink strong Indian tea and weak coffee made with milk. There would be nothing to read but *Reader's Digest* and old copies of *The Lady*. Dispiriting walks would be trudged along well-marked footpaths with Wendy and her characterless labrador.

Wendy took her arm to steer her over to offer her thanks to the Coltranes for coming and Deborah remembered how all her baths contained nasty rubber mats which chafed one's thighs.

'Thank you both so much for coming,' she told Lady Coltrane. 'It was so thoughtful.'

'The least we could do, my dear.'

'The very least,' Sir Bill murmured.

'Bastard,' Deborah thought. 'You're the one that was meant to die!' but she only wrinkled her mouth in humble gratitude and allowed him to press her hand in both of his.

Judith's American friend, Joanna Ventura, was standing in the doorway talking to the chaplain. She had on a plain, black dress made from something diaphanous, like cheesecloth, and had pinned up her mass of hair. She looked Greek; a practised widow. Quite unexpectedly, the sight of her lent Deborah strength.

'Wendy,' she said quickly. 'It was most terribly kind of you to offer but I shan't be coming back with you.'

'What do you mean?'

'At least, I shall come back with you (you must let me pay for the ticket) but I'll be going somewhere else for a while, you see. Not to Gloucestershire.'

Wendy looked furious. This was the last place she wanted to discuss travel arrangements.

'But where else can you go?' she hissed. 'I thought your mother . . .'

'I'm going to my sister's. In Cornwall.' She raised her voice and made an effort to smile. 'Joanna, hello. It was so sweet of you to come. I don't think you've met Julian's mother. Wendy Curtis, Joanna Ventura.'

From the way Wendy's hand stiffened as she held it out, it could have been tightly gloved.

'I'm so very sorry,' Joanna told her, shaking it.

'Thank you,' came Wendy's taut return.

'What have I done?' thought Deborah but there was exhilaration in her panic. She had taken sudden control to change her course but, just as quickly, had relinquished the driving to others.

Seven

With every passing minute of the journey home, Joanna felt that perhaps she had bitten off more than the proverbial mouthful. The flight had been extremely tense, with herself and Mrs Curtis on either side of Deborah. Deborah, it soon transpired, was terrified of flying. At every slight alteration in the aeroplane's position she blanched, clenched her fists and lost her train of thought, which rendered conversation with her deeply unrewarding. Even had Joanna dredged up ten minutes' worth of things to say to Mrs Curtis across Deborah's hunched shoulders, Mrs Curtis was loath to reply.

'Remember she's bereaved too,' Joanna told herself. 'She's just lost her son.'

Then Mrs Curtis would recross her legs in the other direction and brush out her skirt in a certain way that would make Joanna seethe with irritation. Evidently the woman thought she had some prior claim on the new widow and was furious at having been outmanoeuvred.

Joanna glanced across at Deborah who, stiff with fear, was pretending to read a dog-eared inflight magazine. Joanna leant forward and tried out a few polite questions about Gloucestershire, travel arrangements, Mr Curtis and so on. They were met with the shortest possible replies.

'Mrs Curtis,' she asked at last, 'Is there something about me I ought to know?'

'Heavens no, Joanna.' Mrs Curtis's voice was squeaky with

suppressed displeasure. 'Don't be so silly. I'm just, well, rather overtired I suppose.'

She took herself off on a protracted trip to the john, returning with a small bowl of ice and a half-bottle of whisky which she consumed alone in several, quite unselfconscious tumblerfuls before falling into a deep sleep. Soon after, Deborah was persuaded to take some air sickness pills with a gin and orange chaser, so before long she was snoring softly into Joanna's shoulder.

Left in relative peace, Joanna had taken out her holiday reading: Judith's last novel but one, *Privacy*. It had sold very well, and had even been made into an oversimplified film for television. Joanna found all Judith's novels quite unreadable, which Judith understood and accepted, bless her, but which was always a point of conflict when she met Judith's friends and found herself cast in the role of muse-stroke-amanuensis. Their plots, as discussed by said friends or as described on the dustjackets, attracted her (she had enjoyed the film version of *Privacy*) but their execution seemed clogged with wordy abstractions. Also, she felt self-conscious trying to read a novel in the presence of its author, feeling she should be smiling, or at least reacting to it as though it were a play or a piece of sculpture.

'Listen,' Judith would say. 'Don't worry. It's no problem. I like the thought that you love me the me rather than me the novelist.'

But it was a problem and a deepening one. Joanna believed that intimacy should develop naturally with the passage of time and yet each novel Judith had written since they met represented yet another piece of her nature on which Joanna could gain no purchase. She had bought *Privacy* in the airport bookshop on leaving England and had waded her way through almost half of it. As the plane whined home, she read the remainder.

She reached a point, two-thirds of the way through, when the reading became suddenly easier, as though the plot, of which there was very little, were a small motor, laborious to wind up, which could now be released to spend its complex energies. Her thrill at finally reading one of her lover's novels from start to finish and at appreciating with all the sudden force of a revelation the extent of her gift was mixed with a new anxiety. *Privacy* told of one man's obsessive rivalry with another. His envy mounted finally to the level of insane worship as he insinuated himself into the other's life only to confront levels of altruism, intelligence and, most importantly, discretion which increased his sense of his own baseness. Reading it, Joanna was forced to see that the woman she had thought of as a generous creative source, a kind of nurse to joy, was intimately acquainted with hatred, spite, even violence.

Of course she knew Judith was no angel. In their first year together her lover was forever bringing up the subject of her 'past', not realising that Joanna found her attractive precisely because, beneath the cool even schoolmarmish exterior, she was so passionate. (Feeling her writhe on the sheets beneath her she had often sat up in amazement and softly teased her. 'My academic hotbox!' she would sigh, chuckling, and run her tongue along her lover's thigh to rouse her further.) Neither could she have lived with Judith so long and not received wounds from her sharp edges. Judith was quite capable, when goaded, of lashing out with a vicious tongue. Nothing, however, until reading *Privacy*, had been able to sway Joanna's conviction that Judith was fundamentally kind; a cherisher not a breaker. Like a cuckolded husband she had been the last to find out the truth about her beloved. All Judith's readers knew, her faithful following, what Joanna had been blithely ignoring: that deep within her was a seam of negativity. Of mistrust. Filled with a foreboding she knew to be absurd, she wanted to be home at once so as to see whether the woman she thought she knew would seem much altered by the discovery.

If Mrs Curtis seemed less steady when they arrived at

Heathrow, her mouth was no less tightly clipped. They queued in silence through Passport Control with remarkably little wait for Joanna's American passport to be checked, their arrival being in the small hours of morning, then they wound their way through to the monkey house tussle of Baggage Retrieval. Deborah had five pieces of luggage to Joanna's one and by the time Joanna had plunged forward to tug clear the suitcase Deborah had missed on its first trip around the conveyor belt, Mrs Curtis had vanished.

'Oh no,' Deborah wailed, standing on tip-toe to peer about them. 'She's gone without saying goodbye.'

'It's five in the morning, Deborah.'

'Yes but do you think she was awfully offended? I mean it was terribly kind of her to offer to have me to live with them in Gloucestershire and it was only because, well, he's so drunk and frightening and she's a bit, well, you know – but you saw, of course – and they've got the grimmest bathrooms I've ever sat in and I know Julian was terribly unhappy there as a boy. At least, he never talked about it and that's usually a sign, isn't it? But Wendy did fly all the way out to bring me back. Well, she came for Julian's funeral too, I suppose, but . . . Oh dear. Joanna what shall I do?'

Joanna felt the sudden weight of her exhaustion come upon her. She pushed the suitcases together so that a woman could wheel her trolley past.

'Look, Deborah,' she said slowly. 'If you feel so bad about it, if you want to stay with your mother-in-law, all we have to do is shove you on a train. Then you just take a taxi at the other end and cast yourself on her tender mercies. Simple.'

'But I don't think I want to. I *know* I don't.'

'Then shut up.' Joanna grabbed two trolleys and began to load them.

'Oh. Sorry, Joanna. Here. Let me help you with that second trolley.' They walked five paces or so then Deborah froze with fresh horror. 'Oh God!'

'What now?'

'Count five,' Joanna told herself. 'She's a widow. She's your sister-in-law. Count five.'

'I never paid her back. She paid for my flight and I was going to write her a cheque.'

'The post office'll be shut. You can send her a cheque after breakfast.'

'Brilliant.' Deborah actually laughed. Joanna merely grunted.

They off-loaded the two trolleyloads of luggage into a taxi and were driven to Judith's flat on Clapham Common. The drive was thoughtfully silent except for Deborah having a brief weep.

('Sorry,' she said, 'it's so silly but I haven't been in a real cab for ages.')

Mercifully, Steffi the lodger was away on holiday. While Joanna sorted mail and watered plants, Deborah investigated the flat, which she claimed to have never seen. Minutes later, Joanna found her curled up fast asleep on the lodger's stripped bed. She covered her with a blanket, noticing at last a faint likeness to Judith. Deborah's hair had fallen back from her face to reveal a familiar, slightly pointed ear and she slept like her sister with her hands bunched before her eyes as though in the process of warding off a blow.

Having had no sleep during the flight, Joanna's body ached for bed. They could sleep until lunch, have a bit to eat then leave London before the afternoon rush hour. She could not sleep without calling Judith. It was not quite seven. If she waited for five more minutes, she could catch her after the alarm clock. She made herself a cup of tea, raided the lodger's biscuit tin then picked up the telephone.

Eight

Judith finished buttoning the spare quilt into its cover then gave it a thorough shake to spread out the down. She slipped two hot water bottles underneath it; one where Deborah's feet would be, one where the small of her back would rest. The bedding was warm and fresh from the airing cupboard but Cornish mist had a way of percolating through the gaps in the windows and soaking clammily into unheated sheets and towels in a matter of hours. She ran a duster over the bedside table and the looking-glass and spent a few thoughtful minutes selecting her younger sister some books from the shelves that lined the stairs and landing. These, too, were thick with dust. She never noticed dust when she was alone here with Joanna. She blew them clean, making herself sneeze.

'Damn Deborah!' she thought. 'And damn Joanna for bringing her!'

Then she sat at the dressing table, dusting that and feeling guilty for her unworthy thoughts.

The very concept of feeling unworthy had become alien to her life for so long, it was a shock to the system. Only when Joanna had rung up this morning, a call for which she had been lying awake some two hours, had Judith seen the folly of leaving so much unexplained. After the brief crisis of her mother's death and funeral, her family had become a non-subject between them.

'You don't mind my not talking about it?' she had asked once.

'Look, hon,' Joanna assured her, 'I come from a happy, self-centred family of eight who write or ring once a month and who I visit once every eighteen months or so. I've got all the family I need or can cope with. If yours doesn't interest you, it *certainly* needn't interest me!'

'Bless you for that,' Judith had said at the time but now she wished she had told her everything. Joanna assumed that Judith and her sister had maintained some kind of discreet contact, when in fact they had not seen each other since their mother's funeral, had studiously ignored one another's birthdays out of escalating pique and had not sent one another so much as a holiday postcard. For Judith, Deborah was the sole surviving reminder of a past she had hoped to bury beneath her new, unconditionally loving life with Joanna. She had managed to convince herself that, despite her occasional stabs of guilt, their sisterhood was no more than a quirk of biology. It had not been difficult to lose Deborah's change of address cards without copying out the information into her address book. She had quite forgotten what small African state – or was it Middle Eastern? – Deborah had last moved to, and dreaded the subject ever arising to expose her ignorance.

Her brother-in-law's name never sprang easily to mind. They had met only twice, at his wedding and his mother-in-law's funeral, and then only to feel spontaneous, mutual dislike. When Joanna had told her of his sudden death over the 'phone, it had been some minutes before she realised who they were discussing.

'Hello?'

'Hi.'

'Joanna!'

'Did I wake you? I waited until a bit after seven.'

'No. Hello. Welcome to England. How was your flight?'

'OK. Did you get my postcards?'

'No.'

'I sent one a day. They probably haven't even made it to the airport yet.'

'We can read them together next week.'

'Yeah.' Joanna had chuckled. She sounded tired. 'Look, hon, did you hear about Julian?'

'Who?'

'Julian. The thing is I've brought Deborah back with me.'

'Oh.' Judith had thought a moment. '*Oh*! She's with you now?'

'She's fast asleep. Didn't you hear about it?'

'No. What?'

'Julian. Poor kid. She was standing on the porch seeing him off to work and they'd put a bomb under his car. It was meant for William Coltrane, who was staying with them but he was held up so Julian took his car. Deborah's still really disturbed and her face and arms are quite badly scarred. Anyway, I found out from an old paper and went round there just in time to save her from the mother-in-law. I'm starting to wonder why. Judith, she's nothing like you. She's really . . . I dunno. I guess I shouldn't speak ill of the newly bereaved but, well. Has she always been like that?' There was a pause while Judith tried to reconcile her faintly suburban memories of Deborah with terrorist activity and widowhood. 'Hello? Judith?'

'Yes.'

'I thought you'd gone.'

'No. Sorry, Joanna, it's a bit early.'

'Yes.'

Judith had rallied herself.

'So. Tell me. She's with you, and you're bringing her down here to recuperate?'

'That is OK, isn't it?'

'Of course. I mean, we haven't spoken for years but, God, poor Deborah! She must be so . . . What happened to the mother-in-law?'

'Lost her at Heathrow.'

'Fine. I'll get a room ready. How long was the flight?'

'A season in Hell. I've got to sleep a bit but we'll get on the road soon after lunch.'

'Can't wait,' said Judith, thinking, 'Wish you were coming alone.'

'Judith?'

'Mmm?'

'I did do the right thing, didn't I?'

'Of course you did.'

'Of course she did, damn her,' Judith told herself and went out in search of a pot plant to brighten Deborah's dressing table. She had seized on this nightmarish interruption of their seclusion as a welcome diversion from the increasing strain wrought on her by the novel she was failing to write. Throwing herself into a day of frenetic housewifery, she had already made a nut pâté and a comforting bean stew which would be graced, when the time came, with herby dumplings. She took a pretty, variegated tradescantia from the hall windowsill to trail from Deborah's mantelpiece and graced her dressing table with a peppermint-scented pelargonium that had been wintering in Joanna's den. Then she decided to make bread and was soon kneading a large ball of brown dough back and forth on the kitchen table. She had to lean with all her slight frame and grew quite breathless with the effort. She had just loaded more logs into the old stove behind her and the heat was making her sweat. Gingerly, so as not to make it too floury, she unbuttoned her cardigan and laid it over a chair. Then she resumed the satisfying pounding of the dough. Seeing her at this work, Joanna usually made some jibe about it leaving her hands suspiciously clean. As she kneaded, spreading the yeast through the mixture, pausing now and then to scoop in some flour that was in danger of being swept off the table-top, the dough became less and less sticky. Quite suddenly, it always seemed to her, its nature would change, leaving it smooth and elastic as warm flesh.

Her mother had rarely indulged in yeast cookery.

'Too messy,' she said, 'and I can't be expected to sit around half the day waiting for it to rise.'

Only occasionally, perhaps if the weather was bad and Judith stuck inside, she would make Chelsea buns. Brown flour was hard to find then, besides which, Judith's mother declared that it was only fit for communists and vegetarians.

'Cranks,' she would say.

'Like the Protheroes in Brackley Avenue?'

'Exactly, but there's no need to talk about them here.'

She would stir up eggs, flour, sugar, yeast and milk, already muttering that it was far too much bother, and she didn't know why they couldn't buy buns from the baker like everybody else. When it was all bound together she would allow Judith to shake more flour onto the kitchen table from a dredger before she tipped out the dough on top of it and began to knead.

'Go on,' she would say, her glasses misting up with the effort. 'Touch it.' Gingerly Judith would reach out and touch and always her mother would say, 'It's a living thing now, you know. Yeast comes alive when you feed it with sugar.' And always Judith would prompt her to tell her about how *her* mother made bread and buns.

'Granny used to knead prayers into it, didn't she?'

'You know she did.'

'Can you?'

Usually her mother would snort dismissively but sometimes, if Judith pretended she was only slightly interested, she would proceed to say the Lord's Prayer in time to her kneading. Her lurching and pulling made her throw strange emphases on the words.

'*Our* father who *art* in heaven, *hall*owed be Thy *Na*-ame!' Judith never understood why she so wanted her mother to do this; it was so frightening. The smell of yeast, her mother's pounding hands on the off-white dough which looked like old thighs on the beach and the terrible blasphemy of warding off the devil while doing housework were almost more than she could bear. They rarely went to funfairs because they made

Deborah throw up. Making Mother pray over bunmaking was Judith's equivalent to the screaming tension of a ride on a big dipper.

Judith tried it for a few seconds now.

'*Thy* kingdom *come*, *Thy* will be *done* on earth *as it* is in . . .'

The evocation was too strong for her, however, even with brown flour. She tried singing instead. She had never been musical and her voice was reedy and uncertain but some songs, once learnt, were fixed firmly in her mind, like bright rags of poetry. Joanna would joke that she could divine her lover's mood from which of her short repertory of songs rose unconsciously to her lips. It might be 'Da Doo Ron Ron' or 'Jerusalem' (which she always started too high and had to break off towards the end) or, when she was drunk, 'Blue Moon'. Now, perhaps because she was thinking about Deborah and childhood, maybe because its rhythm went well with kneading, she came out with a song learnt in primary school: 'Tell Me Fair Ladies'. An opera lover with whom she had once had an affair had been most upset when he heard her sing this in the bath.

'How could they!' he exclaimed, when she explained how she had picked up her bastard version of his favourite aria. 'It's Mozart!' and he had climbed into the bath with her to teach her the Italian words. Miss Caster of IIE had got there before him, however, and all Judith could remember of his efforts were, *Voi che sapete*. Still, she slipped these five alien syllables amongst the English words to spice them up a little and to honour a not unpleasant memory.

Having pressed the dough into tins to prove beside the stove, she wiped the table free of flour and grains then rubbed it over with a damp cloth. Drying it, she thought again of her growing novel, of Edgar brooding at his mother's kitchen table and of the feel of her mother's own against her cheek. She turned the radio on, finding a broadcast of wild, West Indian dance music.

'Bloody Deborah,' she said out loud, scrubbing the mixing bowl clean under a running tap. 'Shitty well damn her!'

Judith's father used to beat her once a week, sometimes more if she had committed some misdemeanour. The activity was ritualised. They would be in the process of clearing the dining room after dinner and he would turn to her and say,

'Go and clear the kitchen table, Judith.'

She would have to clear the table of schoolbooks, pens, her mother's magazines and, knowing what was coming, stand beside it while Deborah and her mother walked in and out with plates and cutlery. Then they would have to sit quietly on two chairs by the wall while her father made her lie across the table and lashed her. Then the four of them would drink coffee in the drawing room as though nothing had happened. He made her wear thick, boy's trousers at home which he said was to hide her 'shame' but which she soon realised was to lessen any marks his blows might inflict. Just once her mother took her on one side and said,

'You do know, darling, don't you, that Daddy has to do what he does? It's to make you grow up properly. But a lot of silly, common people wouldn't understand because they don't have the same standards so you must give me your word as a young lady that you won't talk to anyone else about it. It's no one else's business, you see, and it would only embarrass them.'

Judith gave her word. She had no desire to tell anyone. After the first four or five times (when she had vomited secretly from fear and confusion) she had felt less and less outrage at his beating her for no reason, for she came to feel that it gave her a role within the family. With childish sexism she thought that it was like being a boy; every family's needing a boy so as to have someone who was brave. From an early age, unnerved by the screaming matches her parents threw after tucking them safely into bed, she had been terrified that some event would separate them all. If her silent, domestic suffering could provide the bond that would hold them around her, she saw no reason why it should not continue.

Her father's fatal heart attack in her late teens, ironically, proved her right. With him and the beatings gone, the family fell apart. She found herself free to go away to university (which he had expressly forbidden). Deborah, who had always made a pretty pretence of stupidity, suddenly insisted on being sent away to an expensive, socially pretentious boarding school, whence she returned as rarely as possible, arranging for most of her holidays to be spent with friends. Their mother was glad to see the back of them, 'Beauty and Bluestocking both'. She welcomed her widowing as an absolution of all responsibility, making no attempt to disguise the fact that she had found motherhood an unrelieved burden on her strength of character. She promptly moved into a smaller house where, the third bedroom being stacked high with packing cases and excess furniture, her daughters' visits could only coincide with inconvenience.

Over and over, in the years that followed, Judith told herself that there was no reason to blame her sister. Younger and weaker than she, childish for her age, Deborah could hardly have been expected to intervene, intercede or even seek outside help. (Doubtless she was given the same strict instructions to keep such things secret from 'silly, common people'. Deborah had been obedient to a fault.) Their father was an object of understandable fear, even for grown women; an unpredictable giant of a man whose temper, Judith perceived with hindsight, was fed by alcohol. Yet whenever, pen poised over Christmas card or hand over telephone, she pursued this line of reasoning, Judith returned, over and over, to images scorched onto her memory: Deborah seen from behind, walking between her parents holding each by the hand and looking proudly up at each in turn; Deborah, blonde curls bouncing as, slightly too old, she squirmed for coy delight on Daddy's knee; Deborah, in her early teens, weeks before her father's death, watching him beat her sister with a look of studious curiosity beyond the call of mere obedience. Weighed against a pan empty of all but the most hackneyed gestures of affection, such evidence of connivance came to smack (unfortunate word!) of collusion.

Judith walked to the chair by the stove and softly brushed the rising dough with sunflower oil to keep it soft. Once again she saw its swollen and puckered resemblance to greased, elderly flesh at the seashore. She washed the oil from her palms, peered at her cross face in the mirror then hesitated. The house was tidy, dinner was made (green-speckled dumplings and fat Bramleys stuffed with mincemeat waited their hour of sacrifice on plates in the fridge) and she was not due to feed the cats and call in on Esther until late afternoon. There was nothing but to return to her novel. She played for time, making herself a cup of coffee to carry over, and allowing herself to be briefly diverted by the crossword's two remaining clues. Then she clicked on the answering machine, pulled Joanna's raincoat about her shoulders, and took herself and her coffee out to the barn to face again the problem of Edgar, his cocoa-sipping mother and the knife.

Nine

Twenty minutes of grief-stricken monologue from Deborah as she took her bath on waking was enough to drive Joanna to strong measures. While Deborah was picking through her sister's wardrobe in search of something warm, Joanna busied herself in the kitchen stirring a good teacupful of Steffi the lodger's sweet sherry into some tinned tomato soup. As driver, she held back some unlaced soup which she hastily heated for herself having taken Deborah's bowl to the table.

'There you go,' she told her. 'Soup to warm you up, toast and cheese to fill in the gaps and an apple to take away the taste.'

'Oh, but I'm not really . . .'

'Deborah, I'm mothering you. Enjoy.'

'Actually I *love* tinned tomato soup,' Deborah chuckled guiltily, lifting her spoon. 'I've always had to eat it in secret. Julian didn't like it if he found any in the larder. He said it was common.'

'He would.'

'What?'

'Would he?'

'Yes. He often said things like that. I suppose he was an awful snob, really.' She lowered her spoon and sighed. She looked, Joanna reflected, really cute when she wasn't crying. Cute *à la* Shirley Temple.

'Deborah?'

'Hmm?'

'We're not going until you've eaten. All of it.'

And sleepily, Deborah had eaten all her soup and rather stale toast and mousetrap cheese like a good girl thus enabling Joanna to drive down the M4 and M5 like a demon with her slumped, oblivious in the passenger seat, skinny Judith's Aran jersey clinging snugly to her most un-Shirley Temple-like breasts.

'Home,' Joanna thought as they passed signs welcoming them to Wiltshire, Avon, Somerset and Devon, 'Home. Home. Home.' The motorway scenery was ugly compared to that on the more southerly route favoured by Judith, but Joanna carried a full colour map in her head and it was enough for her to see evocative signs as they sped by motorway exits. She could picture soft south-western hills beyond the muddy verges and concrete embankments; the Cotswolds on their right then the Mendips to their left, then the Quantocks to the right again and, after a while, the Blackdown Hills to the left.

'You miss Hampshire your way,' Judith said. 'And Stonehenge, and you don't see Dorset at all.'

But, quite apart from the speed, Joanna preferred the motorway for the suddenness of the plunge into countryside when it petered out at Exeter.

She had bought the place in Cornwall six years after moving to Europe, four (or was it five?) before meeting Judith. Like many of her compatriots she had no sooner arrived in England than she fled to Paris. England's weather depressed her as did its obsession with class and the deceptive similarities of its language. Happier in Gigiville (as her sisters called it), she lived in a commune off the Rue de la Roquette. She learnt most of her French in bed or over shop counters because her fellow communards were either American or keen to improve their English. She discovered dope, politics and Jean-Luc Godard (all of them passing phases) and sex with women (which was not). Already a keen amateur photographer, she learned her trade taking photographs for a radical, multilingual 'newspaper' which nobody read but everyone was seen to carry. When its one gay writer sold out to the enemy, taking a job on an American fashion magazine, he dragged her with him and she found she was grateful.

A staggering number of the luscious models she was sent to photograph were involved with other women and, before the year was out, she was ensnared by one too. DouDou was Moroccan, slender as a thigh bone and the first woman Joanna had met who matched her height. DouDou was permanently stoned, spoke no English and lived for money and frocks. DouDou had a fabulous apartment and moved like a cobra but all her talk was small. DouDou drove Joanna to distraction and ultimately back to a reappraisal of London.

She rented a slum with high camp plasterwork in Notting Hill. It was three minutes' walk from a clothes market where she spent most of her change, and a repertory cinema where she spent the rest, learning discrimination through mass exposure. She worked for a while for the London office of the same New York fashion magazine but tired of frocks and colour. Successfully fishing for more commissions from newspapers, she specialised in interesting photographs of boring people. She won a prize for a picture of some property developers. Then, with barely three weeks' notice, her mother died and she had to go home.

She had been exchanging sporadic letters and postcards with her family ever since she came to Europe but it was only when she was back in Montana that she realised how far she had grown apart from them. The only one she had been truly close to was Ma, who had happily acted as a bridge between daughter and family. Now the precious, undervalued bridge was gone. Joanna had become an aunt several times over but the children cried whenever she held them. Her father had gone into a sympathetic death-like state by way of mourning and the long, monosyllabic evenings alone with him made her feel like a caged beast. She was long out of her radical phase but her eldest brother, Perry, who she had always idolised was, she now saw, an unashamedly far-right capitalist. As for the rest, unanimously married, they had discovered Jesus and/or shopping. The pictures she took of them and their children and developed in a local studio went down well, not least because they could tell their friends that the photographer had worked for *Vogue*. Shortly before Ma's cancer took hold, however, she had made the mistake of sending her a long and joyous declaration of the brave new horizons of her sexuality. Ma had duly passed this around the clan and, although they were far too polite to take the issue up with her, she could tell they were aching for her to leave.

Ma's legacy had been considerable for she was the sole survivor of a family of Swedish cattle ranchers. As her favourite and the only child yet to be 'settled', Joanna received the lion's share. She promptly sold this off to her brothers and sisters with the exception of a field which she kept on as a token gesture.

'It'll keep me American,' she told them, feeling less American by the minute.

She had not been back in London three months when she and a journalist were sent to cover the seventy-fifth anniversary of a Cornish music festival. The nearest Joanna had been to Cornwall was Hitchcock's *Rebecca*, which gave her some idea of the romance of the county but little inkling of its variety. The precious musicians and administrators she was expected to photograph at Trenellion, most of them from London, did little to endear her to the place. However, the journalist steered her out to lunch on a balcony overlooking the harbour at St Jacobs and she was lost.

Since her inheritance was farming money she had always felt that Ma would have approved of her buying an out-of-the-way smallholding with it rather than a pokey, gardenless flat in the capital. By comparison with London, the cost of living in Cornwall was so low that she found she could spend more time on less lucrative, more personal work there. Her bread and butter money still came from interesting photographs of boring people and no one had yet asked to publish a book of her work, but her haunting landscapes and curious still lives were slowly gaining attention. A gallery-cum-restaurant run by friends in Notting Hill had twice sold out of her work and she had exhibitions in two Cornish galleries every summer. The last showing had aroused the interest of the owner of a dockside art centre in Bristol. He was looking into the possibilities of a regional tour.

She stopped the car soon after Exeter, to fill its tank and buy herself a coffee and Danish pastry. She always stopped at the same café, one of an unpretentious chain found on A roads and dual carriageways, whose perky uniforms, cleanliness and cheap efficiency were the closest she had found in England to the perfection of the wayside diners in the US of A. Its management understood that the tired driver should be humoured like a nervous invalid, left at perfect liberty to order a large fried breakfast at tea-time or chocolate cake with hot fudge sauce and ice cream at eight a.m. as her whim dictated.

Deborah was still fast asleep so Joanna let her lie, locking her in the car, safe from marauding lorry drivers, and went to order coffee and Danish for one. She sat at a stool in the smoker's area, watching the car through the drizzle. Deborah seemed suddenly very small and very frail.

'Just imagine,' she thought. 'If I lifted her out, very, very gently, and laid her on that verge beside the trash can then drove off without her. She'd be lost. She couldn't cope at all. She'd probably hitch a ride with the first man to notice her there. You wakes the lady: you takes the lady.'

She stirred her coffee, took a bite from her Danish (which was astonishingly sweet even by her standards) and thought how strange it was to hear so many paltry details about a dead man from his grieving wife — his tastes in soup, after-shave, toothpaste, his sleeping habits and his sundry disapprovals — and yet be left with the sense that one had heard nothing at all; that the wife knew as little about him as oneself.

Ten

When Deborah woke from what seemed like hours of half-sleep, she found the car plunged in gloom, and driving rain being sluiced first one way then another by the windscreen wipers. There was no sign of any other traffic. No sign of life at all. The headlamps and thin, dusk light picked out the occasional tree, short and bent. Here and there she could see dark forms which could have been cows or sheep, only Joanna was driving too fast for her to identify them. From time to time the road would lurch between high, rocky banks, overgrown at the top with trees whose branches almost met, like black claws, overhead. A nightmare landscape. When Joanna had first mentioned Cornwall she had pictured brightly painted fishing boats, lobster pots and whitewashed cottages in the sunshine, or emerald green fields above the sea with ruined tin mines on the horizon. These were preconceptions born of a holiday she had taken once with a friend from school whose family had a certain intellectual reputation and were rather too musical, thereby not what Deborah's mother found 'altogether nice', but who had a distinguished holiday house and unlimited good will towards any friend of their daughter's. But then, Deborah consoled herself, that holiday had been in August and this was late February. Even in February, even in England, the sun shone sometimes.

'Raining,' she observed out loud.

'You've woken,' Joanna observed back. 'You've been dead to the world for hours.'

'I haven't seen rain like this for, oh, months. Years even. It never rained in Seneca; we just had very cold dew that was gone before breakfast. Where are we?'

'Nearly there. We've just crossed the county line. We're just past Launceston.'

'Oh. You drive so well.'

'You mean I drive so fast. I'll slow down if you like.'

'No, don't. I like it,' Deborah lied.

'Have you got your licence with you? It could come in handy down here. We're very cut off.'

'I don't drive. I mean, I can't.'

'*What*? How old are you?'

Joanna slowed up violently for a tractor that had suddenly loomed out of a field in front of them.

'I'm thirty-five,' Deborah confessed.

'Never! Start lying, Deborah. You could pass for twenty-eight.' Deborah said nothing. 'I mean it,' Joanna added.

'For what it's worth, with scars like these.' Deborah's little cuts ached. They always did when she had just woken up. She passed her hand over the scab that ran across her forehead.

'I've got time on my hands. I'll teach you. It can be your therapy.'

Deborah was terrified at the thought of finding herself behind the wheel; she always had been. She changed the subject.

'You said this place we're going to . . .'

'It's a farmhouse.'

'Yes. This farmhouse. It belongs to you?'

'Sure it does.' Joanna grinned. 'Every beautiful brick of it. I bought it for next to nothing, mind you.'

'It must be strange, living so far away.'

'Far from what? London?'

'Well. Yes.'

'The way *I* see it,' Joanna flapped a hand against her heart for emphasis, 'London is far away from *here*.'

'But the people. I mean . . . Did you have any problems? You know? Living on your own together?'

Joanna chuckled as she answered: 'Well, there's a strong Edwardian precedent for women to live "on their own together"; all those toothsome young widows. Christ! Sorry.'

'What? Oh. That's OK,' said Deborah.

'I'm just a widow,' she thought. 'I'm scarcely toothsome.'

'I think the locals take one look at us and assume we're plain unweddable,' Joanna laughed. The tractor pulled off into another gateway. 'Thank Christ for that,' she sighed, accelerating. 'And if,' she continued, 'you're thinking of us as two hapless chickens on a moor full of marauding foxy men, think again. Martyrstow is like something from a 1960s B-movie: *The Land Without Men*.'

'How do you mean? No men at all?' Deborah shuddered.

'Very few. It's never really been a man's place. In fact some old girls claim that Martyrstow is actually a bastardisation of Marthastow – Martha's place. Obviously there were men here once. They mined tin, and dug up some slate and they started a china clay works that's still going after a fashion. But the tin ran out on them and the slate quarry collapsed – I mean, really collapsed – and then the wars came along. Apparently not one Martyrstow boy who went to fight in the '14–'18 war came home in anything but a box and the last war took away most of the next generation.'

'Maybe they found jobs in London,' Deborah suggested weakly, peering out at the mist that now swirled around the car, and sympathising with such duplicity.

'You're as cynical as your sister. I think it's a great creepy story. There's a huge war memorial in the village square. They added another name to it a few years ago when a local farmer's son joined up and was blown apart at Goose Green. You should see the procession on Armistice Day. Miss O'Keefe the butcher plays the last post and all these women stand around in silence and their best hats. You see there's more to it than the wars. People never seem to have sons here. Judith says there's something in the water and that we're the subject of some nefarious Ministry of Defence experiment. And if people round here do have a son and he lives, he tends to head East as soon as possible, to Bristol, Exeter or Plymouth – somewhere where the work doesn't involve sheep and cows and where they don't have all those hungry females commenting on how nicely they're growing up. There are some men, some, but the doctor's a woman and so's the minister and the greengrocer and the mobile librarian and the pharmacist. Married men get uncomfortable here – and I reckon their wives get more so – so they move house. They don't go far; just closer to Launceston where there are pubs and supermarkets and less gossip and more men. So, no, in answer to your question. We don't have any problems as two lone females.'

Joanna fell silent and so did Deborah, who had never felt especially comfortable in the company of women, even at school, and was beginning to wonder whether she had done the right thing in refusing a recuperative spell in Gloucestershire. Wendy would have cosseted her, after a fashion, and Gilbert would have flirted with her hamfistedly whenever Wendy was out of the room. Instead she was going to a village of widows and spiteful spinsters to confront Judith who had not seen her since she was newly-wed and was probably rejoicing over her misfortune. Worse still, Judith probably couldn't care less. The house would be cold and boring and far from anywhere and Deborah would be ignored and neglected and unable to escape.

'Stop this,' she told herself. 'Stop this fantasy now.' She was tired. She was tired of travelling and, although she had barely woken, tired of Joanna's talk. She had a headache and she wasn't ready to meet Judith again. She wasn't ready for anything. All she wanted was to be allowed to climb into a warm bed in a silent room to enjoy the sleep of the dead.

'Oh Julian,' she thought. The lack of him came in great

waves when she was least prepared to withstand it. She felt it so strongly she half-expected Joanna to feel it too and turn to her as though she had spoken. 'Oh Julian.'

Joanna flicked on the radio, briefly twiddled it through four or five channels of chatter and loud music then impatiently flicked it quiet again. She snorted, uneasy.

'I dunno,' she said.

'What don't you know?' Deborah asked her.

'Your family's so weird. I can't believe you've never been to stay here.'

'I didn't know the address.'

'But that's what I'm getting at. What kind of family is it where the sisters don't let each other know where they are?'

'I told Judith when Julian and I were moved to Seneca. At least, I sent her a card.'

'Oh. So she's the one that hasn't kept in touch?'

'But I'm not blaming her or anything. She and Julian so obviously had nothing in common.'

'Yeah but what about she and you? You're sisters aren't you? Look.' Joanna slowed slightly to concentrate on the point she was making. 'Let me explain. I come from a big farming family; three sisters, three brothers. My Ma's dead but my father's still very much alive. I can't pretend that we have much in common – they grow wheat and farm cattle and I take pictures – and one of the reasons I came to England was that even on another side of the States that family was so big I didn't feel I'd really gotten away. But I see them once in a while, they write me and I ring back now and then. That's all. But I care if they live or die.'

'Why?'

Joanna laughed to herself and slapped the steering wheel.

'Jesus but you're like her! "Why?" They're my flesh and blood, that's why. There. You smiled so I know you didn't really mean it. Mind if I light up? We're nearly there and Jude doesn't like me to smoke in my own kitchen.'

'She smoked all the time when we were young. She used

to hang mothballs in her cupboard to cover the smell on her clothes.'

'Yeah? Well she's a very ex-smoker now. Ms Macrobiotic and all. Did you always tell tales?'

'No!' Deborah felt herself blush. 'May I?'

'Be my guest.'

Deborah helped herself to one of Joanna's cigarettes. Julian didn't like her to smoke either. It was a habit she had got into after the move to Seneca, encouraged by long dull spells when she would drift into the kitchen and would talk to the maid and cook; Gauloise girls both.

'Filthy habit,' she sighed. 'I ought to stop,' she added automatically. 'I only smoke when someone else does.'

Joanna caught her eye.

'Don't worry,' she told her. 'I won't tell.'

'Thanks.'

Joanna reached for a small atomiser in her bag and squirted herself behind each ear. A delicious scent of orange and vanilla briefly cut through the smell of tobacco.

'Delicious,' said Deborah.

'Like it, huh? I get it mixed for me by this really cute herbalist who has a stall in the market. We should go there. He stocks all sorts of healing oils and stuff. But go on. Tell me before we get home. What is it with you two? Let me tell you now, Judith never, but never, talks about family. She says her childhood was dull and family talk bores her.'

'I must make the effort to talk,' Deborah thought. 'I've been so rude sleeping all this time while she drove.'

'I suppose it was quite dull,' she said. 'Our parents were very quiet people. I suppose one would call them respectable. He was an orthodontist.'

'That's like a dentist?'

'Yes. In a way. A bit more so, I think. And she didn't do anything much. She arranged flowers a lot and cooked. She adored him.' She had said this automatically but was still surprised when Joanna caught her out.

'Not what Judith told me,' Joanna said.

'Well Judith never really understood them,' she snapped back. She felt her rare temper flare.

'Sorry I spoke.'

'God. Sorry Joanna. It's only that I . . . well.'

Deborah reached for that morning's wet handkerchief and blew hard. Her nose was painfully sore, as if she had a cold.

'Colds and grief,' she said, surprised at her own wit, 'no cure for either but time,' and she blew again.

'Oh don't cry, honey,' Joanna pleaded. 'I'm sorry. Too many questions.'

'I'm not crying.' Deborah wiped the tip of her nose dry. 'It's perfectly all right. Not used to these cigarettes, that's all.'

'They are on the long side. I find long ones save on lighter fuel. Time to stub out anyway,' Joanna added, doing so. 'We're there.'

She swung the car off the road and onto a rough track with grass in the middle. Deborah peered through the mist and saw several low-slung windows lit up, two hundred or so yards away. Another light was turned on as she saw someone walk from one room into another.

'We were just a very normal, British family, I suppose,' she said to calm her nerves as Joanna honked the horn and they drew near. 'I think Judith was so much brighter than we were, so much more imaginative. That probably made our life feel rather small to her. I think she always wanted to break away. She was always the naughty one; always getting into scrapes and getting punished. I expect she's told you I was always Daddy's little girl.'

Eleven

Deborah looked awful. The healthy head of golden waves which Judith had once found so demoralising had turned a lifeless shade of ash. Either Deborah or the hospital had cut it short and almost straight which emphasised the foolish roundness of her face. Two deep anxiety lines had settled on her forehead and she had lost too much weight which went badly with her soft, still childish features, giving her gloomy dewlaps on either side of her mouth. Her face and what was visible of her hands and forearms were shockingly peppered with little red-brown scabs. A gash on her forehead, nearly four inches long, had begun to heal but was sure to leave a scar.

In the heat of her preparations, Judith had momentarily forgotten that her sister would have aged since her wedding day and that she was a recent bomb victim. Shocked, she greeted her without thinking, kissing her cheek then drawing her into a close hug. It was only when she turned to welcome Joanna too and realised that she was embarrassed to greet her as warmly as she would have liked that the situation's multiple awkwardness returned to her.

'You've gone a wonderful colour,' was all she could think to say to her lover as she contented herself with merely hugging her. Joanna smelt of cigarettes mixed as usual with the scent she sprayed on in an effort to smother one smell with another one. Meeting Judith's gaze, she smiled sexily with one corner of her mouth and raised her eyes ever so slightly to heaven. 'You must both be exhausted,' Judith told her. 'Supper's all ready for you.'

'I am starving,' Joanna said, emphasising each word. 'Here, hon, if you want to show Debs her room, I'll get the other bags out.' She opened the door again. 'There are quite a few.'

So Judith found herself alone and shy with her sister.

'Sorry,' she said. 'Joanna tends to shorten names automatically. If you'd rather she didn't, just tell her. She won't care. She probably didn't even notice herself do it.'

'I've been "Debs" since breakfast.'

'Oh. Do you mind?'

'I'm not sure, yet.'

'I'll show you your room.'

She led Deborah out of the kitchen, across the sitting room, where a fire was burning, and through the strange, low doorway onto the back staircase. 'You've got your own stairs,' Judith said over her shoulder. 'From that door onwards, this is all your own territory and we won't even come in with a Hoover unless invited.'

The staircase, narrow already, had been made narrower still by having its walls lined from floor to ceiling with bookshelves. Like all the shelves in the house, these were packed, extra books lying horizontally across the tops of rows wherever there was no more space. Deborah stopped to stare.

'They always used to tell me to borrow books from the library rather than waste my pocket money on things I'd never read again,' Judith reminded her. 'But I always insisted on having my own. I still do and they were right – I hardly ever get round to rereading anything.'

'Julian never let me buy either,' Deborah told her. 'Or only paperbacks and I had to give those to the hospital when I'd finished with them. These are nice.' She touched the spines in passing. 'The colours make it feel warm.' Looking down on her from the landing, Judith suddenly heard her mother's

voice at its rare, loving pitch; so rare that in time she had
come to think of it as deceitful.

'Sorry,' said Deborah following her upstairs, 'I'm dawdling
as usual.'

'Here's your room.' Judith gestured. 'I hope it's warm
enough. You'll probably feel the cold terribly after . . . after
Abroad.'

'It feels fine.' Deborah sat on the bed and smiled gamely.

'I've been airing the bed all day but you might need
another hot water bottle when you turn in. And there's a
little bathroom through there. Joanna converted this place a
few years before I moved in. There are bathrooms everywhere
with incredibly powerful showers that use up just as much
water as a bath, which I thought rather defeated the object of
the exercise. I'd always thought showers an economy measure
but apparently they're a pleasure in their own right.'

Judith heard herself beginning to witter and began to back
towards the door.

'It's a lovely room,' said Deborah. 'It's a lovely house.
Mummy . . . she never came here, did she?'

'No,' Judith said, thinking, 'But she's here now.'

Deborah ran a hand over the quilt beneath her.

'I can hardly wait to climb into bed,' she said. 'You're
sure I'm not messing up your sleeping arrangements? Is this
normally your room? Seeing all those books on the way up I
thought perhaps . . .'

'No. Our room's over on the other side. You go back through
the kitchen, through the hall where the proper front door is
which we never use, and it's up some stairs off Joanna's den,
straight ahead of you.'

Deborah visibly gulped.

'Oh,' she said, blankly. Then with altogether more understanding, 'Oh! God I'm stupid.'

Not ready to deal with the substantial penny she heard
dropping, Judith resumed her brisk hostess tone.

'That's right. So if you need us suddenly in the night,

that's where we'll be. Now I'd better see if Joanna needs a hand. Towels and things are in the bathroom. Help yourself to anything you find in the cupboard that takes your fancy – probably all a bit herbal for your tastes. And supper'll be in around twenty minutes. OK?'

'OK,' said Deborah who now seemed to be clutching her bag defensively to her chest.

Leaving her sister to unpack – no mean feat judging from the quantity of luggage which Joanna had piled discreetly at the foot of the staircase – Judith hurried to their bedroom. Joanna had collapsed on the bed. She smiled in exhausted welcome without opening her eyes. Judith pulled off Joanna's suede boots then climbed onto the bed beside her. She gave Joanna a perfunctory kiss then flopped back on the pillows with a sigh. Joanna opened her eyes and raised her head slightly.

'Look what I brought you back,' she said.

'Where?'

'In a yellow paper bag on the floor someplace.'

Judith slid off the bed and rummaged amongst the half-unpacked jumble of clean and dirty clothes. She found the bag and in it a beautiful, loosely-cut silk shirt. It was the colour of dried blood and had black embroidery at the collar and cuffs.

'You shouldn't,' she said.

'But I did,' Joanna retorted sleepily.

'Thank you. It's lovely. I'll wear it tomorrow.'

Judith climbed back onto the bed and kissed her again. She lay back against the pillows and let out another heavy sigh.

'What is it?' asked Joanna.

'Deborah.'

'Did I do wrong?'

'No.' Judith shook her head and reached out to run a hand across Joanna's thick hair. 'No. You did right. Very right. But there's so much about her I'd forgotten until now.'

'Oh? Like what?' Joanna slid a hand around to the nape of Judith's neck and began to massage it softly.

'Like her being my *younger* sister.'

'She doesn't look it.'

'Oh I couldn't care less about the age difference. What I hate is that old feeling – you had younger sisters, you must remember what it was like – of having her trail around after me like a pet dog that's also somebody's spy.' Judith snorted self-mockingly. 'She's grown up to look so like our mother! It's almost sinister.'

'Reincarnation?'

'Precisely. For a moment on the stairs to her room, I almost expected her to ask me, no to *tell* me, in the nicest possible way, to dust my bookshelves before my father came home and she felt compelled to show him what a slattern I was.'

'Were you?'

'No more than any other child. "Mummy" was obsessive about dirt. We had special indoor shoes we had to change into in the kitchen to spare the carpets. When friends came to play they had to take their shoes off too and borrow our slippers.'

'Weird!'

'They didn't come very often. I was too embarrassed. And I hated the thought of stories going around school about what our house was like. Deborah used to insist on having nightmarish birthday parties with jelly and balloons. "Mummy" would organise long games which she took far too seriously. There was always a quiz with questions lifted from the encyclopaedia, which were far too difficult. She always lost her temper. The only time I got into a fight at school was the day after one of dear little Deborah's parties, when I caught another girl standing on a desk and imitating my mother doling out prizes.'

'Who won?'

'I did. I always pulled hair. If you pull someone's hair hard enough they can hardly move for the pain.'

'Ooh!' Joanna breathed and running her fingers through Judith's hair, gently tugged her head back before taking little nips at her chin and neck. Judith laughed and pulled her tightly against her, legs wrapped around her thighs. She shut her eyes as they kissed deeply, relishing the weight of Joanna's body against hers. Aroused, she slid down slightly and began to nuzzle at her lover's breasts, easing her nose between the buttons of her shirtfront. Joanna allowed this for a minute or two then, tired, rolled back onto her side, gently pulling Judith's head level with her own again.

'It's good to be back,' she said, and kissed her nose.

'Good to have you,' Judith replied. 'I *hate* it when you're away.'

'Glad to hear it.' Joanna smiled and shut her eyes. 'Don't let me fall asleep,' she said, 'or I won't wake till tomorrow afternoon.'

'Sleep then.' Judith stroked her glorious red hair across the pillows. Sometimes she did this while Joanna was still deep in slumber, fanning the hair out around her face, turning her into something by Rossetti or Augustus John. 'Sleep if you need to.'

'No.' Joanna yawned. 'I must get up and eat with you.' She opened her eyes. 'Can't leave you to face Miss Moppet on your own.'

'Has she been crying much?'

'Off and on. It's going to get a whole lot worse before it gets better. She's still in shock. Imagine if you'd had to watch me blown apart by a car bomb just after breakfast.'

'Don't!' Judith frowned and looked away to where a spider's web, loosed from its moorings, was shifting in a draught. 'I only met him twice,' she said quietly. 'He struck me as such a creep.' Joanna planted a kiss on her ear. 'Did you talk about us much?' Judith asked her.

'Not really. I mean, she wanted to know how I knew you and so on.'

'How we met?'

'No. Just how I came to know you. I explained that we shared a house.'

'I have the most awful feeling you see,' Judith turned back to her, 'that she didn't realise you were my lover until a few minutes ago. I thought that, before she died, "Mummy" would have been sure to tell her – anything to stir up animosity – but I don't think she can have done. Deborah was always shielded from unpalatable truths – I think we were just one more.'

'Oh Christ,' Joanna groaned.

'Still want to join us for herby dumplings and stew?'

Joanna sat up, tidied her hair with a few slow gestures and rubbed her eyes.

'Dear heart,' she said, reaching for her boots once more, 'I want a ringside seat.'

Twelve

The bed and window of the spare room faced east, so the mounting sun, when there was any, fell directly upon the occupant's face. When she opened her window the night before, Deborah had failed to draw the curtains again. She had been woken early as much by the bleating of nursing sheep as by the watery sunlight, and the rapid recollection of her sad position and strange surroundings roused her further. Sitting up against her pillows, she stared despairingly at her alarm clock then around her at the room.

The walls were roughly panelled in wood which had been painted white. The floor, too, was white but was scattered with thick, brightly coloured rugs not unlike the ones sold in Seneca. There was an old pine chest of drawers and a wardrobe prettily painted in grey and pale blue. A battered mirror hung over the chest of drawers while the wall opposite it, on her right, was barely visible beneath some thirty or forty watercolours of the seaside. She had no idea how far away the sea could be. She had an image in her mind of Cornwall as the 'foot' of Britain but no inkling of whether this house was at its toe, heel or instep. She wondered where all these objects came from. When their mother died, Deborah had divided her belongings between them so as to be seen to be fair. Judith had not wanted anything in the end and Deborah could not now remember what she had persuaded her to take. So far she had seen no piece of furniture, no painting, not so much as a cushion she remembered from her childhood. Her own share, judiciously edited on receipt by Julian, was still in Seneca awaiting instructions. Deborah had been too tired to take things in when they stopped off in Clapham; perhaps Judith's share was kept there.

She might have been doing her sister an injustice, but she suspected that the pile of books on the bedside table had been carefully selected by her according to what she thought Deborah's mental powers could compass. There were several children's novels – *The Secret Garden*, *A Dog so Small*, *Stig of the Dump* – which she had indeed glanced at with a pang of nostalgia but there were also *My Golden Book of Puppies*, *Quickie Recipes for Lasting Romance* and a lavishly illustrated biography of Clark Gable. The last three belonged, she assumed, to Joanna. A fleeting probe of the small library on the stairs had confirmed that Judith continued to mark her every book with her name and its date and place of purchase.

A breath of cold wind puffed out the curtain. Deborah shuddered, began to slide back beneath her quilt then decided to get up. She pulled her dressing gown about her and shuffled to the bathroom. She sat to pee in the semi-darkness then fumbled for her toothbrush and the light switch. Her face in the brutally well-lit mirror there was a shock. Her hair was badly in need of a new blonding rinse; its customary gold, which had suffered so in the Senecan sun, had faded almost to the point of greyness. Curled in sleep and fixed in sweat, most of it stood on end. One cheek bore marks from her pillow's creases and her eyes were pinched and gummy, like a cartoon drunkard's – a resemblance abetted by her generally battered appearance. After brushing her teeth, she filled the sink with hot water, soaked her flannel in it then began to splash and rub her waking skin, feeling little crusts of scab wash away.

Until recently she had never thought it possible to cry in one's sleep. The morning after Julian's murder she had woken unable to open her eyes and a nurse, drawn by her frightened calls, dabbed them clear and gently explained that they had been quite glued up with tears. Deborah found the discovery comforting. It seemed to prove that her grief was no mere indulgence of the conscious mind but a bodily function. She liked the thought that her whole body – fingers and heart, liver and lights – suffered from Julian's death, that it mourned on a night shift, shedding tears on her behalf while her grieving mind rested. At times, without warning, she had been disconcerted by twitches of something far from mourning – something shameful bordering upon relief – at the violent divorce fate had granted her. The fact that she could cry over Julian in her sleep was a vindication of her fidelity, tangible evidence of what she was *really* feeling.

She dressed carefully, pulled back her quilt to air, then made her way down the creaking, book-lined stairs. The stove was still warming the kitchen deliciously. Having divined that it also heated the water for tea, she filled the kettle which she set on a hotplate to boil. Waiting, she tracked down the teabags and a mug then stole a biscuit from a generous jarful and looked out of the window over the sink. Although the sky was still leaden with cloud, the drizzle had stopped. The kettle still felt stone-cold so she stole another biscuit, borrowed some boots and a coat and let herself out.

The house was a long building of whitewashed stone, one room deep. Its roof, which dipped and rose alarmingly, was made of some of the thickest, broadest slates that she had ever seen. The kitchen door gave onto one end of a puddled, gravelled yard. Straight ahead, a track led over a cattle grid and down a steep hill between high-banked hedges. Even though the day was hardly clear, Deborah could see over miles of fields from the doorstep. These were not huge, squared-off expanses like the Wiltshire fields of her youth, but a random affair of odd-shaped, smaller patches, defined by turf-topped walls or thick hedgerows. To her left, across the yard was an old barn, again with a thick-tiled roof.

She walked around the house in the other direction, beneath her bedroom window, and was surprised to find that the building was perched on the very edge of a high moor. A low, winding wall defined a paddock, which seemed to belong to the house, and beyond that, invading a system of other walls fallen into disrepair, and stretching as far as the eye could see, was an astonishing wilderness. Her mind was still used to the sands, ochres and palms around Seneca. The only grass there, around the wealthier houses and scattering of consulates, had been an unconvincing product, imported by the homesick, rarely walked upon, and fed by their sprinklers beneath the stars. Here she climbed a slate stile set into the wall and found herself at the edge of mile upon mile of coarse wild grass, thickened by the cropping of cattle and, she assumed, plenty of drizzle like yesterday's. There were gorse bushes, the odd twisted thorn tree and, here and there, a patch of dried-up heather but the general impression was one of uninterrupted rock and grass. The rock was everywhere; inexplicable outcrops varying in size from a footstool to a large car. There were two high hills in the distance, iron grey with the stuff, and it looked almost as though the boulders Deborah was walking past were the result of some ancient volcanic eruption. Only they were solid granite, not lava. Early lambs, muddy and elastic, wobbled amongst them, warned by their mothers of the approach of a stranger. Deborah watched one being suckled, watched the frantic flicking of its skinny tail as it butted and drank. She sought an enchanting diversion in this from the louring landscape but the ewe stared at her out of unsentimental snake's eyes, bleated and ran from her sight behind a gorse bush.

Deborah walked on and came across a stone circle. This was nothing on the Stonehenge scale – the rocks were no more than three or four feet high – but its lesser scale and tidier arrangement made it seem more plausible and, therefore, more frightening. She was not surprised to see a hollow in its centre, charred by bonfires. Conjuring youthful memories of running widdershins around a church, she walked to the blackened earth and turned slowly in a half-circle until she was looking back towards the farm-house. No sheep had strayed within the ring. One, passing, paused to catch her eye and bleat with manic insistence. Her nerve failed her and Deborah walked swiftly back the way she had come.

The kettle was boiling fiercely. She wrapped her hand in a cloth to protect it from the steam then poured it over the teabag she had set out in a mug. As she reached into the jar for another biscuit she was startled by Judith calling out from upstairs.

'Oh God! Oh! Oh! Oh no! Oh yes! Yes! Jesus I love you I love you I *love* you!'

Deborah froze, listening, her hand nestling amongst the biscuits. She heard her sister's ecstatic moans subside into indistinct mumbles then bubble up into laughter. Joanna's deeper voice joined in. Then there was a pause before Joanna began to speak. Her words were distorted – it sounded as though she were trying to talk and lick at the same time.

'What?' Judith laughed.

'I said,' Deborah heard Joanna chuckle quite distinctly, 'sister, you are *still* my academic hotbox!'

Slopping hot tea on her wrist as she fled, Deborah hurried to the comparative security of her bedroom. She tore off her clothes, pulled her nightdress back on, folded her clothes and jumped back into bed. There she lay sipping the scalding tea and shivering.

She had come across several married homosexual men in diplomatic circles, but she had never knowingly met a lesbian. Now, in little more than twenty-four hours, she had come to have two in her life; one for a sister and one for an abductor-cum-hostess. Once Judith left home for university, she had never come back for more than a minimal weekend, but Deborah had found no difficulty in sniffing out evidence that she enjoyed a full sex life. A normal one. With men. Julian had taken his young wife to a rowdy London party once where pornographic videos were being watched by a furtive gathering around a television. Julian had been busy in another room which left Deborah free to watch and learn. The sporadic lesbian scenes made it clear that women could pleasure one another more than adequately – but it was made just as clear that the arrangement was only a makeshift one rendered redundant by the timely arrival of an interested man. In what little communication they had shared before it petered out altogether with their mother's death, Judith had been brutally honest about the ease with which she passed from one man to another. With hindsight Deborah wondered whether this had not been a smokescreen of bravado.

The idea of her sister indulging in lesbian sex disgusted her even though she could see that it was perhaps the natural expression of Judith's rebellion against those who had loved and nurtured her, against home, family and all these stood for. Deborah found that it also dismayed her, for it bore no recognisable relation to the social forms upon which her life had always been founded. Were Judith and Joanna a firm couple, mimicking the stability of a man and wife? Or were they, like the women in the videos, sexual parasites who would batten onto whoever entered their sphere? If an available man came to stay, would the configuration change? Would catfights ensue? At supper last night she had studiously avoided any reference to sleeping arrangements, marriage, men or even Julian for fear of initiating the difficult conversation which she sensed could not be held off indefinitely.

Worst of all, as she huddled against the pillows, Deborah felt that Judith's perversion lent an extra weight to her grief. With her man torn from her she felt that fate would implicate her in the terrible sadness of these other manless women. Without Julian she felt she had lost her definition; imprisoned by embarrassment in this lonely, female household she feared her carefully achieved edges would blur still further.

Thirteen

The cat was a female tabby, wretchedly thin, her lank coat matted with splashes of mud. She was hurrying back and forth along a line two feet from the plastic bowl Judith held out to her. She mewed on every other turn, pausing to stare at the food she wanted so badly but was too afraid to approach.

'Come on,' Judith coaxed. 'Eat. I won't hurt you. Come on.'

The cat paused again, mewed once more then, risking all for hunger, darted forward and began to eat. Purring, she seized a mouthful of sardine then backed away with it. That mouthful gone, she darted forward for another which, with a flash of grey-green eyes at Judith, she ate on the spot. Her tail ceased its twitching as she fed.

'Good girl,' Judith whispered. 'Isn't that good?'

The cat had almost finished its second fish. Judith held the bowl as still as she could, listening to the crunching of tiny bones. Perhaps now that she had eaten, the tabby would relax sufficiently to wash herself. For all the poor condition of her coat, her markings were attractive. Not a great cat lover before, Judith had not noticed until she began work at the sanctuary that tabby markings were perfectly symmetrical. Ever since Esther had pointed out how one half, from nose to tail, was a hair-for-hair repetition of the other, Judith had found herself examining every tabby she saw, seeking an exception to the rule.

The cat was licking out the bowl now, still purring. Very slowly, Judith reached out her free hand and began to stroke her, feeling the bones beneath the skin. At first the cat seemed to enjoy this. She butted Judith's palm with her head and stretched herself slightly as Judith's hand ran along her spine. Then, suddenly outraged or terror-struck, she let out a low yowl and slashed the side of Judith's wrist with a forepaw. Judith recoiled, sucking the scratches while the tabby retreated into the farthest corner of the pen, ears flat, tail lashing. Two other cats, shyer still, watched this exchange from the gloom of a cardboard box a few feet away. Chastened, Judith let herself out and fed the rest of her charges. She had recently freed three of them. They had become quite tame, if not house-trained, and it seemed cruel to continue to keep them in cages. Until a home could be found for them she would allow them to roam the neighbourhood. Trusties, they showed little desire to stray far and had been waiting for Judith when she arrived. She had fed them first and now they followed at her heels as she moved from cage to cage, slipping between each other and purring their cupboard love. With luck they would charm their way into local households or at least find an alternative food source. It was surprising how people were quite prepared to set out food for a cat every day without the admission that they had adopted it. Once she had finished her round, she held and stroked each in turn. She did not want them to become unused to the sensation and revert to savagery.

'How's Catwoman?'

Esther had ventured downstairs and was sitting at her desk. She was picking through the overflowing contents of a drawer which she had pulled out and set on the top of it.

'Fine, thanks.' Judith sat heavily on an armchair, raising a small dustcloud which made her sneeze. 'Bleeding to death.' She held up her wrist which she had wrapped in a handkerchief. Esther sucked in the air between her teeth.

'Nasty,' she said. 'Which brute did that?'

'The new tabby. Michelle told us about it when she brought the post this morning. Some little boys had it tied up in Ted Varney's cowshed. Her little brother had been shown it after school and was too scared to set it free himself. It was half-strangled, of course, and petrified of being trodden on. It looked as though they'd got bored of feeding it too.'

Esther shook her head and continued to pick through the envelopes and packages before her.

'What are you looking for?' Judith asked.

'An old leather writing case. Not very thrilling in itself but it had some old photographs inside which I wanted you to see.'

'What of?'

'That would spoil the surprise.'

'Pictures of your childhood?' Judith drew her legs up beside her.

'Let's say of my heady youth. Old, *old* pictures.' Esther chuckled. She gave up on the drawer before her and slid it back into the desk, scattering papers as she did so. She was looking weak today; her normally lively face seemed tired, its skin slacker than usual. 'Damn!' she said. 'I suppose I should try this one.' She tugged out another drawer. It seemed to be full of bills and bank statements, many of them unopened. 'I really ought to be throwing this lot out. My father brought us up to be so careful about money and accounts. I've always kept everything in case the Tax Man or my solicitor wanted to know something from ten or twenty years ago, but they never have. When you get to my very great age, Judith, you'll find that your commonest emotion isn't regret for missed opportunities but irritation at hour upon tedious hour of wasted effort. Until I was forty I used to cut out every delicious recipe I came across in a magazine and stick it in a file. That file is fat and probably fascinating now but I swear I never used it. Not once in twenty-five years of cookery. You know why? No bloody index!' She laughed bitterly as she took up a handful of papers and began to pick through them. 'My God.'

'What?'

'I quite forgot to ask you about your sister Dorothy.'

'Deborah.'

'How is she?'

'Pretty much a wreck. She hardly leaves her room.'

'Dreadful thing to happen, especially if she's as feeble-minded as you make out. Things will get far worse before they get better, you know. Shock deaths are always the worst because they're so hard to accept. You'll probably find that now that she's got peace and quiet and is far away from it all, the full horror is only just dawning on her.'

Judith sat thinking about this while Esther rummaged.

'I've hardly seen her today,' she said. 'Whenever she tries to talk it makes her cry. When I took some lunch up to her room, she'd been crying so much I hardly recognised her. I tried to touch her but she sort of shrank away. I suppose I should have ignored that and forced a hug on her or something. I felt so helpless confronted with that kind of, well, I suppose it was despair. I don't know her really. That wouldn't matter − comforting strangers is usually easier − but the trouble is that all I know is how she was when she was younger and I hated her then. Loathed her precious guts. She's too distant from everything I know and love for me to hate her now, but I don't like her. Not at all.' Judith ran out of words and sat picking at her cuticles and picturing Deborah's near-hysterical tears. Guests always introduced different smells into the spare room: disinfectant, bath oil, athlete's foot powder, hair gel, mouthwash, dope. Deborah's smells − lavender bags and an expensive scent Judith could not place but which Joanna had called 'Hetero No. 5' − seemed more alien than the usual ones. At least, they emphasised the void between them to which neither sister had openly alluded. She had mentioned this to Joanna over lunch.

'Can't you just see the blurb on the paperback edition?' Joanna had quipped. '"Born of one man's sperm, they had evolved into creatures as utterly opposed as cat . . . to *dog*!"'

'Want some whisky?' Esther fished a half-bottle out from among the papers. 'There are some cleanish glasses in that corner cupboard.' Judith blew the dust from two old crystal port glasses, which were all the cupboard contained, and Esther splashed a tot into each of them. '"Like" doesn't come into it with family,' she went on. '"Like" requires freedom of choice. You can't like people who are thrust upon you unless they leave it entirely up to you. And that's not how most families behave. Oh blast this rubbish!' With a flip of her hand she sent a sheaf of bills spinning to the floor then she replaced the drawer.

'Esther, don't bother if it's just for me.'

'It isn't just for you. *I* want to see those photographs! I can't think why I hid them so well. Or maybe I can. Maybe it was the last time I had someone to stay — years ago probably. People are so bloody nosey.'

'Sorry.'

'Not you, you goose. People. There again, I might always have just put it down somewhere unlikely without thinking. There's a mysterious tide in this house that sweeps things away and they don't resurface until years later, by which time one has lost all need of them. They go to what my late young husband called the Land of the Single Sock. Are you warm enough sitting there?'

'I'm frozen.'

'Let's go upstairs. You can crouch by the fire with Bunting while I try the bureau in the bedroom. I should have looked there first.'

Bunting was hogging the electric fire as usual. He rolled his eyes at Judith when she came in and thumped his tail on the carpet but clung stoutly to his warm advantage. She pulled her chair closer so that she could at least thaw her knees. Glasses on the end of her nose, Esther began her assault on a Dutch bureau on the other side of the fireplace. Judith sipped her whisky.

'So what about your family?' she asked. 'Did you like them or were they too much thrust upon you?'

'My husband mercifully had none to speak of but as for my own, well, until I met him they were fairly inescapable. I had a brother and a sister, both much older than me which was excellent, one of each parent and a convoy of redoubtable married aunts. Being a daughter I was of no consequence whatever until of marriageable age. I was taken in to say hello to my parents at breakfast and hello it's me again at bedtime and I was wheeled out for the aunts to inspect but otherwise I was left in peace. So, I spent most of my infancy trailing round after the gardener getting absolutely filthy, then I was parcelled off to a boarding school in Hampshire where I spent most of my time sloping off from lacrosse to learn how to prune roses and so on from the groundsmen. My mother died when I was fourteen, which meant almost nothing to me, I knew her so little. She left me this ring, though. I'll need to sell it soon. My fingers have got so stout they'll have to cut it off.' She was lost in silent contemplation of her hands.

'What about your father?' Judith prompted.

'He started taking an interest in my fate a couple of years later and I can tell you *that*,' Esther raised a hand for emphasis while continuing with her search, '*that* was a revelation. All my childhood he was no more than a bogeyman – someone who said grace when we ate together on Sundays, pinched my cheek in passing and was wheeled out as a threat if I misbehaved. And suddenly I was expected to drink sherry with the silly man and take an interest in what he had to say.'

'What was he like?'

Esther paused, momentarily distracted by a mound of exercise books she had discovered.

'Pompous ass,' she muttered and chewed briefly at her lower lip. 'Just like my brother, George.'

'What happened to George?'

'Senior civil servant. Married a pale, manageable thing from King's Lynn. Coronary the week after he retired. Out like a light. No great loss.'

'And your sister?'

'Serena? Moved to New Zealand and married a sheep farmer. Wise girl. He never came to much but at least she got away. Nothing like geography to make one's feelings felt.'

Esther was becoming more and more embroiled in what she was finding, her tone, less and less focused. Judith fell silent for a minute or two, bending forward to stroke Bunting who gave her all his attention, rolling on his back and happily baring a fang. Their encounters often ended this way, with Judith sensing that she needed the conversation more than Esther did, and humiliated that she could have thought otherwise.

'I must go.' She stood.

'Must you?' Esther waved a pink notebook. 'But I was going to find you those wretched photographs. I'm sure they're in here somewhere . . .' She resumed her search.

'I thought we agreed that you were looking for your sake not for mine.'

'You'd be interested. I know you would.'

'Of course, but don't turn the house upside down.' Judith laid a hand on Esther's bony shoulder then withdrew it, remembering that they never touched. Bunting had risen finally and was having a scratch and a stretch in preparation for lying down once more to toast the other side.

'I'll stop soon and scrounge something to eat. I'm pooped. I promised old What'sherface I'd draft her a letter to send to Restormel Council about the badgers. Must you go?'

'Yes.'

'Well hang on a second.' Esther closed one drawer and opened another which was filled with old jars, lipsticks and what looked like a hoard of powder puffs. 'Give this to that poor sister of yours with my love. Give it to Deirdre.'

'Deborah.'

'Quite. Give it to her and tell her I know how she feels.'

'But it's lovely.'

'So? I never use it. It goes with the brush and those other

things on the dressing table but I kept knocking it off. She can fill it with flower water of something.'

'Esther, she'll be thrilled.'

'Bye, then.'

It was a cut-glass cologne bottle with a silver stopper and a little pump to spray the contents into the air. Judith was tempted to keep it for herself – Esther would never have known. On her return she climbed the spare room stairs to ask what Deborah felt like eating for supper however, and the muffled, childish sobs from behind the door dispersed her envy.

Fourteen

For the next two and a half weeks, Deborah's hostesses went about their usual business. Judith tried in vain to dissuade her novel's hero from matricide, even going so far as to rewrite large portions of the extant manuscript – something unheard of when she was still at work on a first draft. Then she resorted to diversionary tactics borrowed from the detective fiction she had read in Joanna's absence. Abandoning Edgar, knife in hand, half-way up the stairs, she pursued an adultery, a furious marital confrontation and a promising piece of pent-up confessional; all three simultaneous developments in the lives of her other characters. Every afternoon, of course, she went to feed and muck out the cats in the sanctuary then spent time talking with Esther. Esther made no further mention of her old writing-case or photographs; she had apparently given them up for lost.

Joanna was asked to make day trips to take photographs in Bristol, Cardiff and a hotel on Exmoor. On the mornings when she was at home, she retreated to her dark room to spend frowning hours developing the fruits of these commissions and her portraits of Seneca's working children. Emerging at around one, she would eat a light lunch with Judith, then retreat to her den to relax with a cup of coffee and the day's newspaper. Unless there was torrential rain, Judith would hear her emerge after forty minutes or so and stride across the yard to open the barn doors. Joanna would saddle up her mare,

Fleet, and ride across the moor, returning two hours later with a high colour, soaked jeans and an air of animal exhilaration that left Judith feeling more than ever slight and brown.

Deborah was not ignored in all this, but left in peace. As Esther had warned might be the case, she suffered a delayed reaction. Julian's funeral and the business of packing up and leaving Seneca in such a rush had temporarily submerged her grief. Thrust into Joanna's quirkily glamorous company, she had remained as far as possible on what she thought of as her best behaviour; behaviour that would not have embarrassed Julian. Now that she had come to a rest at Martyrstow, however, and found herself surrounded by silence and mists and as back of beyond as she had ever been in her life (including Julian's deeply minor African posting before Seneca), she gave up. She retreated into her thoughts. Occasionally she could be found in the kitchen, making herself cups of tea and painfully tidy plates of bread and butter or washing her used-up stocks of handkerchiefs at the sink. She declined all offers of excursions, walks and rides with faint horror, pleading exhaustion. Pretext became truth and she found herself dozing her days away in her bedroom armchair in between outings to the kitchen. With remarkably little discussion, Judith and Joanna found they were treating her as an invalid, as though it were the most ordinary thing in the world for a woman in her thirties to shun fresh air and daylight and confine herself to her room.

'Am I being terribly rude?' she asked Joanna one morning, caught washing up her breakfast things after eleven.

'Debs, we asked you here so you could unwind. Stay in your room if it helps you relax. Stay in bed, if you like. If you suddenly need company, you know where to find us, and if you can't find us, just pick up the kitchen intercom and one of us will answer. OK?'

She rarely got out of her nightclothes, shuffling forlornly around in dressing gown and slippers, and had often had to leave the table during meals as a fit of crying swamped her.

'I'm sorry,' she would shudder as she retreated back to her room.

Half an hour later, one of them would leave her uneaten meal on a tray on the landing for her. They would tap on her door to let her know it was there.

Judith couldn't help but notice the similarity between Deborah's behaviour and that of the cats in her care. Evening after evening, the new tabby female would allow herself to be stroked and petted only to retire in sudden, spitting confusion on recalling her half-wild state. Deborah's halting attempts to behave normally, defeated by insuperable emotions, were like the stray's tentative bids for friendship. Although she thought it fairer not to brood too much on the similarities between her mother and sister, she could not help remembering how her mother had acted after their father's death. Apart from the one instance when they moved house, and had been forced to do without baths and eat several meals on packing cases, this had been the only time in her memory when family propriety had been abandoned.

Her father died from a heart attack in his sleep. Deborah was the first to be told and her screams woke Judith. Undertakers took his great, thick body away the next morning, under Judith's fascinated gaze. For the next three days and the week after the funeral their mother took to her bed. She cried wildly, even shouted obscenities whenever Deborah tried to go to her, so it was left to Judith to carry in her meals on a tray. Excused school 'until you feel ready to return' the teenaged sisters had sat around downstairs, unsupervised. Judith kept to the kitchen. Deborah sat in their father's armchair in the sitting room and watched more television and ate more unsuitable food than in her entire life. Apart from a brief, terrifyingly controlled, appearance at the funeral, their mother lay in bed, hair unbrushed, nightdress splashed with food. She wept, she kept the curtains drawn, she wrote long, furious letters which she tore up and burned in the bedroom grate and she slept hour upon hour, snoring into the increasingly fetid air. For eleven unforgettable days, after which she acted as though nothing had happened, spick and span Mummy went wild. This weird spell was etched on Judith's memory less from the trauma of losing her father than because in those hours spent waiting at the kitchen table, she had written her first published story.

She commented to Joanna on the similarity between Deborah's mourning and her mother's but took the point no further. Joanna's curiosity had not abated, but even benevolent discussion of Deborah while she was in this state of half-collapse was, obscurely, a transgression, like speaking ill of the dead. So for two weeks Deborah had barely impinged on their lives, surfacing only briefly in the half-whispered conversations of the night.

The cloud had cleared suddenly and the cold seemed fresher without its misty dampness. They were eating a breakfast of rolls heated in the stove and the sole surviving pot of last summer's strawberry jam. Their coffee frothed with the unpasteurised milk that Joanna bought every morning through the back door of a nearby dairy, heated and whisked. Judith had thrown wide both halves of the kitchen's stable door to let in the unexpected sunshine that dazzled on the dew. They had been laughing at a sheep that had made its way from the orchard on the other side of the house and came to stand, at once silly and accusing, before the doorstep.

'Guess what?' Judith asked.

'What?' Joanna knew it was something bad; Judith always assumed a perky tone when she had something to get off her chest.

'I think I've got writer's block.'

'You're kidding! You've been shut away over there ever since I got back. And I've heard your printer clicking.'

'I've been writing letters.'

Joanna raised her eyebrows.

'All week?'

'Long letters. And I've been re-writing bits here and there and printing out finished parts to give me something to do.'

'You never have writer's block. You can never stop.'

'Well I haven't exactly stopped now.' Judith frowned down at a piece of buttered roll. 'It's just that my lead character wants to stab his mother and that's not what I had in mind at all.'

'Well take the knife out of his hand. You're the boss, after all.'

'It's not as simple as that.'

'Don't snap at me.'

'Sorry. Was that a snap?'

'Yes.'

'Sorry. I'm just so frustrated.'

'Is it . . . you know?' Joanna jerked her head in the general direction of the spare room.

'No. It started while you were away.'

'It'll come.'

'Mmm.' Judith looked doubtful and chewed. The sheep bleated then lost interest and walked away. 'I read some of your detective stories while I was away. *Hand in Pocket* and *Body Jam*. They were gripping.'

'I'm always telling you so and you just sneer. Anyway, I went one better than that.' Joanna smiled smugly. 'I read one of yours from cover to cover.'

'You actually finished one?' Judith's face lit up with happy surprise. 'Which?'

'*Privacy*.'

'My favourite!'

'It was fabulous. I might even read another.'

Judith leant over and kissed her. Her lips tasted of strawberry jam. There were footsteps on the spare room stairs. They sat back in their chairs and were suddenly at a loss for words.

Deborah was almost transformed. She had washed her hair and fluffed it away from her face and she had left off her disastrous grey eyeshadow which, on eyes swollen and red from grief, had given her the look of a boxing casualty. The dressing gown and slippers had at last been discarded in favour of a smoke-blue woollen suit and cream silk blouse; crazily smart for Martyrstow, Joanna thought, but a distinct improvement.

'Morning,' Deborah said with a smile.

'Hi,' said Joanna.

'Hot rolls in the stove,' Judith told her. 'I'll fetch your coffee.'

And Joanna knew at once that Judith preferred Deborah in a state of half-collapse.

Deborah walked over to the open door to look out across the fields.

'I had no idea it was so beautiful!' she said, turning.

'The weather scarcely gave you the chance,' Joanna told her. 'When it's as clear as this you can see for miles. If we take you up one of the tors you'll be able to see both the county's coastlines like a map.'

'Really?' Deborah sounded almost girlish. Joanna gained the impression she was trying to make amends for something.

'Come and eat your rolls while they're hot,' called Judith. 'I've forgotten: how do you like your coffee?'

'White and two sugars. Please.'

'You should cut down.' Judith stirred in her disapproval with the sugar. 'Think of your heart.'

'Must I?' Deborah turned, still in the doorway. 'I have so few vices.'

'Yeah,' Joanna joined in. 'Think of *your* heart and leave her be.'

'There's someone riding a bicycle up your drive.'

Joanna opened out her newspaper.

'Is it a gingerpop with pink cheeks and a navy-blue donkey jacket?' she asked with little interest.

'Yes.' Deborah had taken fright and come to sit at the table with her back to the door.

'That'll be Michelle the postperson. She comes here at the end of her round so she can stop off to groom and muck out

Fleet in return for a quick ride. She's kinda local, but she doesn't bite. Here. Have a roll while it's hot.'

There was a clatter as a bicycle was allowed to fall to the ground and the ginger-haired girl appeared.

'Hello Michelle,' said Judith going to meet her. 'Are those for me? Do I have to sign? No? Lovely.'

'What's wrong with Madam?' Michelle asked, as Judith, who had fairly snatched her parcels, stalked off to the barn.

'Oh, nothing much,' Joanna told her. 'Work problems maybe. Anything for me?'

'No. Don't reckon so.' Michelle turned out her now empty bag. An envelope fell to the floor. 'Oh, wait a bit.' She stooped to pick it up. 'No. Just another one that's misdirected. Unless it's for whoever lived here before.' She set the letter on the dresser. 'I'll take it back down with me when I go.'

'Cup of coffee?' Joanna offered.

'No thanks.' Michelle rubbed her pink hands together. 'I'll just go out and get young Fleet ready, if that's all right with you.'

'Help yourself. Take her out a bit longer if you like. It's a beautiful morning and I'm not sure I'll have time this afternoon.'

'Oh. Well.' Michelle's face lit up. 'I probably will then. Lovely job.'

She retrieved her bicycle and sauntered off to the stable.

Deborah who had been pretending to read the paper, rose and went to examine the letter.

'It's not misdirected,' she said. 'It's for me. Who knows I'm here?' She brought it back to the table. 'Oh God, it must be from Wendy!'

'Your mother-in-law? She never gave you time to give her the address, remember?'

Joanna grinned in expectation. Deborah saw her and half smiled back.

'You know what it is!' she exclaimed and began to tear the paper. 'Whatever . . . ?'

'I sent off a cheque the day we got here,' Joanna told her, clearing the breakfast things. 'You don't have to do anything about it if you don't want to. I just thought it might be fun to have one in your bag.'

It was a provisional driving licence. Deborah looked astonished as she realised what it was.

'But don't these cost money?'

'Not much.' Joanna waved away her objections from the sink. 'When's your birthday?'

'It was in November.'

'Well there you are. It's a late birthday present. Like I say, you don't have to use it but it's there in case you do. If you would like to have a go, I've got nothing to do this morning and there's a disused aerodrome about a mile down the road. Lots of potholes but, for your first few lessons, all that matters is being away from other cars.'

Suddenly Deborah was hunched over the piece of green computer paper.

'Oh Debs honey, don't cry.' Joanna came over and rubbed her shoulder. 'Don't cry. You don't *have* to drive.'

Deborah shook her head, and wiped her eyes on the sleeve of her jacket.

'No,' she said. 'No I want to. It's just that . . .' She broke off to blow her nose. 'It's just that it's so kind of you. You hardly know me.'

'Sure I do.' Joanna handed her a piece of paper towel from a roll on the dresser. 'I must have watched you cry for a total of eight hours or more and blow your nose some six hundred times. I know you very well.'

Deborah laughed which made her nose run which made her blush. She stood and helped herself to another piece of towel.

'It's very sweet of you,' she said.

'Whatever. You want to drive this morning?'

'Well . . .' Deborah hesitated.

'The idea scares you shitless; am I right?'

Deborah nodded, smiling, found out.

'Me too. Do what you need to do and we'll go.'

Deborah hurried off to brush her teeth *et cetera*. Joanna pulled on an old tweed jacket then went to wait outside. Michelle had led Fleet from her stable in the barn and was giving her a thorough grooming. Fleet's breath formed small clouds. She saw Joanna and snorted in greeting. Joanna stared back. Sometimes the horse seemed vast; the most perfect animal alive. She fed her a piece of apple and rubbed and kissed her above the nose.

'Hello, gorgeous,' she said. She called out to Michelle, 'It's going to stay clear today. You can leave her in the field when you get back.'

'Lovely job,' said Michelle.

Joanna returned to the kitchen and picked up the intercom. After a moment, Judith picked it up at her end.

'Hello?'

'Hon, it's me.' Joanna manoeuvred a cigarette from a packet with her spare hand. 'Debs's provisional licence has come and I've persuaded her to come out for a lesson on the aerodrome.'

'Oh. Fine.'

'Then I thought I'd drive into Launceston to do a food shop and let her take a look around.'

'OK.'

'You need anything?'

'No.'

'You working?'

'Trying to.'

'You OK?' Joanna smiled sexily to herself.

'I'm fine.'

'You sure?'

'Yes, Jo.'

'I'll see you later, OK?'

'Bye.' Judith hung up.

Joanna lit her cigarette and went to lean against the car,

watching Michelle and Fleet again. Deborah was whistling as she used the bathroom. It was one of her less endearing habits; breaking into a nervous, not altogether tuneful, whistle the second she entered a bathroom and stopping the second she left. She whistled nowhere else. Evidently she was unaware how far the noise carried. It reminded Joanna of her least favourite younger brother, Gray, who had married the heiress to a bowling complex. She took a drag on her cigarette. Deborah's hand appeared, opening a window and the whistling abruptly stopped.

'Remember,' Joanna told herself. 'You owe her one.'

Fifteen

Joanna had left Deborah in the town centre and had driven off to a supermarket, arranging to meet her in a café in an hour. Once she had got over a niggling worry that Joanna might have got her alone on the moor with the full intention of seducing her, Deborah had found driving unexpectedly exciting and surprisingly straightforward. Julian had always pooh-poohed her suggestions that she learn, and spoke of the activity as of some mastercraft beyond puny feminine capabilities. She had been lulled into acquiescence by her natural laziness and the luxury of a consular chauffeur. But, on the old Davidstow aerodrome, after hesitantly picking up the positions of the gears and the principle, at least, of clutch control, she soon found herself driving a manly Land Rover at some speed. Stopping gracefully had been less simple and at one point she had lurched them in and out of a pothole so fast that Joanna had struck her head on the windscreen and become (for Joanna) quite cross.

Exploring had never been Deborah's strong point. Her father and Julian in turn had been born to instruct and guide. On those occasions when she was expected to explore without them she had always resorted to a guided tour or at least a dictatorial but easily understood guidebook. English market towns were far harder to enjoy convincingly than their foreign counterparts. Abroad one could meander through markets or go window-shopping, basking in the strangeness of a language and lapping up a culture through its commerce. Newsagents, agricultural supply shops and faded haberdashers were scarcely on a par with the Medinas and souks of North Africa. She ventured a little way into Launceston market but the despairing cries from the cattle pens were too much for her. She followed signs to the castle with relief, only to find herself trailing round little more than a fortified grassy mound. She raised her flagging spirits with a swiftly eaten bun from an excellent cake shop then was prompted by a resurfacing dictum of her father's.

'If you find yourself stuck in a strange town, Deborah, with time on your hands, visit a church. England teems with untrumpeted architectural delights.'

Trying to ignore the looks of pitying curiosity cast at her scarred forehead, Deborah asked the way to the church.

Her immediate reaction to the place was fear. Evidently very old, though she had no eye for period style, it was built from a dark stone, almost black. It crouched long and low. Every available inch of exterior masonry was grotesquely carved, giving it a carbuncled, diseased appearance. A bespectacled couple were standing admiringly outside the porch.

'Pevsner says that the decorative motifs are familiar from contemporary bench ends of the Cornish type,' he said, reading from a guidebook, 'and that, I quote, "The style and the extreme lavishness are not wholly original either". Built 1511 to '24 by one Sir Henry Trecarrel. "Barbarous profuseness" the man says.'

Goaded by this authoritative spur, Deborah let herself in. She read the flower rota and a poster about the church urban fund, then she cast an eye around the interior, lost again for want of instruction. She tried to read stories in the stained glass and was bleakly amused by a plaque placed in memory of a young sailor eaten by savages. The bespectacled couple came in and began to look round. They crossed themselves fervently when passing before the altar so Deborah sat a while on a pew to collect her thoughts for what seemed like a respectful interval. On her way to the door her eye was caught by an elegant Georgian memorial. Georgian was the one period she found easy to recognise, though she was occasionally taken in by fakes. The inscription was elegantly carved. There was an economy to the execution that cleverly conveyed an air of truth. Even a shopping list, she thought, would assume profundity presented like that.

She leant on the end of a pew as she read the poised sentences and she thought of Julian's ashes. These were in an ugly plastic container not unlike a thermos, with an unconvincing bronze finish. She had not dared open the thing yet but she had taken it from its hiding place among her jerseys a couple of times and gingerly shaken it. Just to see how full it was. He had been quite a large man – a rugger player before they left England – but he took up so little space now. Did they give one all the ashes or only a representative shovelful? And if not, what happened to the remainder? Bonemeal, she hoped, for roses. How much would a memorial cost? And would he have liked the idea? The trouble was that he had even fewer roots than she did. She would like the memorial to be somewhere she could visit often but she was still living day to leaden day and had not spared a thought to a suitable future home. His ashes would have to wait, she decided, unless his mother tracked her down and began to bully her with some better idea. Ugly though their container was, she liked the idea of keeping it always to hand.

'Morbid. Morbid,' she thought and drove her concentration back to the Georgian plaque.

Unfortunately its tone unsettled her further still. Bland in its conviction of the existence of a heavenly future for its dedicatee, it ticked off an unctuous list of virtues – fidelity, righteousness, chastity, charity and so forth – which gave no picture of a man's flesh and blood. The inscription could have been written by someone who barely knew him – a solicitor perhaps, or even the stonemason. Not even his corpse or ashes were there. The plaque merely recorded his death and gave a long low bow to the felicities of his existence.

Deborah signed the visitors' book, felt in her pocket for some small change and bought herself a postcard of the church. Then she sat back in the porch and tried to compose a memorial for Julian on the back of it. A *truthful* memorial.

'In loving memory of Julian Curtis,' she wrote. 'Diplomat, sportsman and husband, who was accidentally murdered at 39 and left a grieving, disfigured widow, Deborah, 35. Keen to succeed, ever anxious to avoid embarrassment, he honoured the rich and powerful and rarely remembered the poor save to condemn the impracticality of their ways. Though deeply loved, he reined in his passions until they were least expected. A model of decorum and rectitude, he will be sorely . . .' She broke off. She had written too large and already filled the card. She stuffed it in her jacket pocket, returned the pencil to the visitors' book and left.

There was a butcher's shop across the way. She paused to stare as a plump-faced assistant reached with a pole to unhook a pheasant from a rack above the window. Then she drew near and stood by a small puddle of congealed blood that had dripped from the dead birds. Sausages, black and white puddings, steak, lamb, pork and tripe had been arranged to form a simple flower pattern on the sloping marble slab. Her father had taken her to admire just such a display in the Harrods' food hall on a rare girlhood trip to London. She examined with meticulous revulsion the heaps of purple, pink or bloodless flesh artfully laid out before her then found herself doubled up and vomiting into the gutter.

'Quick Henry, take my bag.'

A hand pressed itself against her forehead while she continued to retch. She tried to shake her head to show that the kindness was beyond the call of duty, but was clutched by another bout of heaving.

'Here,' said the same woman's voice, 'take some of these,' and she was passed some paper handkerchiefs.

'Thank you,' Deborah murmured, and wiped. When she raised her head she saw it was the couple from the church.

'Excellent timing,' said the woman briskly, frowning as she examined Deborah's face. 'You could have been taken like that in a dress shop. Bag, please, Henry.' Henry passed her the bag.

'So kind,' Deborah said again. Wondering what to do with the handkerchiefs now.

'Food poisoning?' asked Henry.

'Shock,' said the woman. 'White as a sheet. Come along, then. There's just the man for you around the corner.'

'Oh, but I feel fine now,' said Deborah. 'Thank you.'

'Nonsense. Come along. He's a herbalist. None of those poisons a chemist gives you to rot your stomach. Nature's remedies. Always the wisest choice. This way.'

She had taken Deborah by the arm and steered her back towards the marketplace, Henry bringing up the rear. She stopped on a corner.

'There he is,' she said, pointing. 'The stall on the end.' Deborah looked through the crowds. 'Well go on,' said the woman.

Deborah started across the square. She glanced back once and saw the bespectacled couple still watching her from the corner. There was no escape.

The herbalist's 'stall' was actually a van with a hatch that opened along one side; the sort that had sold roast chicken and *ersatz* hamburgers in Seneca. There were rows of small-bottled, mud-coloured liquids and paper packages that might have held tea leaves. All were tidily labelled by hand. There was quite a queue. Deborah waited at the back. Even from there the smells were delicious. Rosemary. Orange flower water. Thyme. The first woman in the queue was merely asking for things to cook with – vanilla pods, bouquets garnis, dried sage and rosemary – but those that followed each gave a detailed medical complaint. Having answered several questions they were handed a package.

As she drew near the front, Deborah could see the man serving them. Her first reaction, Julian's reaction, was that he was a typical hippy. His clothes were unironed and battered, except for a vivid green, baggy jersey, which was plainly hand-knitted. His black hair (probably dyed) was long; worn in a pony tail tied with a red leather thong. She glanced across the square. If the bespectacled couple had disappeared, then so could she. They had, but she looked back at the herbalist and decided to stay. Unlike most of what Julian had called 'dropouts' he had no beard. Indeed, his long, finely boned face was so smooth-shaven there was not even a shadow where a beard would be. His teeth, when he smiled, looked truer and whiter than Deborah's own, and his hands were soft-looking and scrupulously clean. Suddenly it was her turn and she found his strange, tawny eyes turned on hers, eyebrows raised in enquiry.

'I . . . er . . . I've just been sick,' she confided.

'How do you feel now?' His accent was subtler than the postgirl's had been. It sounded more intelligent, less stagey.

'Still a bit shaky, actually.'

'Have you got a moment?'

'Um. I suppose so. Yes.'

He turned to the back of the van where an electric urn was steaming. Then, having spooned something from a jar into a perforated metal ball, he plopped the latter into an incongruous Coalport teacup which he filled with hot water.

'Let it stand for a minute or two,' he told her, sliding it across the counter to her. 'It's too hot to drink straight away in any case.'

'Er . . . What is it?' she asked, not wanting to appear rude.

'Chamomile's the main ingredient. It tastes a bit like pond water but it works straight off. You might like a little of this in it.' He slid her a honeypot shaped like a beehive. The teaspoon was silver and worn thin with age. She stirred in a spoonful then used the spoon to lift out the curious metal infusing ball for the water was now the colour of rotten straw. He took both from her and, as she sipped her first, hesitant mouthful, she found his eyes searching her face again.

'Have you been in a car crash?' he asked, less sympathetic than honestly interested.

'Not exactly,' she said and saw him waiting. She took another sip to play for time. All she could taste was honey, but she felt better already. 'A bomb went off near me,' she said. 'I was standing by a glass door. I suppose I was quite lucky, really.' She remembered bits of Julian landing on the consular flowerbeds and hastily drank some more.

'This cream's good for cuts,' he said, reaching below the counter for an attractive blue-glass jar, with tiny writing on its label. 'A lot of people buy it after operations.' He took down a brown paper package from a shelf behind him. 'And you should put equal quantities of this and salt in your baths; about a tablespoon of each. You'll smell delicious afterwards.'

'Oh,' she said, unsure of herself. 'Lovely.'

'You must be under a lot of stress still. Those scars are fairly new.'

'Well. They are quite.' She was aware of new people waiting beside her. She moved over to give him room to serve them but he continued to give her all his attention.

'The baths will help you relax a little but you really need aromatherapy and massage. Do you have someone who could give you massage?'

'No. Not really. I'm staying with my sister over at Martyrstow.'

'Who would that be?'

'Judith Lamb.'

'I know.'

'You know her?'

'Of course. She helps Esther with the cats. She writes too, doesn't she?'

'That's right.'

'But she couldn't massage you?'

Deborah felt herself grow quite alarmed at the idea.

'Heavens no! I mean . . .' she gabbled, 'she has far better things to do.' The old man beside her gave a belly laugh which threw her into confusion. She glanced at her watch and saw she was already late for meeting Joanna at the café. She scrabbled for her purse. 'I must pay up and let you get on,' she told the herbalist.

'Right you are, then,' he said and totted up her bill.

'It's worked beautifully,' she said, handing him her empty cup and she smiled as much as her scars would allow to show him she was not quite such a startled chicken as she must have appeared.

'Come back if I can help again,' he said, passing her the change. 'There's my card in case you need anything before Saturday.'

'Saturday?'

'The next market day. I'm only here on Tuesdays and Saturdays.'

'Oh, of course. Sorry. Goodbye.'

She turned back into the crowd and spent a few moments finding her bearings again and, with them, the way to the café. Joanna had yet to arrive. Deborah bought herself a hot chocolate to take away the strange aftertaste of the tisane and frantically sucked a peppermint in case she still smelled of sick. The café was thick with steam and men who, judging from the state of their boots, were fresh from the market. She chose a table close to the door, stirred a quite unnecessary sugar into her chocolate, then felt in her pocket for the herbalist's address. The card was rough. It was probably home-made from recycled paper and printed by hand on a small press.

'Harvey Gummer, Herbalist and Aromatherapist,' she read, 'Treneglos Mill, Martyrstow Road, Treneglos, Cornwall. Dried or growing herbs, herbal preparations and essential oils.'

'Harvey,' she thought to herself, 'Harvey the herbalist' and for the second time since leaving the house she smiled.

Sixteen

Judith and Joanna were in the sitting room. Joanna was neglecting her after-dinner coffee as she greedily read one of Judith's earlier, funnier novels. Judith was sipping peppermint tea and growing increasingly restless, irritated by an article on the woman's page of Joanna's newspaper. Deborah was upstairs, pointedly taking a bath. Judith had been behaving badly, and felt Joanna's mute condemnation. Neither of them had remembered to sweep the grate and make up a fire this morning, and neither was going to bother to do so now for fear of the other waiting until it was lit to announce that they were going to take an early night.

Deborah's driving and shopping trip had continued the process of recovery first evident at breakfast. She had returned laden with shopping, having made her insistent contribution to the housekeeping budget. Then, with great deliberation, she had set about cooking dinner. Retreating back to the kitchen from her ever more dispiriting work on the novel, Judith had found Deborah actually giggling with Joanna, as she tried to find her way around the larder and store cupboards. Her sense that she was dampening their high spirits inflamed her already kindled jealousy and drove her, door-slamming, out again.

Joanna had always preferred eating to cookery so Judith, who found the demands of recipes therapeutic, tended to treat the kitchen as her domain. Since leaving London, she had become quietly obsessive in buying only products that were kind to the environment and in cooking only foods that were kind to the body. While not a vegetarian, she confronted Joanna less and less with red meat and tended to favour home-grown yogurt over cream. For this evening's dinner (and it was definitely a dinner, not a supper), Deborah had presented them with a *crème vichyssoise* then steak and kidney pie followed by chocolate and sour cream pavlova. When Joanna had reacted all too honestly as one presented with a rare treat, Judith had felt goaded to season the meal with sarcasms about white flour, over-refined sugar and 'recipes learnt at Mummy's elbow'. Deborah's touching attempt at convivial good humour steadily lapsed into a tone of quiet apology. She had even tried to wash up, until Joanna intervened.

'Well, I think I'll take a bath, then,' Deborah had said and gone off to do so leaving Joanna to radiate dissatisfaction from the sinkside and Judith to tend her ugly mood.

At last Judith cast aside the newspaper. She sighed heavily as she did so but Joanna would not be diverted from her reading. Judith drew breath.

'We've got to talk,' she said.

Joanna lowered the book to her lap. Nonchalantly she reached for her cooling coffee and took a sip. Then she lay back against the sofa arm so as to look at Judith over her shoulder.

'You first,' she told her, raising an eyebrow. 'I'm one big ear.'

'About Deborah.'

'Uhuh?'

'The thing is . . .'

Judith broke off, interrupted by Deborah's footfall on the stairs overhead. Deborah was dressed again. Her cheeks were pink from the steam and she brought a hot, flowery smell into the room with her.

'I feel better for that,' she said, standing awkwardly at the foot of Joanna's sofa.

'And you smell fabulous,' Joanna told her. 'Is that the stuff young Harvey mixed up for your baths?'

'Yes. I was meant to put in salt too, but I forgot to buy any.'

'You should help yourself to ours. There's a great jar of it by the stove.'

'Oh, well. Thanks. He says it helps heal scars.'

'Are you sure it isn't an aphrodisiac?' Judith put in. 'Certainly smells like it.'

'Oh no,' Deborah muttered with a confused smile. 'I don't think so.' She continued to stand, picking at the fluff in a sofa button.

'You know he's a witch?' Judith went on. 'Esther's convinced of it.'

'I thought male witches were called warlocks,' said Joanna.

'Warlocks do different things,' Judith told her. 'Anyway, Debs,' (she could not help spiking Joanna's pet abbreviation with irony) 'you be careful. He's very attractive and surprisingly well-off . . .'

'I thought he was a hippy,' Deborah said.

'He is, but don't let that fool you. He's surprisingly well-off and he's one of the few available men around the village. There's a platoon of reluctant virgins queuing up for one of his "massages" who'd soon be on the warpath if an outsider like you were to start toying with him.'

'Well I'm not a reluctant virgin,' Deborah snapped. 'And there's no need to talk to me like a child. Just because Julian's dead doesn't mean that I'm going to start prowling around for someone to take his place and, even if I did, it would hardly be after some long-haired junkie in a grotty provincial town like Launceston!'

So saying, Deborah slammed the kitchen door behind her. Joanna flung Judith an incredulous glance to which Judith shrugged her shoulders.

'Deborah?' Joanna called out. There was no answer. They heard the clunk of the back door being opened. Joanna scrambled off the sofa. 'Debs?' She hurried into the kitchen. 'Hey,' she continued softly. 'Where are you off to at this time of night?' The piqued air of girlish sacrifice in Deborah's response awakened long-buried scenes of irritation in Judith's memory.

'I thought I'd go for a walk.'

'Want me to come too?' she heard Joanna ask.

'It's all right, thanks.'

'No? OK. We'll leave the door unlocked for you.'

'Thanks,' said Deborah, her voice glassier still.

Judith heard the back door close then Joanna returned to the sitting room and sat on the sofa to face her.

'You were saying we needed to talk,' Joanna said.

'Yes.'

Joanna thrust her hair back; a warning sign Judith knew of old. She was clearing the way for her rage. This was always a moment of relief for Judith. Cowardly about initiating confrontations, she had always relied on sullenness and withdrawal to rouse Joanna into bearding her still wordless grievances. Joanna slapped the sofa arm beside her.

'What has gotten into you, Judith?' she shouted. 'I mean, what has she *done*, for Chrissakes? Tried to be more sociable? Done a little shopping, huh? Made dinner for us? Would you rather she was sticking in her room and snivelling to herself all day long?'

'No. I . . . Joanna you don't understand.'

'Quite right I don't. You're so goddamned scornful of her, like she's something one of your mangy cats has sicked up! She's your kid sister and her husband's been blown up right under her nose – Jesus knows what's going on in that weird little, stiff-upper-lip mind of hers – and I'd like to know what makes you think you have the right to walk all over her like this.'

'Well if you'd just . . .'

'You're so goddamned *scornful*!'

Judith was shocked to see tears on Joanna's cheeks.

'If you'd just shut up for a moment,' she shouted back, 'I could tell you.'

108

Joanna dabbed at her eyes with a sleeve.

'So tell me,' she said.

'It's . . . It's not easy.'

'You can do it,' Joanna snapped. 'Is it something she's said when I haven't been around?'

'No, nothing like that. It's nothing to do with her now. Well it is but not so much.' Judith looked up and met Joanna's waiting gaze. After I've told her this, she thought, she'll never look at me in the same way. 'Our father used to beat me.'

'Well? So did mine.' Joanna laughed. 'If we did something wrong, he'd thwack us with an old slipper.'

'No. This wasn't like that. No old slippers. He'd use a leather belt. Sometimes he used a cricket bat.'

'Jesus!' Joanna exclaimed but made no move. She's scared now, Judith thought, she's scared to touch me. 'What had you done?'

'Why should that make any difference?'

'Well if you'd stolen something, say, or . . .'

'Joanna, I hadn't "done" anything except be born maybe, or not been a boy or not been Deborah.'

'How do you mean?'

'He never beat *her*. She was the "good" one, the pretty one. He actually used to call her "Daddy's little girl". She never got bad marks, at least not for behaviour. She never got into fights or came home with mud on her dress. He never let me wear dresses or skirts. He said I was too "bad" to. As soon as I came back from school I had to take off my uniform and change into trousers. Have you never wondered why I swim so badly?'

'Why? I don't see . . .'

'He never let me. None of the costumes was "modest" enough. Oh they were fine for Deborah; pre-pubescent bikinis for *her*. I had to sit beside him at the baths wearing trousers and watch her swim up and down.'

Now that she had finally started to talk, Judith found the telling easier. The hard nuggets of secret fact spilled out and she felt herself lightening for the loss of them, becoming smooth in her truthfulness, approachable, attractive even. She thought of old Bible illustrations of exorcised women having small black devils pulled, claws scrabbling, from their mouths and scaly worms from their private parts.

Still Joanna stayed on the sofa. Her anger had been diverted.

'What about your mother? Didn't she try to stop him?'

'Of course not. She thought the world of him. She believed everything he told her so if he said beating was good for me, she believed it. She never forgave him for dying because it robbed her mean little life of purpose; she had no one to tell her what everything meant. Oh, she felt sorry for me but she never lifted a finger while he was in the same room. He'd only have beaten her instead. She knew when she was well off. She'd cry, of course, and hug me afterwards if she could do it without him seeing. It wasn't like a straightforward punishment, you see. Because I hadn't done any specific wrong, there was never any sense that his beating me had wiped my slate clean. Because he was beating me simply for being there, punishment came to be my family role. I was the "bad" one. I knew my place.'

'What about Deborah?'

'She used to watch. He made her.'

Joanna shook her head in disbelief.

'Poor kid,' she sighed.

'Poor kid? *Her*? What about me?'

'Well yeah, you were the one getting beaten but you're not suggesting she enjoyed watching it night after night? It must have screwed her up rotten. She probably feels guilty about it.'

'She loved him. I can never forgive her that.'

'But . . .'

'Joanna, she never once acknowledged that those beatings happened. He lost his temper with her once and threw a plate across the room. It didn't even hit her but she went on and on about it as if she was about to call the police. But when he hit me with a broom once, in the garden, hit me so hard that the handle broke, all she did was hide until I'd stopped crying. She watched it night after *night*, Joanna, and she never once came up to me in my room afterwards and said, "Christ, you poor kid, that must have hurt." She just watched like a good girl then drank her cocoa. I think all she ever felt was relief that she was the pretty one and just a spectator.'

'But she was younger than you. It's hard when you're the littlest.'

'Not so much younger. Anyway, she grew up. She's grown up now. She never said a thing. She could have told someone at school. Even in those days they knew child-battering when they heard about it. It wasn't the Dark Ages.'

'You could have told someone, too. You could have run away.'

'You don't understand.' Judith shut her eyes against the tears that were starting to flow. She held a handkerchief against them and laid her head back on the cushions. She breathed gently in an effort to calm herself. 'I didn't want it to stop.'

There was a dim rustle then Judith felt the sofa give as Joanna sat beside her.

'Here. Come here,' Joanna murmured.

Judith slid sideways and Joanna wrapped both her arms and legs around her, kissing her hair, her ears, her neck as she wept.

'Thank you for telling me that,' she told her and Judith thought she could hear shock in her voice, and loss of innocence. Joanna softly rocked her dry of tears then led her across the kitchen, through the hall and up to their bedroom. Judith allowed herself to be undressed and led to bed. Her cheeks felt hot against the pillow. She lay there, chilled by cold bedding, and listened to the inexplicably comforting sounds of Joanna riddling the stove then stoking it up for the night.

Seventeen

Her dinner-time sarcasms had not wounded her sister in the way that Judith had intended. Deborah had realised even before setting the first dish on the table that her style of cookery was more suited to consuls and schoolchildren than the health-conscious. Unwittingly, Judith's drawing attention to the food succeeded only in filling Deborah with wave upon desolating wave of nostalgia. The mild cream of the soup, the rich sogginess of gravy-soaked suet pastry, the meringue's dizzying sweetness were painful reminders of the confident security of her childhood. Inevitably they reminded her, too, of Julian.

On leaving school she had completed a course at an Oxford secretarial college, then shared a London flat with four schoolfriends. United by their lack of academic prowess and by what they then thought of as worldly ambition, they were frank – in the all-female privacy of their flat – in regarding themselves as groomed and in training for the 'marriage market'. The last of her highly competitive circle to bring home a boyfriend, she was the first to win a husband.

Precisely because of their social constraints and high tedium factor, her years with Julian now seemed a seamless continuation of her childhood and youth. It was only now, in this strange ménage, far from all familiarly comforting references, that she found herself regarding her life to date as an ended epoch, something she could summon up and scrutinise. She had been riding a continuum since birth, her every responsibility shouldered by another, her every decision subordinate to the desires of her peers or of those she still thought of as superiors. The ride had come to an abrupt end and she had been ignoring in vain the fact that she was now both utterly alone and walking.

Just as the reality of Julian's death struck her at unpredictable intervals through every day, the starker for her being among people who barely registered his loss, so the long unfamiliar sight and sound of her sister brought like a kind of repeated throbbing the sense of some resurfacing piece of terrible knowledge. This was something Deborah had long-since bandaged away beyond the reach of memory. She tried to ignore its stirrings but the sensation of having a block of past to scrutinise was too new for her brain to leave it alone for long. Walking around Launceston, driving with Joanna, even sitting in her room or soaking in the bath, she could think of other things, but no sooner did she hear Judith's quiet, clever voice than her mind began teasing her afresh, as a tongue probes a damaged tooth. There was something bad – 'unspeakable' was the adjective which always sprang to mind – trying to break loose within her. It was taking advantage of the powerlessness of her hours asleep, pressing its outline, relentless, through the soft walls of her dreams.

Six times now she had dreamt of the same dog. It was a small, nervous mongrel, black with a short, scruffy coat. It was digging in sand, scrabbling so hard with its forepaws that the stuff shot out between its hind legs and scattered over a slowly growing heap behind it. There was nothing else in the dream – no people, no sea, no story – only the amplified panting of the dog, Deborah's horror of whatever the hateful creature was uncovering and an acute desire to wake up. In her experience, recurrent dreams tended to progress and develop. Their endings would lengthen or alter until, as though a correct formula had been laid out and so had broken a spell, the dream evaporated as mysteriously as it had taken shape. Night after night she had prepared herself bravely, therefore, for the dog to dig up part of Julian's body – his head, his heart or the hand with his wedding ring on it (the ring had never been retrieved after the blast) – but a part of her knew that the ending would be far worse than that.

She had hurried away to 'take a bath' because Judith's voice and cruel stare had made her think of this dream with an unbearable intensity. She was convinced that if she tried to make any further conversation the dog would turn around to face her and start barking in her skull. As she left the kitchen, the tension had brought her to the brink of tears. With two doors closed between her and her sister, however, she found her eyes dry and her mind dog-free and oddly still. Her eye came to rest on the packages bought from the herbalist that morning and dropped on the bed on her return. She became aware that she ached all over. She ran herself a bath and, tearing open the relevant packet, shook a handful of the flaky contents onto the steaming water. To her delighted surprise they changed there from an unappealing brown to various vivid shades of pink, red, purple and green; pieces of petal and leaf. The steam swiftly grew fragrant. She remembered too late that the herbalist had told her to add salt. She was already stripped to her knickers and the bath was too inviting to delay a moment longer.

The scent grew stronger still as she slid into the waters up to her neck. The water was almost too hot. It reminded her of a rich schoolfriend's conservatory where the scent of geranium and jasmine on a sunny afternoon had once sent her disgracefully to sleep during a party. She closed her eyes briefly and took a deep breath, filling her lungs with flowery steam. The bath was wonderfully long, a far cry from the Seneca consulate's hip-hugging, pinched penny affairs. She pictured Joanna clambering into it undaunted to test it for size in a showroom. Though the sexual aspect to their relationship still scared her, she thought she could understand the attraction Joanna held for her sister. If only she weren't American or lesbian, Joanna would have made a perfect Head Girl, inspiring devotion and disarming envy in all around her. Deborah smiled at the thought and opened her eyes. By one of the mysteries of physics, the reconstituted petals had drifted over the water, drawn to caresss the points where her skin broke its surface. She scooped out a handful and laid them across the stitches on her thighs. Could flowers heal? The salt was probably the vital ingredient, and she had left that out. She paddled a hand through the water to wet her shoulders then she picked out pink petals wherever she could find them and diligently stuck them across the scar where her nipple had been.

'My late, lamented nipple,' she said aloud, then stood, abashed, to soap herself vigorously, wondering if the others had heard her.

Far from being drowsy as hot baths usually left her, she had become strangely alert. She hung her suit up on the back of her door to air, convinced that so isolated a house must suffer from moths in its spare room. Then she pulled on some very clean, rather tight, jeans, warm socks, tomorrow's blouse and a thick jersey. She assumed that, left to their own devices, Judith and Joanna would have retired to do whatever they did in their room at the other end of the house. Her plan was to slip out through the kitchen, taking the key with her to avoid being locked out, and walk to one of the nearby villages and back in the moonlight.

It was not as late as she had thought, however, and she was startled to find them in the sitting room at the foot of the spare room staircase. Judith was still in an unaccountably foul mood – doubtless trying to divert attention back onto herself, as she had done all their girlhood – and succeeded in insulting Deborah deeply by suggesting that the mere fact of buying a herbal bath off him implied a sexual fascination with Harvey . . . with Harvey . . . Deborah had quite forgotten his surname; a sure sign that she was not remotely interested in the man. Politely covering for Judith's behaviour, Joanna had offered to walk with her. Deborah had been tempted to accept — she was not remotely sure of her way — but she knew of old that punishing Judith only made her attitude worse.

'It's all right,' she told Joanna. 'Thanks.'

'No? OK. We'll leave the door unlocked for you.'

Deborah had picked up her coat on the way through the kitchen but the night still felt bitterly cold. The sky was clear and spattered with stars. She could not remember ever having seen them so clearly in England before. The lack of any streetlighting or any of the cumulative wash of light given out by a concentration of houses made the night around her seem far darker than usual but made the moon and stars seem brighter and closer. Having buttoned her coat up to the neck, she thrust her hands deep in its pockets, teetered across the cattle grid and set off down the drive. At the lane she was faced with a choice. There were pinpricks of houselight down below to the right and the left and she could not remember which way they had driven to pass through Martyrstow this morning. Julian would have turned right.

'I must let him go,' she thought and turned left.

Even the dead of night in Seneca had been filled with background noise; distant radios, the steady buzz of generators, the barks and clatter of scavenging dogs — 'Don't think about dogs!' she thought — and the insidious clicks of nocturnal insects. Here there was silence. Now and then her footsteps set something rustling in the high hedgerows, once a sheep startled her by muttering in its sleep and twice she stopped, entranced at the call of a barn owl in the trees below the lane. She walked for some time without meeting so much as a car. The houses she was heading for seemed further away than she had guessed at first and she was beginning to wonder whether she should be turning back — the cold was penetrating her coat — when a man overtook her on his bicycle and turned left through a gap in the hedge. She heard gravel ground beneath his wheels and realised that she was passing a house. Curious, she walked on a little until she heard a door open and close then she turned back to look.

The property was densely planted with shrubs and trees but, as a few lights were turned on, she made out a long, low L-shaped building. It was an old pastime of hers, born of her days in London, to peer in through people's windows at night if they had not yet drawn their curtains. She enjoyed the glimpses afforded of other people's lives, their elegant, sometimes hideous, environments. She enjoyed too the sense that she would walk on knowing far more about each inhabitant than they would ever know about her. The little she could make out of this house's interior seemed uninterestingly shabby so she was about to begin the walk home when she saw the inhabitant. It was Harvey . . . Harvey . . . Harvey *Gummer*! Suddenly his surname slotted into her mind and with it a certain curiosity.

She drew closer to the hedgerow and watched. He walked from one room to another on some errand or other. Then, turning on lights as he went, he walked to what was obviously the kitchen. He stooped out of sight and she heard, faintly, the rattling noise that Joanna made last thing at night and first thing in the morning when she did whatever she did to the stove. Then he reappeared in view, carrying something carefully, and let himself out of the back door. He was bearing ashes in a small metal hod. She saw a few embers glowing among them and when he tipped the hod into a bucket beside the back porch a small cloud of ash blew away from it, lit up by the light from the windows. When he stood, hod at his side, he remained on the spot and gazed up at the night sky. Fascinated, she watched him gazing. She shuddered from the cold.

'Perfect evening, isn't it?' he said suddenly. She had not realised he was not alone. She waited to see who he lived with. Judith, in her gibes, had said he was 'available' so perhaps there was a brother or an elderly mother in a chair out of sight. No one replied. Perhaps he had a dog; a border collie with a winning spot over one eye. Or a ragged black mongrel. 'Isn't it?' he repeated, louder, and she realised he was talking to her.

Blushing in the moonlight, she took a few steps back into the lane.

'Yes,' she said. 'I was just admiring the stars. So bright out here. I moved into the hedge in case a car came round the bend and didn't see me in time. I'm in rather dark colours.' He had walked along his short drive and was standing in the gateless opening at its end.

'Oh,' he said. 'It's *you*.'

'Yes.'

'Still feeling sick?'

'Not any more. I took one of your baths. I mean, I took a bath with some of the stuff you sold me in it. It woke me up rather so I came out for a walk.'

'I see.' He nodded. He was smiling. She saw his teeth glitter. He seemed to be waiting for her to continue but she could think of nothing else to say except 'I should be off' and she was not sure that she wanted to go just yet.

'Have you been into Martyrstow?' she asked him, inspired.

'Yes,' he said, still nodding. Perhaps he was slightly simple. Inbred.

'It looks pretty quiet.'

'No pub,' he said. 'Have to go the other way, to Treneglos for that. I was massaging old Esther's bad back.'

'Isn't it rather late for that?'

'No!' He laughed at her. 'She likes it last thing. Helps her sleep.'

'Ah.' She pushed her hands deeper into her pockets. 'I'd er . . . I should be getting back.'

'All right,' he said. 'But there's something on your shoulder.'

He reached his hand over to her shoulder-blade and picked off a piece of old bramble caught on her coat. His jacket sleeve smelled of bonfires. And very faintly of kippers.

'Thank you.'

'Must have attached itself when you left the road to look at the stars,' he said.

'Yes.'

'Goodnight, then.'

'Goodnight.'

As she walked back up the lane she was sure he had stayed where he was to watch her. Was he smiling?

When she let herself in she found that the others had gone to bed. Chilled, she warmed herself awhile by the stove. Then she made a cup of cocoa to drink in her room, washing and drying the milk-pan scrupulously when she had finished with it. As she climbed into bed, she found that someone – Joanna, presumably – had been up to slip a hot water bottle between her sheets. This unexpected kindness together with the lingering scent from her herbal bath made her think again of Julian. She thought of the way he invariably complained of her cold feet in bed and of the way the air in the bathroom always bore a trace of his aftershave until late morning, when the maid expunged it with the plastic lemon scent of her creamy cleanser. Years after leaving boarding school, Deborah found herself bitterly homesick at dusk on Sundays. The consular maid in Seneca had Sundays off so on Sundays Julian's aftershave lingered long enough to become associated with his wife's Sunday evening gloom. It joined the complex of stimuli – the spiced smell of toasted teacakes, church bells, bonfires, the lowing of cattle and the music the World Service played before its late-night shipping forecast – that drew to the surface the tremulous emotion of her early teens.

She sipped her cocoa. For a moment she felt the tightening around lips and nose that presaged weeping, then she sipped again and the feeling passed. She had no religious faith but, since Julian's death, she had resuscitated the bedtime prayers of childhood. God was not mentioned and she no longer ran through a dutiful litany, drawing down heavenly interest on her every friend and relation. Instead she prayed to Julian. It seemed to her that if her bereavement were ever to dwindle to manageable proportions she would have to allot it a parcel of her daily time. For ten minutes or so before she fell asleep, she would force her mind to dwell, without celebration or regret, on some aspect of his personality or person. This was a kind of prayer; it honoured him.

Tonight she thought of his smile. She thought of its various manifestations; the official smile, the smile for colleagues, the smile for his mother, the smile for the maid, the smile for her. It struck her now that he had never opened his mouth when he smiled for her, and yet he had excellent teeth. Perhaps his mother had taught him it was bad manners. The substantial part of her mind which acted beyond her control then thrust forward the image of Harvey the herbalist smiling, his teeth glittering from the shadows. She heard Judith's sneering again and tried to discard the image as quickly as it had come. The very thought that she might try to compare the two men shocked her. She glanced at her alarm clock. Julian's ten minutes were up. She drank the rest of her cocoa, relishing its sweetest dregs, switched off the light, then pulled up the bedding to her ears, discomfited but not altogether unhappy.

Eighteen

Joanna stopped the car in a lay-by, opened her door and walked around to the other side, slapping the magnetic L-plates back on. She opened the passenger door. Deborah was all blonde confusion.

'You're not going to make me drive on a road?'

'Budge over Deborah. It's cold out here.'

'But what if we meet other cars?'

'We will, darling. We will. Shift.'

Deborah made as if to manoeuvre her hips across the gear lever then thought better of it.

'Think I'd better go the long way round,' she apologised. Joanna shuddered from the cold and jumped in as soon as Deborah was clear of the door. There had been a thick frost in the night and the trees and grass still bore traces of its white crust. The car heater was toasting the women's feet but not much more. When Deborah lowered herself into the driving seat there was a drop on the end of her nose. She excused herself and dabbed it away with her hand.

'Forgot my hanky,' she twittered.

'Here.' Joanna tugged some tissues from a box in the glove compartment. Deborah thanked her and blew her nose.

'Now,' Joanna asked her, 'remember the drill?'

'Check mirror, check neutral, check handbrake,' she said, checking each and gently mimicking Joanna's mid-western accent. 'Ignition, gas pedal, into first, check mirror, right-hand wing mirror, look over shoulder and, oh, we're off!' They pulled away with a slight lurch. 'Oh!' Deborah exclaimed. 'I'm driving!'

'Yeah, you're driving. You're driving on a road. Now second. Quickly. Check the mirror first. That's it. More gas. Not too much. That's it. Keep left.'

'But . . .'

'Don't mind him, he's going nowhere fast. Now third.'

'Check my mirror first?'

'Always check.'

Deborah checked, somewhat wildly, then changed up into third.

'How about fourth?' she asked.

'Not here,' Joanna told her. 'Nasty curves coming up. Wait till we're back on the moor. Here are the curves. Foot off the gas in good time. That's it. That's it. Now back on to bring you out of it. Not too much. Great. Now indicate right. Other way. That's it. Slow up a little. Now second. Yup. Now pull into the middle a bit and you'll have to wait for these lorries. That's it. OK. Off you go. And back into third. Listen to your engine. Always listen to your engine; it mustn't suffer. Ever. And *now* you can go into fourth. Open road, Debs. It's all yours.'

Joanna let Deborah drive them, uninstructed now, across the moor. The woman was a natural driver; her nerves, like so many of her 'feminine' characteristics were a palpable screen erected through painstaking tuition to hide capabilities which she had been trained to underestimate. Julian had so obviously been a man of political shifts and social ambition. What could have attracted him to her? Such men never married just for sex and, according to Judith, their father had left little behind him but old shoes and bad feeling. She probably wasn't even very good at sex and it was hard to imagine her as a lady ambassadress. Insecure as a dolly in quicksand. Maybe he had thought he could mould her into some diplomatic ideal. Poor, misguided Julian that he was.

They were reaching Joanna's favourite part of the moor,

where she always brought Fleet to a halt to let the mare catch her breath and drink from an icy stream. It was how she imagined the moon's surface would look grassed over. Treeless, bushless and – rare thing for a piece of the county one local writer had described as 'less a rockery than a boulder-garden' – rockless, its charm lay in the mounds and furrows of a terrain spotted with a network of tussocks formed by coarse bog-grass. The bog-grass was a darker green than the sheep-cropped turf around it and the stream swirled with thick hanks of weed which the sun turned brilliant as lime cordial. One always saw rabbits here, sometimes whole nurseries of them at play. Once, pausing with Fleet, Joanna had watched a fox walk quite calmly to the stream to drink. It had taken the distant shouts from a man to his dog to scare it away again. Through the window to her left now she saw the local farmer rounding up his cattle on horseback. It was one of the few sights here to remind her of home.

'OK. You'll have to stop here, Debs,' she said. 'The road comes to an end. Brake down direct into second. You see? You can do it but you have to brake a bit more first or we get a jolt like that. Now stop on the left here. Don't forget the clutch or we'll stall. That's it. Now. Turn us around.'

'Here?'

'Sure here. We can't reverse all the way back home. Into first.'

'Right.'

'Now softly, softly and swing her out as tight as she'll go. Keep your foot on the clutch. All the control's in that. That's it. Slowly. Now just before you stop, swing the wheel the other way. That's it. Stop. Great. Now reverse. You can undo the belt if it helps you look round.'

'I'm all right, thanks.' Deborah looked over her shoulder. Her cheeks were pink with effort. She reversed, swinging the wheel the other way. 'Now first?' she asked.

'That's right. And pull us up again on the left. There. That's a three-point-turn.'

'Is that it?'

'Well, it's harder with traffic around you, and there's not much camber on this bit. Do that in Clapham and you're *really* driving. How about a coffee?'

'Oh yes,' Deborah sighed. She switched off the ignition, then remembered to pull the handbrake on. Joanna leaned behind them for the Thermos. 'Actually . . .' Deborah wrinkled her nose.

'What?'

'How private is it here?'

'No bushes, but there's a kind of hollow behind us on the other side of the road.' Joanna pointed to a spot to their right. 'Try down there. If that farmer rides this way or if I see anyone else coming I'll honk, OK?' She poured their coffees then sat watching the steam circle up onto the windscreen while Deborah did her stuff. She noticed the sheepish grin as she clambered back into sight, adjusting her skirt and at last understood how she won herself a husband. 'Better?' she asked as Deborah opened the door.

'Much. It's the cold, I think.'

'That and the excitement. Counting that session on the aerodrome you've been driving nearly two hours this morning.'

'What's that curious place way beyond the end of the road?'

'China clay works. If you go closer you can see how the water at the foot of the quarry's turned to a kind of fluorescent milk.'

'Oh.'

'In the right light it looks like a bright blue swimming pool.'

They sat for a few minutes sipping coffee in a silence broken only by the subdued churning noise of the heater. The farmer and his dogs had driven all but one bullock across the road. As the herd moved away towards the edge of the moor the bullock began to follow at his own pace. Joanna wondered how she could broach the subject that was on her mind. She didn't feel her approach could be as direct with Deborah as it was with Judith, even though the younger sister's surface passivity encouraged one to take the lead. Then Deborah eased her way.

'Joanna?'

'Yeah?'

'Does Judith work at her writing every day?'

'Just about.'

'She goes to her study as though she was going to the office, or something?'

'Yes.'

'She isn't,' Deborah picked at the leather on the steering wheel, 'just doing it to get away from me?'

'No. Why should she? She's just a disciplined worker.'

'It was your idea I came to stay, not hers.'

'But she agreed.'

Deborah turned to face her. Joanna expected tears but saw that she was too tense to cry.

'Joanna, she *hates* me. We've never been close. And I often think it's stupid to suppose that being in the same family means that people have to like each other, but . . . I thought perhaps it was just my being married. To Julian, I mean. I thought things might be different now that he's dead. Maybe we could become like proper sisters again. I thought I should at least see. And I've seen and Judith really *hates* me.'

Suddenly all the simpering, the yielding, the pussyfooting politeness had dropped out of Deborah's voice. Joanna drew breath.

'Could it be something in your childhood together?' she suggested. 'Judith has an elephant's memory.'

'I told you. Our childhood was happy.' Deborah spoke as though she needed to say this aloud to convince herself of its truth. 'Very straightforward and a bit dull but basically happy. She was always being told off for being naughty . . .'

'Naughty?'

'Yes. Naughty. But I think that often happens when one child is so much more intelligent than the rest of the family and, looking back, she obviously was. But we were comfortable. When you hear how some children live! We had everything. Was your childhood happy? You're always so, well, not cheerful exactly but so in control.'

'There were a lot of us and I was in the middle, which is never easy.' Joanna thought back. 'Farms in Montana are *big* so I suppose we were very isolated. But we made our own fun and it was healthy and kind of idyllic.'

'Do you get on with your parents?'

'Well my Ma's been dead a while now as I think I already told you. I guess I was closest to her. He's kind of buttoned up but he got where he is from nowhere and I respect him for that. Sure. We got on. He was firm but fair and she was loving and fun and sometimes sort of wild. I think she probably drank a bit when she cooked; she was always more sentimental with us in the evening.'

'And your brothers and sisters?'

'We've got precious little in common – less and less, the longer I live here – but I love my memories of them. We fought, shared secrets; the usual things. We taught each other to smoke.'

'Talking of which.'

'Sure. I'd forgotten.' Joanna dug out a packet and tapped out a cigarette for each of them. Deborah pushed in the cigarette lighter on the dashboard. 'This is one thing they *never* do any more,' she said. 'Last time I went home I had to keep going out in the yard or hanging out of the windows, like a schoolkid.'

'The air's so clean out here, it feels *really* wicked!' Deborah giggled. She wound down her window a little before they lit up. Joanna smiled wryly to herself and inhaled deeply.

'Debs, I got quite a shock from Judith last night. After you'd gone out for your moonlit walk.' Deborah looked at her, blank, waiting. 'She told me how your father used to beat her.'

'She was a tomboy, as I say,' Deborah blustered. 'Always getting into trouble.'

'She said she didn't have to *do* anything, Deborah. She said he just beat her so as to have someone to beat. And she told me how you and your mother used to have to sit and watch. She said how neither of you ever lifted a finger to help her.' Deborah flinched. Or perhaps smoke had blown in her eyes.

'She's exaggerating. She always did,' she said. 'Mummy used to say that the first words she spoke were a lie. She is a novelist, after all.'

'I don't think she was lying.'

Deborah stubbed out her barely-lit cigarette.

'You don't understand,' she said.

'What don't I understand?'

'Anything.'

'Deborah I'm not blaming you, and deep down I don't think Judith is either, but you keep saying your childhood was "straight-forward and dull but basically happy" and I don't think most people would call child-beating any one of those things.'

'Everyone beat their children then. You didn't even think about it. It was just the done thing. All my friends were beaten. Weren't you?'

'Sure I was. My dad used to take his slipper to us.'

'There! You see?' Deborah's tone was almost triumphant.

'But he never made a big deal out of it. It was always for a specific thing we'd done wrong. What's more important, he would never have made the others watch.'

'Well neither did mine.'

'Yes he did.'

'Not every time.'

'Judith says he did.'

'She's lying.'

'She's not.' Joanna took a last drag on her cigarette then stubbed it out too. 'And I think you and she should talk about it with each other. This thing's been buried too long.'

Deborah whipped round.

'Look, just shut up, will you?' Now she was crying. At least, she had tears in her eyes. 'It's none of your business.'

'It most certainly is. I love the woman. I live with her.' Joanna half laughed, 'You're my goddamned in-law. Of course it's my business.'

'Look. I know you mean well but you're just meddling in something you don't understand. You couldn't understand. You weren't there.'

'Wish I had been. I was a big girl. I'd have beaten the bastard back.'

Deborah clenched her small fists and shook them slightly.

'I know what you think,' she muttered. 'You think he was some kind of pervert. A monster taking out his aggression on helpless children.'

'Quite right I do. I think it might help you if you did too.'

'No one understood him. Our mother certainly didn't.'

'What?'

'He was lonely.'

'Give me a break,' Joanna said quietly. 'He needed medical help.'

'Shut up! OK?' Deborah shouted at her. 'Bloody well shut up!'

Joanna raised her fingers in a mute gesture of acquiescence. Then she let her hands fall to her lap. Despite Deborah's slightly open window, the car had become uncomfortably hot. She adjusted the heater's control then became irritated by the noise of its fan and turned it off altogether. She opened her door a fraction, shook their coffee cups dry, then screwed them back on the Thermos. Covering it with the palm of one hand until it was clear of the car, she emptied the ashtray into the wind. A flock of sheep had been drawing slowly closer throughout their conversation. Their inane bleating punctuated the silence.

'Sorry,' Deborah murmured finally.

'It's OK,' Joanna replied. 'At least, it's not but, well, it's sort of your problem.' She laid a hand lightly on Deborah's fore-arm. Its muscles were tensed to hardness still. Surprisingly, given that the woman was obviously unhappy around dykes, they slowly relaxed at Joanna's continued touch.

'Would you . . . ?' Deborah was coming over all frail again.

'Want me to drive us back?' Joanna divined. Deborah nodded. 'You walk around and I'll climb over.'

Nineteen

Judith turned a knob on the side of her word processor monitor which darkened its screen but even then a small red light on the disc drive showed that the machine was switched on. Darkened, it still waited, hungry for her sentences. She swung it to one side, reached over to the table behind her chaise longue and picked up the first weighty volume of her two-volume Proust. Despite occasional foolhardy hints dropped to the contrary, she had never managed to read much more than the Combray section and half the account of Swann's humiliating affair with Odette. The work's massive indolence, however, had always usefully spurred her on to activity of her own elsewhere and she hoped it would not fail her now.

She had begun to re-read Proust last night, goaded by the half-vengeful wakefulness of sexual frustration while Joanna slept, heavily contented, in the shadows beside her. Their love-life had never seemed problematical before. Now, in the light of her still secret insecurity concerning her work and the violently conflicting feelings aroused in her by Deborah's encroaching presence, certain scales had fallen painfully from her eyes. Unlike Joanna, always so convinced in her desires, Judith saw herself as a sapphist made, not born. Making love with Joanna she had always felt completed, utterly natural, but the path to that happy completion lay through many other beds, shared only with men. Although she knew that, by her parents' and sister's standards, her sex-life seemed promiscuous, even depraved, for her it had always represented the sad, cyclical history of the ceaselessly disappointed romantic. From the jealously-guarded sexual awakening of her childhood, she had dreamed of loving only one man, who would adore her, rescue her, protect her from her parents and ask her to bear his children. Was it her fault if she had attracted only the wrong men while it was left to Deborah to be swept away in her virginity? Though she was grateful for it now, Judith's amorous net had caught only terminal bachelors or other women's Julians.

Once they had surmounted her initial embarrassment, there had been no problem with Joanna. Indeed, the bliss of sex with another woman came as a revelation. For the first time in her life she could make love with her not-quite mirror image, whose body she understood and yet never utterly knew, with someone who cherished rather than conquered her, whose sexual sophistication stretched far beyond a well-meaning but impatient search for an on button. And yet. And yet increasingly it seemed to her that she thought of sex more than Joanna did. Joanna was enthusiastically sensual but seemed to be able to switch off her libido when it suited her. So long as it was there when she wanted it, she could take sex or leave it. More often than not she left it. Whether it was simply that Judith had a higher sex drive (wherever *that* was situated) or whether she was more prone to anxiety and frustration and therefore more often in need of release, she frequently found Joanna content with a bedtime kiss and cuddle when she was hungry for more. This had not disturbed her badly until now; she had always fobbed herself off with the old palliative that a partner with identical impulses and appetites to one's own could never fascinate like a partner with her own peculiarities of temperament. But more than ever her timing seemed hopeless; she found that whenever her need for Joanna peaked, her lover was asleep, hard at work or absent. Yesterday she had sat in a corner of Launceston's public library to skim-read a chirpy American manual called *Night after Night after Night: How Sex with One Partner Can Go on Being Great!* She pounced on a section about biorhythms in the hope of finding a method of bringing their sexual highs and lows to coincide the way that their menstrual cycles had done. *'You want it at bedtime and he wants it at breakfast,'* she read. *'You like it in the kitchen in the afternoon but he's always out at work then. Sometimes you want him badly in the middle of the night but you daren't wake him up. Sounds familiar? Has it ever crossed your mind that you only want what you know he can't give?'*

Since Deborah's arrival Judith had repeatedly caught herself wondering what grief did to one's sex-drive and whether Deborah's fantasies now revolved around a corpse. Shocked at herself, Judith had begun to entertain the depressing possibility that on an animal level she was no different from her sister. Was it possible that, like Deborah, her entire sexual outlook had been formed by men, that having once had sex with a man a part of her was conditioned into a hunger that only a man could satisfy? She knew the suggestion was political sacrilege, but that made it no less easy to entertain. In her dreams, in her waking fantasies, even in their pillow talk, Joanna remained for her a kind of goddess, a superior, unsullied creature who had realised her total female potential by never stooping to compromise with men.

'Oh,' Joanna would sigh, slowly smiling, 'you don't know the *half* of it, my dear!'

But for Judith this only evoked a warm-spiced past of passionate female embraces. Joanna's past, she remained convinced, had integrity and pride. Joanna would never have pleaded openly with a man that he take her to bed just one more time. She would never have sat in some man's porch half the night in the vain hope of his arrival. Not for her the letter begging crumbs of worthless male affection or the cringing scenes in party kitchens.

Joanna had driven off up to Barrowcester that morning to

take the bishop's portrait for a magazine. Judith had been half asleep when she kissed her cheek and left. Rising alone (Deborah appeared to be taking a considerate lie-in) she had determined that today would be the day she broke through her novel's impasse. When Joanna arrived this evening, Judith would truthfully admit to having enjoyed a 'good day's work'. Ten pages of Proustian verbiage had their usual effect. Roused, she set the book aside and tugged her work table back to its proper position above her. She stared for a moment, non-plussed by the blank screen then remembered, twisted the appropriate knob, and found herself back in Edgar's kitchen.

Without perusing yet again the latest paragraph, she caused the machine to lift it off into its short-term memory then she began afresh.

Irritated by the buzz of a housefly, she wrote, *Edgar glanced around the room. In a few seconds he had traced the insect to the edge of the ugly tasselled lampshade overhead. He watched as it then flew down to the dresser to feed on something spilt there. Holding his breath, he silently rose from his chair and approached his prey. Then, as he raised his hand to strike, it darted forwards and took refuge in a drawer that had been left slightly ajar. The cutlery drawer. Without even pausing to think what he was about, Edgar opened the drawer and, ignoring the fly, took out the long, dagger-toothed knife. The one they used for sawing frozen meat.*

Then Judith tapped in a few lines of space before recalling the banished paragraph from the machine's memory.

As if it were the most natural thing in the world, she read, *his eyes had come to rest, then lingered, on the cutlery drawer. His head felt pleasantly empty of thoughts. Edgar rose at last, tugged open the drawer and took out the long, large-toothed knife they used for sawing frozen meat.*

The fly was a definite improvement, even if Edgar was still hell-bent on murder. Perhaps she could change Edgar's gender? Make him Philippa. Philippa Clare? She had written no Philippas in a long while. Mother-crushed, stay-at-home librarian spinsters were surely no more commonplace than their male equivalents? No. Edgar felt right. Philippa – lover of horses – sounded too strong. The fly business was a good sign. The text was growing again. If she just waited a while, patiently. No more Proust. No more coffee. No lunch, indeed, until she could write another paragraph.

The intercom buzzed. Deborah must be up, unless it was Michelle with a query about the post or Fleet. Judith glanced at the dechimed long-case clock that ticked at the other end of the room. The morning had evaporated. The intercom buzzed twice more.

'Hello?'

'Judith, it's Deborah.'

'Hello.'

'Am I interrupting?'

'Yes.'

'Oh God. Sorry. Look I'll go away.'

'No. What did you want?'

'Nothing. Honestly. I was just making some coffee and I wondered . . .'

Judith scowled at her screen. The clock ticked a few times.

'Come on up. Bring me a coffee. Black with nothing.'

As she replaced the hand-set she heard Deborah ask, 'Are you sure?'

'So this is where you do all your writing,' Deborah said as she came in. In the time it had taken her to make two cups of coffee, Judith had sought in vain the signs of narrative growth that had briefly made their presence felt.

'Yes,' she said. She tapped the store button, so clearing the fragment of precious text from the screen.

'There's your coffee.' Deborah set a cup on the floor to Judith's left and continued on her tour of the room.

'What a wonderful space!'

'Joanna had already done up the house when I moved down

here. This bit was my contribution. My dowry.' Judith drew her knees back beneath her quilt to watch her. Deborah had walked to one of the big windows.

'And the view! Does it get hot under this roof in summer?'

'A bit. I just open the windows.' Judith sipped her coffee. Deborah had made it far too weak.

'These radiators are extraordinary.'

'Do you like them?'

'I'm not sure. They're different.' Joanna had insisted Judith buy two wildly expensive radiators from a shop in Bath that imported them from France. Painted high-gloss canary yellow, freestanding and elegantly thin, they rose well above Deborah's shoulder height several feet on either side of the chaise longue. Deborah reached out a hand to touch one and recoiled. 'Efficient too,' she muttered, shaking her fingers.

'I didn't want too many pictures or anything in here to distract me,' Judith told her. 'Joanna thought those attractive enough to pass for abstract sculpture.'

'And that chaise longue is enchanting.'

'Yes. Present from Joanna. And now you've admired every object in the room except the word processor, which is scarcely a thing of beauty.'

'Sorry. You want me to go. Shall I take your cup? It was only that I thought we ought to talk.'

'Sit, then.'

Judith pulled back her feet to make room on the end of the chaise longue. Deborah sat.

'Where's Joanna?' she asked.

'She's had to drive up to Barrowcester to photograph the bishop for some Sunday magazine.'

'That's miles isn't it?'

'Some way, yes. She won't be back until well after dark.'

Deborah looked into her coffee mug.

'It's so kind of her to be giving me driving lessons,' she said. 'She's so . . . She's an awfully nice person.'

Judith could think of no reply to that so she nodded slowly.

Deborah looked at Judith's hair briefly which reminded her that she had forgotten to use a comb after washing it.

'I suppose I should be honest,' Deborah said in a rush, standing to examine Judith's photograph on the wall. 'But if I'd known, well, that she wasn't, you know, just your friend, I might well not have accepted her invitation to come and stay.'

'Well you could always leave,' Judith told her.

'Oh no! Don't you see? Now that I've seen you − the two of you − I don't feel like that. Stupid old Mummy never explained, you see. You know how she was.'

'I know.'

'She just said you were living with . . .'

The telephone rang.

'Hang on,' Judith said, leaving her to drift awkwardly, unanchored by furniture, while she answered it. 'Hello?'

'Just thought you ought to know,' began Esther, who never bothered with greetings or introductions when ringing Judith, 'that we've just had a request for cats for a barn over towards Altarnun. People called Trembath. They don't mind getting a whole family so I thought you could take them that fat tortoiseshell creature and her brood.'

'I don't see why not,' Judith agreed. 'They're all grown-up enough to catch their own mice. I'll come over at once if you like. Will you give me the address when I get there?'

'No. I'll give it to you now. I'll be out.'

'Out?'

'There's no need to sound so suburban about it. I'm not an invalid, it's a sunny day and I thought a short walk around the village would clear out my tubes a bit. Loosen up what's left of the old spine after Harvey Gummer's ministrations. I thought it might be fun to check up on a few things. Got a pencil handy?'

'Er. Yes. Of course.'

Esther dictated the address then hung up.

While Judith copied her morning's pitiful work onto a spare

disc which she kept for safety in a small tupperware box in the fridge, Deborah came forward and rested a hand on the top of the word processor monitor. Judith found this triggered territorial instincts in her, which she tried to dismiss.

'Was that your cat woman?' Deborah asked.

'Yes. I'm afraid I'll have to leave you on your own for a bit. I've got to take some cats out to a barn some way away.'

'Couldn't I come too and watch?'

Deborah sounded so pathetic that it struck Judith suddenly that she might be terribly bored. She took no walks and she never seemed to read.

'How strange,' she thought. 'How cruel that my sister should have grown into one of those people who needs constant entertainment.'

'Yes,' she told her, rising. 'Of course you could. Wear something warm, though. There'll be a lot of waiting around.'

Wrapped, at Judith's insistence, in an old duffel coat of Joanna's, Deborah retained the incongruously elegant silk headscarf that had been her own concession to the cold. She tied it exactly the way their mother used to do. Under the lip but over the chin. Judith was amused to see her look appalled at the run-down state of Esther's house and even more so at the smell of the cat sanctuary.

'There were worse things in Seneca, surely?' she asked.

'It's not the same when you're abroad,' Deborah said, wrinkling her nose. 'Judith, you are good the way you do this. Oh!' She trod on an old sardine, scraped her shoe clean on a brick then retreated to watch from a perch on an old garden roller. 'Can I do anything to help?'

Judith had entered an enclosure and, heavily gloved, was trying to capture the lithe spitfire Esther had referred to as 'that fat tortoiseshell creature'. She made no reply. Having thrust the cat to the back of a basket, she buckled it securely behind its wire mesh door, averting her face as she did so to avoid the swipes from its emerging paws. Encircled by the trusties, who were drawn to the smell on her shoe, Deborah clapped as she emerged. Judith surprised herself by giving a little bow and smiling. The 'brood' – two soon-to-be-strapping ginger toms and a silvery queen – were easier to catch. Born in captivity, they came when they were called and kept their claws to themselves. Until they, too, were boxed up. Judith lifted the four baskets into the back of the Land Rover then she and Deborah drove towards Altarnun, the extraordinarily loud wails and mews behind them putting conversation out of the question.

The farmhouse was in one of the low-lying pockets of lush beechwood in which the area specialised. Dry-stone walls had dressed themselves thickly in moss and ferns which had also sprouted on the trunks of the trees. The damp air was filled with the sound of running water. Unusually, the farmer's wife had made some attempt at a garden, fenced off from the mire of the yard. Judith called in to announce herself and to collect some milk to persuade the cats to stay. The family were eating lunch. The small daughter begged to be allowed to watch but her mother told her to finish her food first.

'They won't go scratching her, will they?' the father asked, fetching her an old plastic bowl and some of the farm's own milk. 'She's a terrible hugger.'

'She can hug them all she likes,' Judith assured him. 'Except for the mother. But she's wild and no one can get near her anyway. Just tell her not to stroke them unless they come to her first.'

'Right you are then, Mrs. It's the rats we want them to catch. I'd rather the littlun was scratched by a cat than bit by one of those. The barn's up this back lane a way. Can't miss it.'

Judith poured the milk out first, setting the bowl in the barn's centre. Then she released the cats; the tame ones first. Deborah tried to help, but received a scratch for her pains and, letting fly a most uncharacteristic curse, retired, licking the back of her hand. When all four were free and feeding, Judith joined her on a mound of hay bales.

'Will they have to kill mice and things to survive now?' Deborah asked.

'I don't think so. At any rate, there's a lonely-looking little girl down there who's all set to feed them to bursting.'

'Oh good.'

One of the ginger toms stopped eating, came to sniff around where they were sitting then vanished, in four quick leaps, over the top of the wall of bales behind them. Suddenly Deborah produced a packet of cigarettes from the duffel coat pocket, with the air of someone who has finally made up her mind.

'Do you mind awfully?' she asked.

'Don't ask,' Judith told her, having failed to hide her surprise. (Not only could Goody Two-Shoes swear, but she smoked!) 'Just be careful where you flick the ash, or we'll go up in flames.'

'Oh yes. I hadn't thought of that.'

'Smokers never do. Here. Use this.'

Judith passed her a miniature fizzy drink bottle that was half-buried in the straw at their feet; evidence of the 'littlun's' secret feasting.

'Thanks.' Deborah lit her cigarette with slightly shaky hands. 'Judith . . .' She stopped and stared at the smoke she had just blown. Even out of doors the smoke stung Judith's nostrils. Like many ex-smokers, the smoking of others badly affected her eyes and throat.

'You want us to continue our talk.'

'Yes. Well. It's more me really. That has to do the talking, that is.'

'Yes?'

'And. You see. Now look, I wouldn't want you to think I've been blabbing about it to Joanna or anything . . .'

'Which means you already have.'

'No!' She almost dropped her cigarette into the hay. She took another drag on it to steady herself. Then, in a quieter voice, she added, 'Well yes.'

'I grew up with you, remember?'

'Yes.' Deborah grew animated. 'Remember the cat we used to have?'

'He wasn't ours. He lived next door.' Judith recalled the animal as clearly as she had remembered their kitchen table.

'Yes but we fed him more than they did.'

'Wasn't he called Guzzler?'

'Muzzler. I don't know why we called him that. Ugly cat really, with that fat face and that boxer's neck.' She giggled. 'And those enormous balls!'

'Deborah!'

'Sorry.'

'Don't apologise. You surprised me, that's all.'

Deborah sighed heavily and tapped some more ash into the bottle where for a second it sizzled in some syrupy residue. She took another drag and stared away through the open barn doors to the field. There were signs of fresh mist forming. She sighed again.

'You didn't really want to talk about cats, did you?' Judith asked her, gently impatient.

'No. I . . .'

Judith took her sister firmly by the shoulders. This was the first time she had touched her since the hug on her arrival. She felt surprisingly strong.

'Deborah spit it out,' she said, 'this is making me lose my temper.'

Deborah spat it out in a gabble.

'I just wanted to say that I know you were beaten as a child.'

'Of course you do,' Judith snorted. 'You were there.'

'I mean I don't want you to think that I've forgotten.'

'I should hope not.' Judith let go of her shoulders in time for a short explosion.

'Oh bloody hell, Judith! You're not making it very easy for me.'

'Well, it wasn't exactly a pushover for me.'

'Well, that's not my fault.'

'You watched.'

'I had to.'

'You could have complained. You never stood up for me. Not once. You never even tried to tell a teacher.'

'How do you *know* that?' White from the cold, Deborah's cheeks were turning pink again.

'Well nothing happened, did it? If you'd told someone I'd have been inspected by the nurse or visited by a social worker or something, wouldn't I? You just sat back and watched.' Judith was so angry that she couldn't look her in the eye. 'You just sat back and let it happen.' It felt as though it were not her suffering they were discussing but that of a third party; she was an adult coming indignantly to the rescue of someone else's battered daughter.

'What else could I do? I was frightened.'

'*You* were frightened?'

'Yes. How could I have "stood up for you"? You were my big sister. You were meant to stand up for *me*.'

'It never struck me that you needed much standing up for. You were the pretty one.'

'You had the brains. He gave me hell when school reports came in.'

'Well he never stretched you across the kitchen table and went for your backside with a cricket bat, did he?'

'No.' Deborah drew a breath as though about to say something else. 'No,' she said again.

Then Deborah cried. This was quite unlike her recent repressed sobs and choked-on mewling. She wailed. It was as though something jagged were being torn from within her. Judith thought again of women undergoing exorcism. Blinded by tears, Deborah fumbled the remains of her cigarette into the bottle then let out a kind of roar, clutching the bottle so tightly the bones seemed to stand out in her fingers. The scar across her forehead seemed more livid suddenly. Judith could hardly bear to look at it. It seemed as though it might tear open to let something terrible free. She threw her arms around her, as if to hold her sister's body together.

'Ssh,' she murmured. 'Please Deborah, ssh.'

She was shocked at how warm Deborah's body felt, even through the duffel coat. Looking over her shoulder as she rocked her, she heard footsteps running up the track towards them.

'Deborah. Deborah, quickly. Someone's coming.'

Still clutching the fizzy drink bottle, Deborah lurched to her feet and ran, waving a handkerchief, out of the barn and around to its other side. She scattered the remaining three cats as she went. Moments later the farmer's daughter came in panting from her run up the hill, mousey plaits bouncing on her shoulders.

'Where are they?' she asked.

'Ssh,' Judith stood and raised a finger to her lips.

'Where are they?' the girl repeated in a stage whisper. Judith pointed to the great pile of bales behind them.

'Up there,' she said. 'Can you see their eyes watching you?' Still panting, the girl stared. 'They'll come down if you wait. They haven't finished their milk.'

'How many are there?'

'Four.'

'Four!'

'Ssh. Yes. A mother – she's the fat old tortoiseshell one you mustn't try to touch – two boys and a girl.'

'Which is the girl?'

'The pretty grey one. She's not fat like the mother and she's more fluffy. There she is.'

Obligingly, the young queen had raised her head, inquisitive, over the straw ramparts. The girl stared up at her, hungry with love. The cat mewed and the girl smiled back. Two of her front teeth were missing.

'If you sit here quietly,' Judith told her, 'she'll come down to you. She's just shy because you haven't met before. That's it. You sit and wait.'

The girl sat, entranced. Judith made her way quietly back to the Land Rover. Deborah was waiting for her inside. Eyes puffed, headscarf tightened, she looked every inch the young widow. Judith smiled at her shyly as she climbed up. They drove homewards in silence until Deborah suddenly asked Judith to stop and said she would walk the last stretch of the way and find her own lunch later.

Excited to have something to write, even if it did little to solve the problem at the centre of her narrative, Judith went straight back to her workroom on her return and introduced a new character to her novel. There was now to be a gap-toothed child, daughter to Edgar's new neighbours and not unlike the little girl she had just met at the farm. Satchel on shoulder, she chatted to Edgar at the bus stop every morning. At night he heard her weeping on the other side of his bedroom wall and he became convinced that her parents were mistreating her but could not muster the courage to break through her sunny chatter to ask her. He never even asked her name.

When Judith broke off her writing in mid afternoon, she was uncertain what she would do with this girl but she suspected she might have her hospitalised or even killed. Or maybe, if it could be done without stretching the bounds of Judith's cynicism, she would have Edgar rescue her. Of course Edgar would be a matricide by then so even if he did bring the little girl to a new life he would be unlikely to be allowed to enjoy it with her. Life as Judith had lived it was rarely so kind and never so simple.

Twenty

His house was far smaller than it had seemed by moonlight. Deborah had taken the little she had made out – a low L of three or so rooms – to be but one angle of the property. She now saw it to have been the modest whole. It was not old, in fact it strongly resembled the post-war bungalow in the reading primers of her childhood. Spring being some weeks off, the climbing roses and wisteria he had trained on wires between the windows were doing little to disguise drab brick walls. Only the yellow splash of a winter jasmine lent the place an enfeebled rustic charm. Although the first frosts had eaten back all but the hardiest evergreens, there was evidence of a well-maintained nursery garden to the rear of the house, with a long seasonal greenhouse made from thick polythene laid over a tunnel of metal hoops. Lung-like, it puffed out and relaxed under the play of the wind. She knocked at the front door and stepped back to sniff at the winter jasmine grown around it before she remembered that it had no smell. She was about to knock again when she noticed a piece of wood nailed to the porch. He would seem to have used a hot poker to burn the message onto it.

IF NO REPLY TRY CARAVAN

She looked around her. No caravan. She knocked once more to be sure then walked around the side of the house, past the back door where he had emerged the other night, past a water butt and between a clump of compost bins. She rubbed her fingers in passing on what she thought was a rosemary bush only to find them smelling of curry. Perhaps he grew drugs here? Illegal ones as well as his 'cures'? The greenhouse might conceal a multitude of nefarious cuttings. She had not seen a single policeman since her arrival, not even a village bobby on a bicycle.

The caravan was, not surprisingly, a battered affair on blocks. An electric cable stretched overhead from a hole in its roof to a hole drilled in what she took to be the kitchen wall. A bird she could not identify (it was black with a red beak) was perched on it watching her progress. It flew off, chattering, as she drew near. The caravan windows were clouded with condensation and droplets of melted frost. Standing on tip-toe, she tried to wipe one clear but succeeded only in soaking her glove. She could make out music and the light of a desklamp but the caravan appeared to be empty. It felt stupid to knock on a caravan door so she simply let herself in.

He was lying on a sofa below the window, sound asleep. His long hair was hidden beneath a closely-knitted navy-blue hat. A paper tissue had slid half-way out of a pocket of his donkey jacket and was flapping in the hot draught from an electric fan heater. A radio, tuned to an Asian music station, lay on the floor beside an empty coffee mug, its volume turned low. With his eyes closed, she admired their long, black lashes. In such total repose his lips were fuller than when tightened in speech. He had cut his cheek and seemed to have staunched the bleeding with a piece of cobweb.

Realising that she was letting cold air in, she shut the door behind her. He raised his eyebrows slightly at the noise.

'Er,' she said softly, 'excuse me.'

He opened his eyes slowly and looked up at her, utterly calm, as though she materialised in his caravan like this every afternoon.

'Hello,' he said.

'He's been expecting me,' she thought.

'I'll go away,' she said, not moving. 'I shouldn't have disturbed you.'

'No,' he said, 'thank you for waking me. It was so warm in here after digging outside, I just nodded off. The music didn't help greatly either.'

He switched off the radio, which increased her sense of exposure. He had not yawned once. *Had* he been asleep? His manner was so immediately fresh and alert that she suspected he had not.

'What can I do for you?' he asked, standing.

He gestured to her to sit down on the sofa and pulled an upright chair out from behind the table for himself. As she sat where he had just been sleeping she fancied she felt the caravan shift beneath her weight.

'I thought,' she said, 'that is, your card said that you were a healer.'

'Yes,' he said.

'How do you heal? With herbs?'

'Herbs are more a cure. To heal, I use touch.' He held up white fingers in demonstration and smiled.

'You mean, er, massage?'

'It's not a dirty word.'

'Sorry. Massage, then.' She repeated the word in a more forthright, clinical manner.

He smiled again.

'Not exactly. I just touch.'

'Oh.' The fan was hot on her legs. A trickle of sweat ran down her side. 'You mean like Rasputin?'

'He was a hypnotist. Take off your coat if you're uncomfortable.'

'Thank you.' Deborah stood, removed Joanna's heavy duffel coat then hastily sat again, her legs further from the fire.

'Where is your pain?' he asked. 'Your face?'

'No.' She realised that her hand had strayed to touch her wounded breast through her jersey. She hastily raised it to the scar on her forehead. 'No,' she told him. 'It's more, well . . .'

'Tell me what did that, again,' he asked, pointing at her face.

'Broken glass. Someone blew up a car with a bomb. My husband was killed. I was standing some way off but a window beside me caught the blast.' He was frowning. 'I think he died straight away,' she said.

'Where was this?' His tone was kinder. 'Were you in Northern Ireland?'

'Seneca. Julian worked there. He was the . . . He worked in the Consulate.'

'Ah.'

'So you see, my pain is . . .' She faltered.

'I see. I see precisely.' His tone was kind and she felt immediately that he did see. He understood that the pain of her new widowhood was enmeshed with the ache on her wounded thighs and breast and her embarrassment at the scar above her eyes. He watched her silently for perhaps a minute, head resting on his hands. She felt no awkwardness, looking back quite calmly and dropping her hand to her lap to bare her forehead to his gaze. When he stood, she followed suit.

'Do you want me to undress?' she asked.

'There's no need,' he said, smiling. 'I only touch your head and neck.'

'Oh!' She laughed. 'Sorry. You must think me an awful idiot.'

'Not at all. Sit down again but lean against the side of the sofa. That's right. Put your legs up if it's more comfortable that way.' His accent had grown perceptibly less Cornish. She wondered whether he emphasised it as a defence against strangers, or simply to improve trade on market days. Carefully she slipped off her wellington boots, straightened the thick woollen socks she was wearing over her tights, then raised her feet up before her, knees bent. 'Now,' his voice was suddenly much calmer, as though he were relaxing in sympathy. 'Shut your eyes and clear your mind.'

Her mind filled at once, with images of cats and barns, of

Judith grown up and Judith young and beaten on a kitchen table. His hands came around beneath her mouth to untie the headscarf. She had quite forgotten that she was wearing it and smiled because it tickled slightly as he slipped it off her. The floor creaked as he shifted behind her. The noise of the fan heater acquired a slight rattle. That black bird was back again; she heard it chattering. Then his fingers began to touch her. They touched so softly, their pressure was so slowly applied, that they felt like extensions of her own skin. It seemed that she had developed unnatural muscular control, so that spots of her forehead, scalp and neck depressed themselves of their own volition. Suddenly, unbidden, she saw herself sitting at her dressing table in Seneca, as though watching from a corner of the ceiling. Julian was standing behind her. He was tanned and quite naked except for a fetching bandage around his hair and eyes and he was slowly, lovingly, uncharacteristically, combing her hair. He was using an ivory comb she had never seen before. From her overhead vantage point, she saw her own face in the mirror, tears running down unscarred cheeks.

Deborah opened her eyes to find herself stretched out on the sofa with Joanna's duffel coat arranged over her lap and legs. She was alone. She sat up and stared for a while at the mixing bowl of dark, dried petals on the table. There was a scoop in it. A tray of empty, labelled packets waited to one side. She looked out of the caravan window. At the end of the garden stood the small mill that had given the place its name. The roof had caved in and only the metal framework of the waterwheel remained. Some climbing plants had been allowed to run riot across the old walls – roses, perhaps, or honeysuckle. She tried to imagine it in summer. Gardening required a vision and a patience which she lacked.

Harvey was crouched over a trench, scattering handfuls of something brown from a full plastic sack. She glanced at her watch and was amazed to see that she had been asleep for over an hour. Filled at once with a reflex panic at lost time and an almost sickening hunger for Judith's indigestible but comforting home-made bread, she lurched up, stamped into her boots and pulled on the coat. When she turned from shutting the caravan door she saw him walking to meet her, spade in hand.

'Better?' he queried.

'Quite extraordinary,' she said, unable to think of any more precise description. 'What do I owe you?'

He shrugged. 'You could always buy some more herb tea.'

'No. Honestly. You must let me pay you.'

'Why?'

'It would make me feel better.' She had taken out her purse.

'All right,' he said, taking it from her. He slipped a note into his back trouser pocket then handed it back. 'Do you want to come again?' He picked at a label on the spade's handle then looked up when she hesitated.

'Well,' she said. 'Yes. Don't let me keep you. It'll get dark soon.'

'No matter.'

Once again she felt him watch her until she had walked out of sight around a bend in the lane.

Twenty-one

When Deborah failed to return, Judith supposed that she had taken a longer walk home than she had previously planned – via the pub at Treneglos perhaps. She thought about making supper early but decided to wait until Joanna's return then suggest that she treat the three of them to a meal at one of the few passable restaurants to stay open beyond the tourist season. She took a cup of tea up to her study but found her mind too full of thoughts of Deborah to work. Frightened that if she spoke to her sister too soon she would say the wrong things, she left food on the kitchen table for her then drove back down the hill and into Martyrstow.

She found a parking space in the square, by the war memorial. Unlike Joanna, who was a glutton for local gossip, Judith preferred to do her shopping in Launceston, where nobody knew her. If she had to go into Martyrstow for anything, she tried to go in the afternoon, when its few shops tended to be quieter. Giant supermarkets having reached the area, it was a wonder that any of the small-time, local shopkeepers managed to make a living. Two of Martyrstow's six shops had been starved into closure in the last few years. One of the remainder housed Meg and Dora Viney – stout pillars of the Methodist chapel and the area's undertaker and monumental mason. Then came *Custance and Daughter, Hardware* and their neighbour, *Toby Sawyer* – who had brilliantined hair and a face like a stoat's but sold locally-grown organic fruit and vegetables and free-range eggs. Across the square, boasting a double shop-front, was Mrs Haines' empire. Like her mother before her, the proprietress was the village postmistress, but she also dealt in newspapers, sweets, bread, ice cream, frozen food, biscuits, cheese, and anything that was tinned. Her proudly displayed initials, S.S., her iron grey hair, stately prow and forthright manner had earned her Esther's nickname – Battleship. She dearly loved a challenge and delighted in ordering anything her regulars could not find on the shelves. Thanks to Judith's enquiries hers was probably the first village stores to stock fully biodegradable washing products and lentils in any colour but orange. After the first public announcements were broadcast concerning AIDS, she actually set packets of condoms within easy reach, alongside the chocolate – until a scandalised deputation organised by the Viney sisters persuaded her to move them to a less attractive corner, in between flea collars and medicated shampoo. Judith successfully bought Esther a bag of tangerines with no more than a 'How's you then? Fine, thanks. Lovely job' from Toby Sawyer but then she had to buy stamps.

Even on quiet days – and Martyrstow was rarely abuzz with shoppers – the postmistress was never reduced to talking with her fluctuating team of shop assistants, for she had a small court of female admirers. These hung on Stella Haines's every word and seemed never to run out of licences to buy or complicated postal forms to fill out. To ensure a place at her counter several of them, Judith was sure, had resuscitated post office savings accounts opened for them by their mothers during the war, thus ensuring long discussions with the postmistress and each other of the relative merits of different bonds. Even with a queue before her, S.S. Haines would not stoop to letting the simplest transaction go by without gilding it with her conversation. Conversation, when Judith came before her, consisted of a chain of questions, asked in a tone guaranteed to alert the deafest pensioner.

'Ah Miss Lamb. How nice.'

'Hello Stella. How're you?'

'Not so bad. Not so bad.'

'I'd like fifty first-class stamps, please, and fifty second-class ones.'

'Lovely job.'

Judith had never bought stamps in bulk until moving to Cornwall. Buying stamps in London was not a perilous activity. Mrs Haines spent a needless amount of time finding the right page in her stamp book.

'First class, did you say?'

'Yes. Fifty.'

'I gather from young Michelle that you've your sister staying with you at the moment.'

'Yes.'

'That's nice,' Mrs Haines nodded. 'A bit of peace and quiet should do her good. Poor thing. We read about her sad loss in the paper.'

'Was it in the paper?' Judith was surprised to find that her brother-in-law had been so important. Then she remembered that the Foreign Secretary was involved.

'Oh, of course,' her inquisitor continued, 'I was forgetting that you don't take one.'

'No.'

'We read about it as I say, but I didn't like to say anything to you, seeing as it was so soon after and I assumed you would still be grieving. None of us thought it right to intrude.'

Judith laughed bitterly.

'I rather wish you had,' she said. 'Being so cut off, I didn't hear about it until days after the event.'

'Well now!' Mrs Haines exclaimed and clicked her tongue. 'What a thing! Fifty first class for you and then was it forty second class?'

'Fifty please.'

'Fifty.' Mrs Haines sighed. 'Terrible business. Imagine. A bomb under his car!' She spoke these last words with a terrible emphasis. Judith imagined the shop assistants growing ever more slack-jawed as they listened. Mrs Haines shook her head. 'They should all be shot,' she said, more quietly. 'All of them. And if the bullets miss their hearts, so much the better. And . . . er . . . Joanna – is she well after her holiday?'

'Very well, thanks.' Judith made a stab at conversation. 'She's so brown I'm quite jealous. Well, brown by her standards.'

'Is she now? Well of course, she's got that fine, pale skin. She needs to be careful.' She nodded meaningfully at a bystander who had been pretending not to listen. 'She does. *Melanoma*,' she hissed. 'The American president had it and all those young men who spend too much time surfing. I read it in a book. Sorry, Miss Lamb. You're wanting to pay. Will there be anything else?'

'No thanks.'

'Lovely tangerines that Toby's got in.'

'Yes. I'm taking some to Esther.'

'Oh, that's nice. She's well is she? Well I needn't ask, actually, because we all saw her. Large as life and out and about! She came in here and we had a good long talk about everything. Those cats, I dunno!' She shook her head, chuckling to herself in a way that said she thought it unhygienic to keep more than one, well-neutered animal at a time. 'Well, I mustn't keep you.'

Judith imagined the slipping of tone and telling of truths that would follow on her leaving the shop. Mrs Haines had never said as much, but Judith knew that she knew the extent of her relationship with Joanna and that she heartily disapproved. However she knew also that her disapproval was tidily balanced by her appetite (need, even) for the differences in other people which were the staple of her conversation and the nearest way of bringing her to congratulate herself upon being proudly ordinary. Joanna joked that Mrs Haines had obviously read some extremely outmoded article on role-playing lesbians of the 'you call me Howard and I'll call you Babe' variety as evinced by her insistence upon calling Joanna plain, 'feminine' Joanna but Judith, the stricter Miss Lamb.

Judith drove around the square and out of the village, past the church to Esther's ivy-clad house. More than ever, she was grateful that her old, doubtless once very proper, friend was so unprurient. Esther's sudden show of fresh-air activity had clearly not worn off. Led there by an exhausted, shivering Bunting, Judith found her building a log pile in the coal shed.

'Esther?'

'Hello old thing.' Esther waved with a mossy log. She had on a riding mac, long, with a split up the middle. It was yellowed with age and the labour-in-progress had spattered it with brown and green. Her silver coiffure, ordinarily her pride and joy, was in disarray, strands falling about her face and sticking to her sweaty forehead. 'I know,' she chuckled, following Judith's gaze. 'Do I look a sight?' She pushed some hair back with a mittened hand and left muddy streaks of surprise over one eye.

'You shouldn't be doing this on your own,' Judith scolded. 'Think of your back.'

'Well I'd completely forgotten the bloody log woman was coming. Has she been to you?'

'No. We use Damon Coles.'

'Oh. Well Verity Thingummy is Battleship Haines's sister-in-law and very Jehovah's W. Acts as though every inconvenience is a way of storing up mercies in Heaven. Bunting and I got back all ready for a quiet lie-down after our rather stately walk and found a great pile of the things just lying outside, blocking the pavement. I thought I should get them undercover in case it rained or someone tripped up and felt they could sue me.'

'Well stop. I can do the rest.'

'Nonsense. I'm not quite a cripple.'

'You soon will be.'

'There! How does this look?' Esther had pulled a large,

none-too-clean yellow handkerchief from her mackintosh pocket and had tied it over her wayward hair like a scarf. 'Am I greatly improved?'

'Much,' Judith laughed at her.

'Cats settled in at Altarnun OK?'

'Fine. I left the daughter watching them.'

'Fat little thing with mousey hair?'

'Yes.'

'Apparently she's diabetic, poor lamb. Aggie told me in the fruiterer's. Now look. If you insist on helping me, you can bring me logs in the wheelbarrow and I'll just carry on building the pile. Can't have you being responsible if the whole thing tumbles down. Oh! Oh dear, well never mind.'

'What is it?' Esther was standing by the pile, evidently at a loss, clutching a log in one hand and patting at the logs below. 'Have you lost something again?' Judith asked her.

'No. No of course I haven't.' Esther's denial was quite angry then she laughed at herself. 'The old cat's mind is wandering, that's all. Come on. What's that song the postgirl's always singing? *Work That Body*!'

For the next half-hour Judith busied herself fetching logs. The prolonged stooping and lifting made her spine ache, so she dreaded to think what it was doing to Esther's. Neither spoke; the work took all their breath, but Esther would grunt acknowledgement as she stood aside for Judith to tip each load through the coal-shed door. Deborah's outburst in the barn had disturbed Judith to the core; she could guess how much from the relief with which she threw herself into the thoughtless repetitions of this labour. It grew dark as she was shifting the last few loads and Esther had to light up the shed with a huge, antiquated flashlight.

'It's a work of art,' Judith told her when the pile was completed. Esther had built a perfectly straight wall of uneven logs which held back the more disorganized mass behind like a mortarless dam. It reached to her angular shoulders. 'I just leave ours in a heap any old how.'

'Well, that's all very well when you've got a bloody great barn to do it in.'

'But this is a wonder of engineering!' Judith was truly impressed.

'You can send L'Americana round to photograph it,' Esther said with a grin and rubbed her back. 'You were quite right, of course, I've probably buggered all my discs again but it was an immensely satisfying way of doing it.'

'Let's get back into the warm and I'll make us each a cup of tea.'

'I was thinking more of a tot of whisky. That bottle I found in the desk the other day has got me back onto it. So much nicer than gin. Bunting and I walked all the way to Treneglos and bought a new bottle in the Williams Arms. Superior stuff for once; Battleship Haines only stocks Co-op blended rubbish.'

'I'm driving.'

'One won't wreck you. Come on.'

Judith fed the cats who had begun to mew, frustrated at seeing her walking back and forth with nothing but logs in the wheelbarrow. Then she walked upstairs to where Esther had lit a fire and poured them each a generous tumbler of best malt. She took a few sips to warm herself then watered the rest down at the bedroom sink. Bunting raised his grizzled muzzle at the waft of cat she brought into the room with her then subsided by the fire to toast his undercarriage. Esther sat up on the bed leaning against a nest of pillows. She raised her glass to Judith then drank, shutting her eyes.

'So,' she asked, 'how's Goody Two-Shoes?'

'Better, I think. Certainly less good. She came with me to settle in those cats today.'

'Oh yes?'

'Esther, is it wrong of me to hate her?'

'Is it that bad?'

'If hatred is forever wishing someone elsewhere, then yes.'

'Ah. Is it something she's done?'

'No. Not really.'

'Then you can't help it and she can't stop you.'

'She's trying. She tried to make her peace with me today. It was terrible. I suddenly realised that I'm not a forgiving person. Not at all. Do you think people who lose a leg go through the rest of their lives hating people who still have two?'

'Curious analogy.' Esther finished her glass and topped it up, muttering something about drinking the second one more slowly. 'What does she make of L'Americana?'

'In a weird sort of way they get on. Joanna's teaching her to drive.'

'Yes. You said.'

'Did I? Sorry. I think it's harder for me because she and I have a background in common and all the hang-ups about loyalty that being family is supposed to entail. Joanna and she are so utterly different that they can meet each other on neutral ground. In between. Am I making sense?'

'Mmm.'

Bunting sighed heavily and rolled over so that all four legs were in the air. His lip fell back to expose a yellowed smile. Judith rubbed his stomach gently with her toe.

'I mean, I feel sorry for her being a young widow and so on, and having that cut on her forehead can't make things easier – although she says it'll heal eventually like all the little ones and disappear – but there's something about her I just can't stand. I think,' she adjusted her position, 'I think it's the way she's always on her best behaviour with me – "minding her Ps and Qs" as she'd put it. She acts as though I'm going to bite her head off any moment which only makes me want to. And I know I'm scarcely a paragon of well-adjusted spinsterhood but I find her so . . . so bloody *repressed*. How long do you think we're expected to put up with her? Esther?'

Esther let out a short snore. Her whisky glass, carefully drained already, had rolled out of her grasp and onto the counterpane. Judith lifted it out of harm's way in case she rolled on it, then she shook out a blanket that lay across the armchair and drew it carefully up to Esther's chin. The action reminded her of a dingy Victorian engraving that had hung in her childhood bedroom until she was old enough and brave enough to take it down. Showing a wavy-haired bourgeois maiden arranging a Madonna lily in the grasp of her equally impressive mother's corpse, it bore the legend, 'Duty's Last Gesture'.

Twenty-two

Joanna glanced quickly back at the menu.

'I'll have the prawn thing to start with,' she told the waitress. 'Then the fillet steak – done rare.'

'Vegetables?' the waitress asked.

'Everything you've got going,' Joanna told her. 'Especially that creamy potato thing with the garlic.'

'Fine.'

The waitress made notes then turned to Judith.

'I'll have the prawns too,' said Judith. 'Then the sea bass with leeks and ginger *en paupiette*. Just a green salad for me. No potatoes.'

They waited a moment then Joanna prompted Deborah.

'How about you, Debs?'

'Oh sorry,' Deborah said. 'I was looking at the wine list.' She returned to scanning a menu. 'Er . . . The scallop and bacon tartlet I think and . . . oh dear, it all looks so delicious – things I haven't had for ages! Oh God.'

'Debs, choose.'

The waitress smiled at Joanna's growling.

'Sorry,' Deborah said. 'I'm being maddening. I'll have the pheasant. Please.'

'Vegetables?'

'Could I have a little selection?'

'Of course. And what about wines?'

Deborah handed Judith the wine list. Judith chose quickly, familiar with the selection.

'We'll start with a bottle of number eight and my friends can have a number seventeen with their flesh. And we'd like a jug of water as well.'

'The water's from a spring on the hill above the village,' Joanna told Deborah as the waitress left their side, 'clean as a whistle and cold as ice.' She picked out one of the anchovy hors-d'oeuvres which had been set out on the table when they arrived. Munching, she gestured to the proprietress who, as was her custom on quieter nights, was eating at a small corner table, one eagle eye on her staff, the other on what she obviously regarded as her guests. 'Most of the villagers collect it in jugs but Ottery-Jones there drives up the track with an industrial drum. She uses it for steaming things and such like. When she first set this place up — before she knew better — she tried to charge for it like it was the bottled stuff. Soon saw the error of her ways.'

Deborah looked around her at the pink stippled walls, candelabra and gilt chairs.

'It's very er . . .' she said.

'You could say that,' said Judith.

'Louis Soixante-Neuf,' said Joanna.

'It's so unexpected,' Deborah went on. 'When you said it was "a fish place" by the harbour I'd expected a glorified fish and chip shop with plastic tablecloths. This is, well, grand. I should have changed.'

'Nonsense,' Joanna told her. 'You look fine. I'm in jeans for Chrissakes.' She paused while another waitress, older than the first, poured their white wine. 'Anyway,' she went on, 'it makes Ottery-Jones feel good if she's the smartest woman in here. Word has it that she had never intended this to be a restaurant at all.'

'No?'

Judith grinned and set a finger to her lips.

'Am I shouting again?' Joanna asked her.

'Just a little.'

'Products of a large family,' Joanna explained to Deborah, 'spend their lives shouting to be heard.'

'Anyway,' Judith continued for her, in an undertone, 'it is said that she was an actress in rep before her marriage – hence the flair – then after her divorce she moved down here, with every intention of living in the place to enjoy her alimony.'

'Trouble being,' Joanna cut back in, 'that she wildly over-spent on hiring some fancy London decorator to do it up and it was a question of make cash *pronto* or sell up. Said decorator being no fool, he offered to turn the downstairs into a restaurant provided she ran the business and gave him half the takings. She agreed and now she eats in here almost every night just to show us that it's her home as well as her workplace.'

'How sad,' Deborah said. 'Poor woman.'

'Hardly,' Judith told her. 'She's raking it in. She's long since bought out the decorator's share. She bought the house next door and turned it into an expensive hotel. And Madame Ottery-Jones is no seaside landlady. People drive across counties to eat here then stay for breakfast. It's booked up months in advance in high season.'

Unable to resist, Deborah turned to examine this paragon of enterprise. Used to such curiosity, Sylvia Ottery-Jones gave her a gracious bow in return. She would come over after their main course to ask if everything had been all right.

Judith smiled at Joanna behind her sister's back, wrinkling her little nose.

'How was your bishop? I never asked.'

'Charming,' Joanna told her. 'And vain but very photo-genic. I was through in an hour.'

'Did you have time to explore?' Deborah asked.

'Yeah. I had a bite of lunch in a pub before I set out for home. You know,' she reached out to touch the back of Judith's hand, 'I am *so* glad we don't have to live in a place like that.'

'I thought it was very pretty and unspoilt,' said Deborah.

'I think that's what she means,' Judith told her.

'Sure it's pretty,' said Joanna. 'Even at this time of year. It's like Toytown or somewhere. I kept expecting the Munchkins to come dancing out from the gardens. The bishop said they had the lowest crime rate in England which I must admit I find hard to believe. If I had to spend more than a week in a place like that I'd be reaching for my axe.'

Smiling at this, Judith turned to her sister.

'Didn't you say that Julian's mother lived somewhere near there?'

'Yes she did,' said Deborah. 'I mean she does. Not far from there. In one of those villages that feel so like a filmset that it's a surprise to find people are still there after dark. We had to stay there a few times and, well,' she picked at a piece of rye bread, 'I didn't turn violent, but I came pretty close to it.'

'Well get her!' Joanna laughed at her kindly and Deborah laughed back, her cheeks pink. Deborah's smile receded.

'This is nice,' she said.

'Mmm,' said Joanna.

Judith gave her another of her private, feline smiles and raised her glass.

'Cheers,' she said. Joanna raised hers in return. Deborah joined in.

As Joanna drank she had a sudden realisation. She set her glass heavily back on the tablecloth.

'OK,' she sighed to Judith, 'this is unforgiveable of me but I admit. I had completely forgotten the date.'

'What do you mean?' Deborah asked.

'What date?' asked Judith.

'Oh don't play naive with me. Today's date. You organised this dinner. You remembered.'

Judith laughed for a moment then, in exaggerated shock, touched her hand to her face.

'I didn't,' she said. 'At least, I had the idea of taking you two out but I . . . You won't believe this but.'

'You *never*!'

'I did!' Judith gasped.

'My *God*!' Joanna fairly shouted. 'Well at least that lets me off the hook. Are we getting old or what?' She laughed and reached out to cup Judith's cheek in her hand.

'What?' Deborah asked. 'I don't see.'

'I had completely forgotten,' Judith told her. 'And what is so funny is that it turns out that she had completely forgotten too.'

'*What*?' Deborah begged.

'That today is our anniversary.'

'But that's wonderful!' Deborah cried, and a barely detectable crack in her voice told Joanna that, on the contrary, this other couple's continuing happiness brought a widow nothing but pain. 'We must have champagne.' Deborah hugged Judith, who was still chuckling. 'You must let me pay for a bottle. No. I insist.'

'But we've already ordered your burgundy,' Judith said, ever the stickler for detail. 'And you're both eating red meat for your main course.'

'So?' Deborah went on, unnaturally carefree. 'We can have champagne with pudding.'

And when their first course arrived she ordered a bottle to be put on ice.

Like Joanna, Judith seemed to have sensed now the tactlessness of their celebration. Quietly picking at her cluster of king prawns and *crudités* she tried to draw Deborah out on the subject of her driving lessons. Deborah obliged for a while but then circled back on the matter that must hurt her.

'So,' she asked, 'how many years is it now?'

'Nine,' said Judith.

'Eight,' said Joanna.

'She's right,' said Judith.

'Feels like a whole lot more.'

'Well thank you very much.'

'What I mean,' Joanna said, 'is that after five or six years of living together you stop counting what's behind you and start thinking years ahead of where you are. It's only when you've been with one person that long you can make the final break with family. Leaving home is never enough; it's only when they see you dedicate yourself to someone else that they accept they've lost your first loyalty.'

'Judith and I are all the family we've got left,' said Deborah uneasily.

'Are you sure it isn't nine years?' Judith asked Joanna.

'Positive. I've still got the ticket to prove it.'

'You haven't!'

Joanna reached into her jacket pocket for her wallet. Tucked into a compartment behind an old passport photograph of Judith was a faded ticket for a showing of *La Dolce Vita* at the National Film Theatre. She passed it to Judith.

'Our first date,' she explained to Deborah.

Judith smiled over the scrap of card, shaking her head.

'What do you keep this for?' she asked.

'To stop you pretending I've known you longer than I have. Anyway, what happened to yours? That was the special one, after all.'

Judith dismembered her last prawn.

'You know I lost it,' she said. 'It was in the wallet that got stolen in Perugia.'

'Oh yes.' Joanna drained her glass and looked at Judith smiling over the ticket.

'How did you meet, then?' Deborah cut into their reverie.

'You don't want to hear all that.'

'Yes I do. I'm curious.'

'These things are rituals,' Judith murmured. 'They need retelling at regular intervals.'

'Was it at a party?'

'You wish,' Joanna mocked her. 'I picked your big sister up in a park.'

'No!'

'Not just a park,' Judith qualified. 'It was St James's. Did you ever meet Gus Fleming?'

'I don't think so.'

'Tall, very patrician-looking.'

'Total bastard,' added Joanna.

'As she so rightly says, a total bastard. I'd always known him as one half of a couple then she left him and I found myself homing in to pick up the pieces. Not a good idea.'

'Oh dear.'

Judith broke off while the older waitress cleared their plates away. She poured herself another glass of the white wine before continuing.

'Anyway I had just about finished breaking up with him. No, I *had* broken up with him but we had to meet in St James's for tea so that I could give him back the clothes he'd left behind him in the flat. There were some dirty socks, a tie and a jersey.'

'And so?'

'Well,' Joanna broke in, 'I just happened to be in St James's too. I was taking some pictures of people feeding the birds on the lake and this, well, this vision . . .'

'Ha!' Judith snorted into her glass.

'As I say this vision walked into my viewfinder. I tailed her back to the cafeteria. One look at the expression on her face, that creep she was sitting with and the socks and junk she was handing him told me she was ripe for the picking. I had two tickets for *La Dolce Vita* on my person – I had been planning to take an ex of mine to it actually – so I wrote my phone number on the back of one . . .'

'And you wrote "I dare you",' Judith reminded her.

'That's right. "I dare you." Then I sashayed up to the two of them and pretended I'd known her for years. I said "How *are* you, darling? Mild winter we're having," and all that stuff and I slipped the ticket into her pocket.'

Deborah's jaw had all but dropped. She turned to Judith.

'And you went to the film?' she asked her.

'I was at a very low ebb.'

'Enough of that!' Joanna flicked a piece of bread at Judith across the table. This incurred a pained look from Sylvia

Ottery-Jones which melted into a sickly smile under Joanna's challenging glance.

'Are you very shocked?' Judith asked her sister. 'You are, aren't you? We weren't even introduced.'

'I think it sounds terribly romantic, actually,' Deborah said. 'Because it was different from the way most people meet, you've remembered every tiny detail.' She stopped to admire the food that was being set out before them, watching, fascinated, as Judith cracked the filo pastry parcel around her piece of fish.

'How did you meet Julian?' Joanna asked, ignoring Judith's wince.

It was the first direct question she had asked her about him. She had sensed, rightly it seemed, that Deborah needed to discuss him. Deborah continued to carve at her pheasant breast for a moment, as though she had not heard the question.

'I was set up,' she said at last. 'We both were.'

'How so?' asked Judith, and Joanna could see that, for all her pretended disdain for her late brother-in-law, her writerly curiosity was aroused.

'Well you remember – actually you probably don't – but when I finished my secretarial course at the Ox and Cow I shared a flat in Fulham with some girls from school. There was Tricia (it was her flat) and Emma and Fiona and Charlie and me. The flat was nice but sometimes it was pretty awful, all of us squeezed into it. Tricia was the only one with a room to herself, of course, so if anyone wanted to, you know, bring someone home, they had to bribe her to give up her bed.' Judith groaned.

'What?' Deborah asked.

'Nothing. This just brings back awful memories of my student house.' She smiled kindly. 'Tell us what this awful Tricia did to you.'

'I'm not sure it was just her. I think it was a bit of a team effort. Everyone in our crowd had boyfriends you see. I was always rather, you know, old-fashioned and I think it put people off. Anyway, it had got to be the big joke with them; that I was the maiden aunt who was always on hand to chat to people's mothers and help with the cooking.'

'Ha bloody ha,' said Joanna, pouring them both some more red wine. She offered to pour Judith some of the white but she waved her hand over the glass. She was driving them home.

'Anyway, Emma's boyfriend – he was a merchant banker – came to supper one night. Emma had told him to bring a friend and he brought Julian, who'd been at school with him. Julian and I barely said a word to each other. We were sitting on the same side of the table. I thought he was rather pompous because he talked about politics. Anyway, a couple of days later the girls told me that Julian thought I was wonderful and wanted to meet for dinner.'

'Uh-oh,' said Joanna.

'I remember thinking it was a bit odd of him not to have asked me himself but they said he was quite shy and had asked Emma's boyfriend to ask Emma if she thought it would be OK.'

'Did you go?' Judith asked.

'Yes. Needless to say it turned out that Tricia and the others had told him that I was wild about him and a complete nympho. They'd told him I liked to pretend that I was a wilting violet while what I really wanted was to be, erm, sort of raped.'

'Jesus!' Joanna hissed.

'The joke was on them in the end though,' Deborah laughed gamely. 'Julian was always very direct. Half-way through dinner he stood up and said he couldn't wait any longer and he fairly dragged me into a taxi back to his place.'

'Deborah!' Judith was scandalised.

'What?' Deborah asked.

'You didn't go? After everything they'd made him think?' Deborah had taken a mouthful of pheasant. Her steady chewing raised the suspense.

'Yes,' she said. 'I did. I was so embarrassed and angry with

167

them and it seemed a good way of getting my own back. I'd heard Tricia say she was very keen on him and so on. Anyway, I didn't go back to the flat in Fulham for three days. I didn't ring or anything. And in the end Tricia came round to see if I was still alive.'

Joanna was unsure how to react so she kept quiet.

'You see,' Deborah turned to her, 'Although I'd started out by using him – and I suppose that did shock me rather – after Tricia had admitted she was worried, after I'd won, it was as though I was noticing him for the first time. There was something véry straightforward about it all. At least, there was at first. We got engaged after just a month. Don't you remember?' she asked Judith. 'Tricia and Emma were my bridesmaids.'

Mrs Ottery-Jones had made her silent approach and was standing at Joanna's elbow.

'So nice to see you both again,' she said. 'Is everything all right?'

'Delicious, thank you,' said Judith.

'Perfect,' Joanna added. She smiled but all she wanted suddenly was to be back home. She wanted Deborah shut away at the other end of the house and she wanted to find herself in bed, in the dark, with Judith lying warm between her legs.

Twenty-three

Deborah leant against the stove waiting for the kettle to boil. She had drunk slightly too much at the restaurant as had the others, who had giggled throughout the perilous drive home at something they left unexplained but which Deborah could divine well enough. Flush with the easy money of her day's commission in Barrowcester, Joanna had insisted on treating them both. Although the bill had seemed ludicrously expensive after the restaurants in Seneca, Deborah had protested that it was a good opportunity to pay them back for their hospitality.

'No Debs,' Joanna pushed her cheque book away. 'You save your pennies.'

'I don't think I need to,' Deborah told her. 'When Julian's pension and life assurance come through to me I shall be rather well off.'

Joanna laughed at her and thrust away the money she was offering for the champagne.

'Get you! Well when it does you can treat us to somewhere *far* better than this.' She handed her money to the waitress with a drunken smile. 'Thanks, hon.'

'When your pension does come through,' Judith asked, more quietly, 'what do you plan to do?'

'I hadn't really thought,' Deborah confessed. Joanna hurriedly changed the subject and soon after she and Judith began their prolonged flirtation. Steadying herself by the armrest in the back of Joanna's car as they lurched along the clifftop road out of St Jacobs, Deborah continued to wonder with increasing unease. Julian had always said she was 'well provided for' but she had seen no figures. For the first time since his death she was confronting the possibility that she would have to find a job again. Her only qualifications were secretarial, and those had long since begun to gather dust. The memories of office work stirred up by her reminiscence over dinner were far from appealing. Perhaps Julian had died too young? Perhaps the life assurance would come to no more than a token annuity? Perhaps she was expected to find another man to support her?

The kettle boiled. She spooned some of Harvey's prescribed infusion into a teapot then poured the scalding water over it. A sweet, slightly farmyardy smell rose up in the steam as she carried teapot and mug to the kitchen table. She brought some honey from the larder, set a teaspoonful in the mug then sat to wait for the mixture to infuse.

Water had finished running down the pipes from Judith's and Joanna's bathroom; they were in bed now. The giggling had stopped but occasionally she caught the low murmur of their conversation. It was only in the last few years that Deborah had discovered that anyone took lesbianism seriously, that it actually happened, and between people who weren't necessarily criminal or unattractive. Her mother had only mentioned the topic in terms of abusive suspicion, as in, 'I wouldn't be remotely surprised to discover that Delia Collins was a lesbian.'

For Mother, lesbianism and communism were interchangeable perversions. At school 'lesbian' had similarly been a term of abuse, nothing more. In the bilious letters Mother had written in her last illness, she had broken the news to Deborah that her sister was living 'more than ever in sin' but had given no details. It had always seemed to Deborah that her sister needed to be 'bad' and it had crossed her mind when she first understood the nature of Judith and

Joanna's relationship that, having exhausted the possibilities of the promiscuous enjoyment of men, she had simply gone one step further. It was like what Julian had always told her about drugs; that one started on the softer stuff but ended up having to experience the hard. Now that she had been here longer, however, and especially since she had seen their pleasure at remembering their anniversary, she had begun to revise her opinion. Whereas on the very few occasions when she had been allowed to meet Judith's boyfriends, Judith had worn a contrived air of worldly aplomb, she now seemed natural. It was as though she had found her true self and no longer cared what brave impression she was creating. She was not happy, of course, not being a happy person, but listening to her laughter in the car tonight it had seemed to Deborah that she was now as happy and relaxed as she could be. She wished that Julian were there to explain. She feared she was being misled.

Deborah poured out a mugful of infusion and stirred in the honey. She sniffed it. The smell was less farmyardy now. It had deepened into something warmer, more spicy. She took a sip. Vanilla and cinnamon. A curious mixture and, with the honey, an almost overpowering one. She tried to ignore what she was sure was the squeaking of her hostesses' bed. She drank some more – it had cooled rather fast – and then found her head filled with the image of Harvey coming to meet her outside the caravan, his hands caked in mud, giving her that strange smile. There was something soft about him. She would almost have said that he was feminine, but of course that was nonsense. But he was unlike other men. He was unlike Julian. The smell of the drink reminded her of Harvey's caravan. She drank again and pictured him, as she had done over and over as she walked home that afternoon, pictured him watching her slide into that sleep, or trance or whatever it was, then gently lifting her legs into a more comfortable position on the sofa, arranging her clothes perhaps, then softly draping her with her coat as one draped an accident victim or a corpse.

Disgusted at herself, she stood, walked quickly to open the front door, then tossed contents of both mug and teapot onto the grass. The moon was new and clouds had covered the stars. She stood there looking out at the extreme blackness of the night.

'This is absurd,' she thought. 'I'm acting as though it were a love potion he gave me, not some cranky herbal tea.'

Judith had spoken over dinner of some writer woman she knew who had left her husband to run off with a Devonshire farmhand. It was not as foolishly romantic as people supposed apparently because said 'farmhand' was actually an accomplished, even commercial, potter.

'All the same,' Joanna had added, 'very D. H. Lawrence.'

Deborah had never read D. H. Lawrence, but Julian had taken her to see the film of *Women in Love* so she knew enough to sense that it would be 'very D. H. Lawrence' to be made love to in a caravan by a muddy-handed herb gardener.

She laughed silently at herself and walked back inside. But even as she was washing up the teapot and mug she knew that, drunk or not, she was too exhilarated to go to bed. It was late. He might be asleep. Whatever would he think of some strange female turning up twice in one day?

'Grotesque, woman,' said Julian.

'Harvey can think what he likes,' she thought, ignoring him. 'If there are no lights on, I can assume he's asleep, and come back at once feeling foolish. If nothing else, the walk will make me sleepy.'

There were lights on. The kitchen was lit up and, as she walked along the drive she could see him drinking beer from a can by the flickering light of a television; hardly the picture of alternative healthy living.

'This is entirely out of character for you,' Julian told her and she rang the doorbell.

The bell was a cheap, battery-operated one fixed on the other side of the door. It sent vibrations through her finger as she pressed. The spell was immediately broken and she wanted nothing but to run away. It was too late however.

'It's open,' he shouted. 'Come in.'

She walked through a drab uncurtained kitchen and found him crouched in front of the television, turning off its sound.

'It's you,' he said. 'Hello.'

'I couldn't sleep.'

'It's not late,' he said.

'The others had gone to bed already,' she said. Her knees were shaking so she sat on one end of the sofa. The room had no curtains either, but was beautifully warm. 'Am I disturbing you?' she asked.

'Ssh. Close your eyes.'

Without her asking, he was already touching her as he had that morning. His young hands were so soft. Not gardener's hands at all. She felt herself sway.

'I'm drunk,' she thought. 'I'm not going to go into a trance, I'm going to pass out.' She could smell beer on him. 'I might even be sick.'

He pressed fingertips to each of her temples then slowly dragged his touch back and up across her scalp.

'No,' she said. 'I . . .'

'Ssh. Relax yourself.'

With an immense effort of will she drew herself forward out of his grasp and pushed herself into a standing position.

'I'm sorry. It's no good. I really must,' she said, turning, and found herself standing up against him, the tip of his nose only inches from the tip of her own. They were the same height. She lurched backwards. He caught her. Thoughtless, she pulled him to her and kissed him lightly on the lips. She looked at him, astonished at the sudden clarity of his beauty as much as at her action. Then she kissed him again.

'Heal me,' she thought and he responded with his tongue. She pulled back again, let go of him and touched her hair.

'I'm sorry,' she said. 'God I'm sorry.'

'That's all right.' His eyes shone in the light from the television. His smile was kind.

'I just . . . I can't. Not . . .'

'Don't worry.' He took a step towards her. 'We'll only kiss.'

'No,' she insisted. 'No. I'm sorry. No!' And she fled back through the kitchen, along the drive and onto the lane. She didn't bother to turn. He wasn't following. She wept as she walked, tears of mortified confusion.

Before climbing into bed she carefully folded and packed half her clothes into her suitcase. Then, having lifted a jersey and uncovered the plastic urn of Julian's mortal remains, she less carefully unpacked her clothes and set them back in their drawers.

Twenty-four

'OK,' Joanna told her, 'I want you to pull in at a safe place on the other side of this junction, check the way is clear every which way then reverse us round the corner.'

'What?'

'You heard.'

'I thought it wasn't allowed.'

'You can reverse off a main road, you can't reverse on.'

'Oh.'

'So do it. Uh-uh. Why's this not a safe stopping place?'

Deborah looked around them.

'Someone's entrance?' she suggested.

'You got it. Never mind. Reverse. Slowly.'

'Which way do I turn the wheel?'

'Same direction as you want our rear to go. That's right. Good. Not too close — you're working too hard. That's it. Nice 'n' easy. Now straighten up. Further. Use your mirror. No. This one here. That's it. Slowly. And stop.'

Obediently Deborah braked and shifted the gear-stick to neutral.

'How did I do?' she asked.

Joanna opened the passenger door to gauge their distance from the kerb.

'You're a bit far out but you're straight, which is the important thing,' she said. After a pause she added, 'And there's a joke in there somewhere.'

'Where?' asked Deborah, 'Oh yes!' They laughed.

'OK,' Joanna told her. 'Now you can do something useful with this newly acquired skill and take us to the supermarket.'

'Which way?'

'Er. Bodmin, so left, then left again at the junction and keep straight on till I tell you to stop.'

Deborah took them onto the Bodmin road, calmly executing rather too swift an entry at the junction so as to avoid having to trail behind a laden cattle lorry.

'Did Judith tell you I interrupted her work yesterday?' she asked.

'No. She just said how the two of you went about her cat business together mid morning. Was she mad at you?'

'I don't think so. Well. Maybe. That's why I asked. The thing is, I couldn't help noticing that she hadn't written anything.'

'Maybe she was just starting on a new chapter.'

'Maybe. But she didn't look it.'

'Debs, what the hell are you driving at?'

'Sorry. I mean that once I was up there she seemed glad of the distraction, as though she was having trouble working.'

'She did mention something but I didn't take it too seriously. I mean, the woman's already produced twelve novels – talent like that doesn't just dry up but she's bound to have off days like the rest of us.'

'Perhaps I was imagining it.'

'I dunno. She's kind of secretive about her work. Just disappears up there day after day and then suddenly there's this new novel to talk about. But not until it's done. I think she's superstitious about them the way some women are about the babies they're expecting – not buying clothes for them until the last minute; that sort of thing.'

'Where now?'

'Straight over and on. Watch your speed. There are children here sometimes.'

'Sorry.'

'You never mention her books, Debs. Didn't you like them or something?'

'I know. It's a bit awkward. You see I never read, really. Not much. Well I do, but not proper novels.'

'Only what Jude would call "pulp" huh?'

'Mmm. I did try to read one of hers once – after all not everyone's sister writes novels, and people do think terribly highly of her – but I found it awfully hard. Actually, I gave up on it.'

'Join the club.'

Deborah laughed with relief.

'No! You too? My God, and you're her . . . her . . .'

'Come on, sister. Spit it out.'

'Her lover.'

Joanna cheered. Deborah laughed.

'I thought it was just me being stupid,' she said.

'Uh-uh. I'm stupid too.'

'You're not.'

'Am too.' Joanna laughed at her incredulity.

'But you never sound it. You always have something to say and, well, I mean, last night you were mentioning all sorts of people I'd never heard of.'

'Those were film people. They don't count. Anyone can sit in a pitch dark room, appreciate a movie or two and pick up a few names.'

'But you read, don't you?'

'Yeah, but only murder stories and stuff.'

'Not Judith's?'

'Well, I'm started on a second one of hers. I managed to read one on holiday – in Seneca, that is – and I figured if I could get through one maybe I should try another. Wait for this lorry, Debs. I think his indicator's bust. Thought so. Yeah well, nothing much happens in them but I guess there's an extra fascination for me – seeing as I live with the woman. They might teach me things about her I didn't know.'

'Joanna, there's no way you're stupid. Judith *hates* stupid people. She always has. That's why she hated Mummy. She can't bear women to be just wives.'

'Debs, I may not be "just a wife" – I earn more per hour on a shoot than she does in her hayloft – but I assure you that in academic terms I am one dumb redhead.' Deborah shook her head.

'You're just saying that to make me feel better,' she said. 'I never went to university. I failed the spelling exam at secretarial college three times.'

'So? I've got no degree either. I tell you, you're talking to the woman who barely learned long division, much less graduated out of High School. But if you think I'm bright, I hate to think how dumb that makes *you*!'

Deborah laughed. For some reason she was very easy to amuse today. Joanna wound down her window a little, lit a cigarette for each of them, Paul Henreid style, and they rode the few miles to the supermarket smoking and singing along to an old Tammy Wynette tape Deborah had unearthed in the glove box earlier. The clouds of the night had brought on sporadic drizzle in the morning. They were forced to run across the supermarket car park as the drizzle turned into a full-blown cloudburst.

Deborah was doubly insistent upon paying for this shopping expedition because Joanna had bought their dinner the previous evening. Once she had finished buying cigarettes and having her cheque stamped in advance, Joanna tried to coax her out of her headscarf.

'Makes you look twice your age,' she said. 'Makes you look like some sourpuss farmer's wife.'

'I feel so self-conscious about this,' Deborah flicked a hand towards her forehead.

'Deborah, look around you. These women aren't peaches and cream perfection. If they're young they've got faces like pizza with make-up on and if they're over forty they look like the surface of the moon. You're among a tribe that stuffs junk food all winter and fries itself raw whenever the sun shines.'

'She's pretty.'

'Where? Oh. Her. Well one pretty woman in a supermarket isn't going to wreck your day. Take it off. It's hot in here. You want to broil yourself? Anyway, people are only going to peer at you to see what you've got to hide. You're like some Beverly Hills broad trying to look inconspicuous by shopping in dark glasses. That's it. Take it off. And fluff your hair out a bit. You've got such pretty hair.'

'You sound like my mother.'

'From what I've heard, that's no compliment. Here. You get the fruit and I'll get the veggies.'

'What do we need?'

'One lime, two lemons, three pink grapefruit and three pounds of everything else. Nothing with a label on it unless it's English or Spanish; it'll only be from some place Madam wants us to boycott.'

Having fetched fruit correctly enough, Deborah then contented herself with pushing the trolley while Joanna filled it. She sprang to life in the bathroom section, however, slinging in shampoo, conditioner, medium flow tampons, baby oil and cotton wool buds with gay abandon. Joanna held the latter up for closer inspection.

'What do you find to do with these?'

'Ears,' Deborah told her. 'Ears and tummy button.'

'Ah. I always use my pinkie and a flannel.'

'Oh.'

'I guess yours are more petite.'

They had trundled through the bread and frozen food sections when Deborah asked:

'What's a pinkie?'

'Little finger.'

'Thank you. I've always wanted to ask that. For some reason I thought it was something rude.'

'Want me to explain anything else while we're at it?' Joanna asked her as they joined the back of a check-out queue. 'Cunnilingus? Smegma? Dildo? *Soixante-neuf*?' She winked at the woman in front who had turned round enquiringly.

'Not here,' Deborah hissed.

'Go on. Disown me. I don't care.'

'Ssh.'

'You know Debs, you're so much fun to tease.' She smiled but Deborah was looking earnest.

'Actually, there is one thing,' Deborah ventured once the woman in front had begun to busy herself.

'Enquire within. My carnal knowledge is encyclopaedic.'

'What?'

'Let it pass. You were asking?'

'Well, the thing is, I think someone's interested in me.'

'"Interested"? Who?'

'Harvey Gummer.'

'Harvey the Herbalist?'

'Ssh.'

'Jude was right! How do you know?'

'Never mind. I know. You won't tell her, will you?'

'Not if you don't want me to, no.'

'She'd only . . . Never mind. The trouble is . . .' Deborah fiddled with the knot of her headscarf, pulling the material tight around her neck then letting go. 'He's so young.'

It was on the tip of Joanna's tongue to say,

'So? It's not as though you're really serious about him. Have a fling and no harm done.'

But she saw that Deborah was looking utterly solemn. She looked like a teenager discussing the outcome of an all-important first date. Only Judith had made Joanna feel so calloused with amorous adventure before, and *she* was no cloistered nun. What *was* it about these Lamb women?

A space began to appear on the conveyor belt. Joanna clicked down a Next Customer bar and began to pile up their goods behind it.

'This is really important to you, is it?' she asked.

'I don't know. Not really.' Joanna caught her eye. Deborah smiled then looked solemn again. 'Maybe,' she confessed. 'I don't know.'

'Do you actually know his age?'

'No.'

'You're just guessing that he's much younger?' Deborah nodded and continued the loading while Joanna slipped forward and began filling bags. After a while Deborah joined her with the empty trolley and helped. 'I can tell you, up on that moor a lot of those villagers are related by blood as well as marriage. Half the births registered are the fruit of incest passed off as the grandmother's without fooling a soul. What's a little age difference? At least he's not your brother. Take control for once, Deborah. Be your own mistress. You want something? Why shouldn't it be yours?' She swung the last bag into the trolley. Deborah wrote out a cheque. As she joined Joanna by the door she shook her head sadly. 'Not that simple, huh?'

'No,' she said. 'Not really.'

'Want to talk about it?'

'Not really. Sorry, Joanna. You are a help. You've cheered me up. But I shouldn't have mentioned it. My God, poor Julian's only been dead a matter of weeks. I must be mad. Thanks, though.'

'Any time.'

Deborah kept her mouth shut as she concentrated on driving them back towards Martyrstow. The cassette, left in the player from their drive over, began to play 'D-I-V-O-R-C-E'. Joanna lit them each a cigarette and let Tammy do the talking. Neither of them sang along.

Twenty-five

Judith worked through what was normally her lunch hour, claiming over the intercom that she had come down and snatched an apple and some cheese while they were out shopping. Joanna resorted to an old standby for cold lunchtimes — tinned sweetcorn and tinned cream of chicken soup whizzed up in the blender then heated — and made toast from stale bread. Evidently regretting her hasty confidence re Harvey Gummer, temptation posed by, Deborah had reverted to polite conversation. Preferring offended silence to studiously banale twittering, Joanna passed her half of the newspaper to shut her up then retreated with her share of the soup into a long article on American foreign policy. Then, leaving a still taciturn but less poker-faced Deborah curled up in a sitting room armchair, torn between attempting one of Judith's easier, early novels and watching a video from Joanna's collection, she retired to her dark room and locked herself in.

She had finished processing her Seneca films within days of her return, but, through lethargy but more through distaste, had so far avoided looking at the results. She began to wind one through her enlarger, subjecting each image to scrutiny as it scrolled into view on the white paper beneath. She lit a cigarette. Apart from her den, her dark room was the only spot in the house where she could freely smoke. She was resolutely ignoring Judith's frequent claims of late that the fumes seeped up through the ceiling and onto their bedroom staircase.

The first three shots taken of a diminutive roadside tea-vendor were spoilt because his eyes were shut, but in the fourth he stared out at her from the shade of his stall with a look of superb gravity. She filled the four trays beside the enlarger with fluids from the bottles on the shelf above – developer, fixer, a stop-bath and a wash – then switched off the desklamp and bathed the room in red safe-lighting. After slipping a sheet of photographic paper into place, she adjusted the enlarger's timing mechanism then set it to print.

She could tell that Deborah was obsessed with the idea that she had been unworthy of her late husband. Perhaps Deborah even blamed herself for his death. She had a tendency to assume responsibility for mishaps. When Judith had dropped and broken a saucer the other night, Deborah, who had just washed it up, apologised. The ultimate in quirks of fate, Julian Curtis's accidental assassination had just the bungling quality that appealed to her low self-esteem. She probably felt that the easiest way to compensate for the negative effect she had taken on his lifetime was to remain true to his memory after his death. The longer she could wait, the easier she would find it to keep any new male approaches at a respectful distance. She was already using that headscarf and her (fairly insignificant) scars for just such a purpose; it was extraordinary that young Harvey Gummer had managed to penetrate the young widow's *pudeur* as far as he had.

Joanna slipped the embryo print into the tray of developer and watched carefully for the right moment to fish it out again. Slowly the boy reappeared, with his steaming tea-urn, corrugated iron shelter and soulful stare. She waited until his eyes were just dark enough then tweaked the new print clear and slipped it into the stop-bath to halt its growth. Tongue thrust into her cheek with concentration, she transferred it to the tray of fixer then left it submerged in the final wash, glancing at her watch to see when she should take it out to dry. Although, like all conjuring, she knew it to be a matter of meticulous preparation, she had never ceased to marvel at the seemingly magical process by which she could summon stolen images out of stiff white paper. She had once come second in a portrait competition sponsored by a magazine. The second prize was an excellent camera, to be presented at the end of a guided tour of a factory where photographic paper was made. Superstitious that certain mysteries should not be revealed, she had cried off the tour, pleading indisposition, and had the jury send her the camera by courier.

She wound on the developed film, making several prints in succession: two of the belly-dancers she had found, one of the carpenter, also a street-cleaner, some tiny girls weaving, a black boy unpicking wool from an old carpet and a wall-eyed blind urchin who cleaned the shoes of passers-by. This last one shocked Joanna's work to a halt. As she watched it appear beneath the surface of the developing fluid, she recognised a glimpse of the British Consulate beyond the dusty tangle of traffic that had made such a din behind the boy's indifferent back. She tried to remember at what stage in her holiday she had taken the picture. It was obviously before her visit to Deborah's bedside – her stock of film had run out by then – but she wondered whether, when she crouched on that particular stretch of pavement, Julian had already been destroyed. No. She looked closer and saw that the consulate Union Jack was still at full-mast. Julian might even have stopped the consulate car there that morning and paid the urchin to clean his shoes.

When she had set a bemused Launceston travel agent to buy her a return flight to Seneca, Joanna had done so with no thought of Julian. In fact, until she opened the out-of-date newspaper in the Senecan-French restaurant that morning, she had quite forgotten that he was the local consul. Had she remembered, she would have bought a flight elsewhere, to Mozambique perhaps or Mauritius, in an effort to let unpleasant memories lie. As she sat reading of his disgusting demise the possibility had crossed her horrified mind that some small, subversive portion of her brain had remembered every detail of his latest appointment and had steered her to the Hotel Continental with every intention of allowing a fresh encounter to occur.

She had met Julian seven years ago, after his marriage to Deborah and after her own embarkation on the liaison with Judith. The American magazine for which she was then the London-based staff photographer had sent her to photograph an extraordinary lunchtime gathering of lady ambassadors in some elegant rooms off Whitehall. Julian had been there to receive her, guide her around, introduce her to people and stop her photographing anything she shouldn't. When he quietly suggested they meet for a drink when she had finished, she said yes without thinking. Neither was it a matter of intellect or even taste when she said yes to his urgent suggestion that they check quickly into a room of the hotel where they were drinking.

She had not had sex with a man since her late teens. The experience was no more subtle than she had remembered but Julian had exhibited less greed and more ardour than her scrabbling high school beaux. It was only lying back on the pillows in the over-heated room, watching him hurriedly dressing, that she took time truly to observe him. She had indulged herself in him the way she very occasionally dined on barely-browned slabs of steak; all the while diverting her mind from what her body was so rapaciously doing. Still emerging from a daze of satiety, she felt less guilty than curious as to what she was feeling.

'Would you like to meet again?' she asked.

He stopped buttoning his fly to look up with an expression in which need followed hard on surprise.

'Would you mind?' he asked.

'If we didn't?'

'If we did.'

'No,' she told him. 'I'll ring you at work.'

'No!' A note of panic. 'I'll ring you.'

'Impossible.' She pictured Judith at work in bed in Clapham,

Judith reaching out to answer the telephone, Judith frowning, puzzled. 'I live with somebody.'

'Here then?'

He pushed a lock of hair off his ungiving, boyish face. His need was so palpably stronger than hers that it aroused her dangerous curiosity.

'Yes,' she said. 'Lunchtime tomorrow. Keep the same room. I'll be here at one.'

He had kept the room, had paid for its keeping, for five days. Monday to Friday. On Friday she had walked to the hotel — yet another Hotel Continental, she now recalled — rehearsing a short speech.

'This is the last time,' she intended to say when he had once more rolled, panting, from her side. 'I hate hotel rooms and I suspect, if we were to spend any length of time outside one, that I'd find I hated you. I have no love to spare and my body has been lent, not given.'

He spared her speechifying. No sooner had he penetrated her than he pinned her wrists above her head and, after a flicker of smile, hawked then spat in her face. She kneed him twice in the groin, the second time sharply before his hands had time to protect himself. Then, once his hands had rushed instinctively down, she punched him hard on the cheek, so hard that she bruised her knuckles. While he writhed, she snatched her clothes and ran without a word to lock herself in the bathroom. She washed his spit off her face, showered, dressed then sat on a bunch of towels against the bathroom door until he had stopped crying and left the room.

It was only that evening, watching Judith talk to her in the interval of some new play, that she realised how appalled she would be ever to learn that Judith had effected such a betrayal. But Judith wouldn't, she realised. She saw that now; Judith never would. The less surprising that sex became between them, the more fiercely Judith clung to the evolutions of their relationship. Judith had done all there was to do with men or, Joanna imagined, had it done to her, in the years before they met. When they met, when Joanna had taken her photograph among the geese in St James's Park then walked boldly up to her and falsely introduced herself as an old acquaintance, way back then, Judith was busy getting herself wounded by the last in a long line of unworthy men. For Judith, Joanna knew herself to represent refuge, a kind of completion and pure, womanly integrity. Raised on the Godless certainties of *National Geographic* and the *Encyclopaedia Britannica*, Joanna found her lover's idolatry perplexing and just a little scary.

Joanna glanced at her watch then lifted several prints clear of the wash, shook them free of droplets and hung them back-to-back on an overhead line. She heard Bette Davis's clipped tones of chin-up martyrdom coming from the sitting room and a sudden upsurge of music that placed the film at once. Deborah was watching *Now Voyager*.

Julian had given Joanna no more details of his wife than she had of her 'somebody'. He sensed perhaps, as she had, that their intercourse was enabled solely by this lack of particulars just as the thrill it gave him (independently of any contribution from her) arose from its being professionally ill-advised. Two years later, not long after their move to Cornwall, Judith's mother had died. Judith had attended the funeral alone – protecting, jealously as ever, the divide between home and family. She had returned angry, triumphant and slightly drunk that night clutching an electric tin-opener for the cat sanctuary and a box of her mother's belongings apparently forced on her by the mysterious Deborah. This box had lingered for days, unopened, on one end of the dresser. Then Joanna tore it open impatiently one morning to find a canteen of silver, a sky blue cashmere twin-set, mugs commemorating three royal weddings and a silver jubilee, a toast-rack and, in a heavy silver frame, a photograph of Deborah and Julian on their wedding day.

'Sod the picture. Keep the frame,' Judith had exclaimed, weighing the object in her hand when she finally came to pick over the dingy trove and Joanna grudgingly let her have a scaled-down self-portrait for it. She kept the wedding picture too, however, retrieving it from the kitchen trash can and secreting it in a file in a corner of her dark room. As a picture of Deborah it represented a thin light shed on the murky territory of Judith's family, as a picture of Julian it was a reminder that Joanna Ventura *née* Verdura was not as 'sunny side up' as her mother had always maintained.

She shook out the prints of the shoe-shine boy and hung them up to dry alongside the others. She picked her cigarette out of the ashtray.

'You'll have to tell her,' she thought, imagining the sisters, as she did increasingly, as two faces of one barely decipherable coin. Deborah she had to tell if she was to save her from starving to a sexual death during sentry duty outside a whited sepulchre. Judith she had to tell, because, with the exception of her account of one week of lunchtimes, she had made it the cornerstone of her love always to tell Judith everything.

Twenty-six

Deborah had chosen to watch a video rather than read her sister's book. There was a fire made up in the grate beside her but, rather than waste fuel (there being only her to enjoy it), she had fetched a blanket from her bedroom and wrapped herself in that. Joanna had amassed a substantial collection. Meticulously labelled, they filled a large bookcase where they were tidily arranged according to director and date. With a few exceptions, which Deborah suspected would shock or frighten her, they were all tapes of films made before 1960. Most of the titles were unfamiliar but she soon discovered that Joanna had glued photocopies of each film's entry in a film guide to the front of its box, giving cast, plot outline and terse critical comments. There were few horror films and no Westerns, with the exception of *Cattle Queen of Montana* which formed part of Joanna's near complete Barbara Stanwyck library. Deborah crouched on a stool for a while, reading the stories, amused at their telling repetitions. Browsing through the George Cukor section, she was tempted by the plot of *The Women* until she saw that it was a comedy. Instead, she opted for *Now Voyager*.

She avoided black and white films as a rule; she found the lack of colour sinisterly reminiscent of dreams and the poor quality of so many of the soundtracks left her with a headache. *Now Voyager* seemed fresher than most however, and from the first shot of Bette Davis's sensible shoes descending the stairs, she was hooked. Charlotte Vale's transformation from lumpen depressive to high-heeled sophisticate and the scenes where she bested her tyrannical mother (especially the one where the mother died) were compelling. With the heroine's breaking off her advantageous engagement to a wealthy widower however, and that for a man who could give her nothing but the occasional well-mannered visit and the loan of his pudding-faced daughter, Deborah's sympathy withered. The admirable woman had turned out to be nothing but a sentimental martyr, albeit a wealthy one. Deborah reached for the remote control panel and switched off the video, feeling obscurely cheated.

There were footsteps on the kitchen flagstones. She looked over her shoulder and saw Joanna who was leaning on the metal rail that ran the length of the stove. She was staring down at the gleaming hotplate lids as one might gaze through one's reflection in a pond.

'Did the noise put you off?' Deborah asked her. 'It's finished now anyway.'

'No, no,' Joanna called back, not turning. 'That place is pretty much sound-proof. How's about some tea?'

'Lovely.' Deborah began to rise from her armchair. 'Let me help you.'

'I can boil a kettle, Deborah.'

'Sorry.' She sank back and pulled the rug about her again. Rain was being blown hard against the windows. Some soot fell into the fireplace. Joanna brought in teapot, cups and a cake on a tray. She pushed the door shut behind her with her foot.

'Tea,' she said, setting the tray down on the low table between them.

'Should I call Judith?'

'She gets her own when she's ready.'

Deborah munched slowly at a slice of cherry cake pausing to sip the steam off her teacup. Joanna ate a slice too then poured her own tea (she liked it strong) and sat back on the sofa to break the silence.

'Do you mind if I ask you a personal question?'

'No. Well. No. What?'

'How well did you know Julian?'

'Very, I should hope.'

'Do you mind my asking?'

'Not at all. It's good for me to talk about it. Him.' Deborah sipped. 'I knew him very well,' she went on. 'His parents were rather formal you see and he was an only child. So I often felt I was a sort of younger sister to him; someone he could confide in without having to impress. Although he did impress me, of course. And sometimes he did talk down to me rather but that was because he was older. And I can be so silly sometimes. You know?'

As when they had asked her to talk about him at the restaurant the night before, she was struck by the way that her words seemed to lay him to rest. Each careful sentence she fashioned was like a hand combing the dead man's hair, arranging his final button-hole, smoothing his deathbed suit. As after the death of her father, she felt beneath this sense of the dead man's impotence against her quiet, taming phrases, a disturbing temptation to lie. No. It was less a temptation to lie than an uncertainty as to whether she had lied already. Words tidied Julian, committed her to a version of him which she must be careful not to vary.

'Did he,' Joanna asked, 'go out with many girls before he met you?'

'Oh yes. At least, he was engaged once before. She broke it off because a previous boyfriend had moved back to England from Hong Kong or something.'

'But after he met you . . . ?'

'Oh no.' Deborah was vehement. 'Definitely not.' And with her vehemence came insinuating doubts. 'Although,' she added, 'I was always afraid of it. I think that's how I can be so sure; I'd have noticed it straight away. Besides, he was too busy. I think mistresses take up a lot of time. Aren't they meant to be more demanding than wives? I know I would be, in that position. It's the lack of security, I suppose. They need so much assurance.'

Joanna drained her cup before setting it back on the tray.

'Debs, you mustn't be so sure,' she said. She pushed back a handful of glossy hair and looked her straight in the eye. Deborah liked Joanna more each day, but not when she played woman of the world, not when she patronised. Americans could be so superior. Julian had always joked about them in private, calling America 'Our Atlantic Colonies'.

'I don't see why not,' Deborah told her.

'Look, he's gone. He can't come back and criticise you. You can admit it now; he was only human. He was just a man. You've got to be careful, Debs, or you'll trap yourself. You're still so young. I can't stand to watch you honouring his memory like he was some war hero. Like you were, I dunno, some Vestal Virgin.'

How *dared* she?

'Oh yes? And what experience do you have?' Deborah stood and walked to a window. 'You've never been married have you?'

'No.'

'And apart from your mother, all your family are still alive, aren't they?'

'Well yes. Look. I'm sorry.' Joanna shrugged. 'I'm not trying to get at you or anything.'

'You could have fooled me.' Deborah picked at a bowl of shells on the windowsill.

'Well I'm not.' Joanna held out a hand in a pleading gesture then let it fall to a cushion. 'Sit down, for Chrissakes.'

Deborah sat and poured herself another cup of tea. It had begun to stew but she sipped at it anyway.

'I'm not a Vestal Virgin,' she said quietly. 'But he did die horribly and I had to watch it and I know it will take me a long time to get over that. I know you're trying to help, to make me fall into the arms of Harvey or, or someone else who comes along, and that's sweet of you. But Joanna, I need time. Of course I need to honour his memory. He wasn't perfect – neither am I – but if I don't honour what I can remember of him, I don't have much left. Don't you see?'

'Yeah.' Joanna cut a sliver off a corner of the cherry cake and picked at it. 'I see. I'm sorry if I made you mad. It was just . . .'

'I know.'

'. . . after what you started to say in the supermarket this morning . . .'

Deborah tried to silence her.

'I know. I know,' she repeated. Joanna fell silent and ate the rest of the sliver she had cut. Deborah waited, letting her own anger subside to reveal, in all its wearing inevitability, the unwelcome plot-twist which Joanna was raising between them. 'So you'd better tell me,' Deborah said, 'everything you can.'

'Debs, I don't think . . .'

'*How* did you know him? You weren't at Mummy's funeral.'

'I used to live in London. We did, before we moved down here. I knew a lot of Londoners.'

Deborah picked at the buttons on her cuff.

'And one of them told you something about him and . . . some woman.'

'Not exactly.'

Deborah's impatience made her angry again.

'Tell me, then. What did he do that I don't know? Spying? Drugs? Small boys?'

'No, no.' Joanna all but laughed at her. 'It *was* a woman.'

Deborah felt queerly relieved.

'Oh,' she said. 'And what makes you so certain this was true?'

'Remember him coming home one evening with a badly bruised cheek?'

Deborah thought back. November. There had been a fireworks party.

'I remember. He was punched by a drunk who asked him for money outside the tube station.'

'He was punched by me.'

Deborah felt a sudden warmth in her gut, as though she had just gulped neat whisky.

'How long?' she asked.

'A week. A working week. Five days.'

She remembered Joanna, a weird, uninvited apparition at her bedside in Seneca. She remembered how Joanna had wept with her.

'Would you mind very much,' she asked deliberately, 'leaving me on my own for a bit?'

Joanna murmured something like, 'Sure', and walked into the kitchen closing the door softly between them. She had left the tea things behind her. Deborah wanted to cry. She wanted to cry so much. She tried staring hard at a sofa button, holding her eyes wide and unblinking until the effort stung them. Not a tear. The rain had stopped and, with the slick rapidity of a children's cartoon, the clouds had broken into ribbons against a sky of brilliant blue. A sheep bleated and, to complete the scene, some birds began to sing. At a loss, she cut herself a large slice of cake — twice the size of her original portion — and walked up the stairs to her bedroom, biting ravenously at it as she went.

Twenty-seven

In her more morbid moments when she assembled dialogue in her head for this scene, Judith had always given herself stage directions to pull the word processor from its trolley and hurl it in a satisfactory blast of sparks and broken glass at the floor. Or, depending on her mood, at Joanna. Her soul had proved prophetic in that the scene was indeed taking place in her study, but she found herself incapable of violence. Instead, like one of her stunted creations, she gently reached out to the keyboard and tapped the button marked EXIT. Joanna had been standing beside her but now, anticipating an assault no doubt, she retreated to a distant windowsill, where she sat. Judith watched her.

'Why him?' she asked. 'Of all the men in the world, why him?'

'Does it matter?'

'Yes. It smacks of conspiracy.'

'He wasn't "him" at the time,' Joanna protested. 'Not to me. I didn't realise until I saw their wedding photo.'

'But why?'

'Believe me, hon,' Joanna's voice was low, 'if I knew why, it would never have happened. I saw him. That's all. I saw him, he saw me and . . .'

'Stop. I don't want to know. How long?'

'Five days. Five lunchtimes. It didn't mean anything.'

'It never does.' Judith made a fist and punched the back of

the chaise longue rather than the word processor. A terrible thought entered her mind. 'But you went to Seneca on your own. You laid such an emphasis on the importance of going on holiday on your own and then you chose Seneca *knowing* he was there.'

Joanna grimaced.

'You'll never believe this but I had honestly completely forgotten that they were based there. Jesus! You had too, Jude. Remember? That change of address card Deborah sent you got thrown in the bin after breakfast. You knew I was going to Seneca and you didn't say anything. You didn't even joke about "Give my regards to my sister" or anything. You'd forgotten.'

'So it was just fate, then? A horrible shock for you?'

'Yes. I'd been talking about going there for ages after we saw that documentary on the women working in those dye pits.'

'All right. I believe you,' Judith conceded, not quite sure that she did. 'But to do it with a man. I thought you were better than that.'

'"Better"?'

'And such a stuck-up, right-wing, pompous little *git* of a man! Tell me why? *Why*, Joanna?'

'You tell me. You're the expert.'

Judith paused, momentarily winded.

'All that was before I met you,' she said.

'So? Didn't we always agree that men didn't count? Didn't you always insist that infidelity with another woman would hurt you so much more? Didn't I always tell you that men were no competition?'

'Yes. Yes.' Judith began to cry, which made her words sound all the more childish to her. 'But it was all very easy to say; I never thought you were ever going to be interested in them.'

'I wasn't. I'm not. Julian was my first since, since . . . Jesus! . . . since Peter and Ricky Gruber in high school.'

'Then *why*?'

Joanna stood and walked over to one of the tall, yellow radiators which she clasped with both hands.

'I'll resist the temptation to say "Why not",' she said, quietly. 'Look. You've always treated me like I was some kind of sapphic goddess or something. I used to think it was a joke – it still is a kind of joke – but then I began to see what lay behind it. You think . . . You thought I was better than you because I'd never had sex with a man. Why the hell? *I* never said I was better, did I? If anything, I felt *you* were better. I felt you were the stronger one because you were making a conscious decision to change rather than,' Joanna shrugged, 'I dunno, following the dictates of your pussy or something.'

Judith felt that her every surface was raw. Joanna's words stung her even as they sought to soothe. The very sound of her speech caused her pain. Her cheeks were streaming with tears. She ached for Joanna to take her in her arms but knew she would flinch furiously at her touch.

'I love you,' Joanna said. 'If I didn't I wouldn't have told you this. I'd have let this lie grow hard between us. Worse still, I'd have left you to find out through some crummy hint of Deborah's.'

'She wouldn't have told me,' Judith wailed. 'I'd never have known.'

'Well think how I felt. It only lasted five days – probably not even five hours if you just take the time we actually spent together – but I've bottled it all up so it feels like I've been deceiving you for years. *Years*, Judith. As though the fucking affair was still going on. Christ I love you. I love you so much. I've never stopped.' Joanna never cried, yet even she was beginning to sound tearful.

The telephone rang. Judith jumped as if it were a firecracker. She stared as it rang five, six, seven times.

'Answer that, will you?'

If Joanna had a pet hate it was unanswered telephones.

'I can't,' Judith muttered, dabbing her cheeks finally with her sleeve. 'Deborah will get it.'

'I don't think she will.'

Judith sniffed fruitily then reached out for the receiver.

'Here. Let me.' Joanna took it for her. 'Hello?' Her tone was brusque. 'Er. Yes. This is the cat sanctuary, I guess. How can I help you? . . . Well why not go right on and shoot it? . . . Oh. I see . . . She did? Well give me your address and so on and we'll see what we can do.' She took Judith's pencil and scribbled on a notepad. 'Uh-huh . . . Uh-huh . . . Fine . . . Yeah.' She hung up.

'Who was it?' Judith asked.

'Some farmer. A Mr Penry? Says he thinks they've got a feral cat killing their chickens. He thought it was a rogue badger but his wife pointed out that it's been getting in through the chicken run roof and badgers don't climb. He was going to shoot it but your friend Esther told him to ring you. Said you would trap the thing and have it put down humanely.' Judith held out a hand. Joanna ripped the address off the notepad and passed it to her. Judith stood and made for the stairs.

'Bloody Esther,' she muttered. 'I hate killing them.'

'Hey!' Joanna chased her to the door. 'I love you.'

Judith gave her a perfunctory hug but the combination of relief, spent tears and the desire to punish left her feeling deeply uncomfortable so she broke away. She wound down the Land Rover's window as she started the engine.

'This could take an age,' she called out, then drove away, glad at the distraction of a demanding chore. She glanced up at the mirror and saw Joanna watching her from the yard. The fresh sunlight flashed from the puddles around her and made her hair glow against the stone of the barn.

Twenty-eight

As the initial shock of what Joanna had told her passed, Deborah sat on her bedroom windowsill feeling hemmed in. She had thought of walking across the yard to talk to Judith, but she had sensed that Judith knew nothing of what had passed between Joanna and Julian and there was no way she could tell her how she was feeling without betraying Joanna's guilt. Then she heard the Land Rover starting up and saw Judith driving away from the house. She was uncomfortable at being left alone with Joanna, besides which the house was growing uncomfortably warm now that the sun had come out. She pulled on a light coat then waited at the foot of the spare room stairs to listen. Joanna was in the kitchen. Deborah heard the clink of bottles as she opened and shut the fridge door. She heard her unscrew the lid on what was probably the jar of biscuits then clunk the kettle down on the back of the stove when she had made herself a cup of something. Deborah peered around the door's edge and saw her walking out into the hall. A door opened and closed. Deborah waited until she was sure that Joanna would not reappear then walked briskly to the kitchen and let herself out by the back door.

She had no plan in her head save to escape the house and walk in the sun for a while, but once she was striding down the hill between the high hedges, the sun on her back while she breathed in the sweet stenches of silage and wet earth, she decided to walk all the way into Martyrstow. She hesitated at the end of the lane, tempted by the turning to Treneglos and Harvey's caravan, but she remembered that it was market day and he would not be home. Besides, she was too confused by what Joanna had told her to feel sufficiently the mistress of her actions. If she found that by chance he had come home early, if he looked at her the way he had when she kissed him last night, she would almost certainly find herself without last night's resolve. Something had stopped her packing, after all, and she suspected that it was more than her characteristic indecision.

In the market square at Martyrstow she went into the village stores to buy herself some bars of chocolate – a commodity sorely lacking from Judith's larder. A well-upholstered woman behind the post office counter at the back of the shop was deep in conference with two scrawny, younger customers with badly permed hair. Deborah could not help hearing them mention 'Mad Esther', which pricked her conscience. Soon after her arrival, when she was barely able to hold a conversation without breaking down, much less leave the house, she had been touched by the present of an old cut-glass scent bottle sent her by Judith's friend – presumably the 'Mad Esther' under discussion. Handing over the money for her chocolate supplies, she asked the salesgirl the way to the cat sanctuary. Her words silenced the postmistress's conversation, although not spoken especially loudly, and three heads turned in her direction.

'Cross the square,' said the salesgirl, evidently less interested than her employer, 'follow the road out towards the church and it's the big house covered in ivy and that, on the right-hand side.'

A small crowd of shoppers and some schoolchildren were waiting to board a bus in the square as Deborah passed. One of them, a striking old woman with a slight stoop, swathed in an antediluvian riding coat, called out as she passed,

'Excuse me, but aren't you Judith Lamb's sister?'

Deborah halted, surprised.

'Yes? I'm Deborah. Deborah Curtis.'

The woman held out a wrinkled, bony hand.

'Esther Gammel. How d'you do.'

'Hello. I was just coming to find you, as a matter of fact.'

'Really?'

'Yes. I feel so awful. You gave me that enchanting little scent bottle weeks ago and I still haven't thanked you.'

'You liked it. Good. Only old junk really. My house is piled high with the stuff.'

'It was sweet of you to think of me like that.'

Esther Gammel peered at her, searching her face.

'You don't look much like her,' she said. 'But there again, I knew it was you straight away.'

The rest of the small queue had boarded the bus.

'I think they're waiting for you,' Deborah said.

'Oh yes.' Esther glanced round. 'I'm going on a jaunt. Come too.'

'Well, I don't . . .' Deborah began, then thought she might be sounding impolite, so asked, 'Where are you off to?'

'Not far. Tintagel. I suddenly realised I hadn't been there in ages. The bus stops there for forty minutes while the driver has her tea then it comes straight back – end of the line, as it were. Have they taken you there yet?'

'No. They haven't taken me anywhere much,' said Deborah, feeling a twinge of disloyalty. 'But I really ought to be getting back. I never told anyone I was . . .'

'It's a terrible dump really,' Esther went on, impervious to the driver's revving of the engine and the impatient glares through the bus windows. 'Full of tourists in the summer, but it's a ghost town at this time of year, and the castle's extraordinary. Come on.'

Something in her bearing and face reminded Deborah of a favourite teacher – a French teacher – who had made a pet of Deborah despite her being one of the least adept girls in the class.

'Are you sure it turns round and comes back in just forty minutes?' she asked but Esther had headed up the steps and was already buying her ticket. Deborah glanced around the square then climbed up after her.

'End of the line and back again,' she asked. 'Please.'

The bus was too full for them to sit side by side which was something of a relief. (Deborah had always been abashed at the nakedness of conversation on public transport.) They sat on either side of the aisle, Esther a few rows in front. Esther turned from time to time to smile at Deborah, nodding as though to reassure a nervous child. The driver, a barrel of a woman, drove like a Senecan taxi driver, reckless speed evidently the only thing that made her job worthwhile, and seemed oblivious of any children or hens that ran squawking out of her path. She wore her blonde hair in two stout plaits on either side of her face. Deborah fancied she saw them swing as the bus careened around corners. Several of the passengers seemed to live at houses even more isolated than Judith's. The bus would stop to set them down by cattle grids or gaps in the hedge, where the only signs of life were milk churns on a slate shelf or weather-beaten signs pointing the way to a farm. Slowly the land around them grew less rural. The ancient hedgerows and wind-distorted thorn trees gave way to the occasional caravan park and to bungalows with hectic colour schemes. Some of the unnaturally orderly front gardens they passed seemed to have abandoned planting altogether in favour of inanimate ornamentation; seashells, plaster animals, the inevitable gnomes and even shards of mirror. House after house announced bed and breakfast services, flats, rooms or mobile homes to let and soon Esther was turning more and more often to point with an ironic leer at sights like *Ye Olde Smuggler's Chippie, King Arthur's Café* or *Queen Guinevere's Filling Station*. After winding along a street of gift shops and cafés which were mostly boarded up behind vivid blue or orange shutters for the winter, they lurched to a halt in a deserted car park bordered by a bowling alley and a chapel of rest.

'Tintagel,' announced the driver as the doors hissed open. 'Just in case anyone hasn't noticed. Bus sets out again five o'clock sharp. Thank you very much. Not at all I'm sure.'

'Told you it was a dump,' said Esther as they left the car park. 'Look at that!' She pointed at a bucket outside *Lancelot's Rock Shop*. It was filled with multi-coloured plastic swords and a paper flag which fluttered in the breeze bearing the legend, EXCALIBUR 50p. 'Castle's down here.' She plunged down an unprepossessing alleyway behind some public conveniences. It opened out onto a track.

'Oh!' Deborah exclaimed. She had not realised that Tintagel was on the sea.

'What's up?'

'Nothing. It's just so nice to get away from all the houses.'

'Quite. From here onwards it only gets better.'

The track led steeply down into a gorge where a brook ran noisily to spill over the rocks and onto a beach. The beach had some golden sand but was made gloomy and forbidding by the walls of overhanging rock that shadowed it. Deborah followed Esther across a bridge over the brook then up the steep hill on the other side. The combined forces of wind, rain, housebuilding locals and dramatic subsidence had caused many of the castle's walls to collapse to a height of little more than three or four feet. Deborah had never been good at reconstructing ruins in her mind's eye and these ones were more challenging than most since the original castle seemed to have been the size of a small town. The large promontory, which had once been entirely fortified against anyone foolish enough to brave the boiling seas beneath it, had subsided in its middle. Visitors now had to cross onto its tip by way of a hair-raising flight of steps stretched out along the thin spine of rock that was all that remained to link the two sections. Deborah looked around her as she clung to the iron rail on her left, at the seagulls wheeling overhead and the surrounding fields which sloped crazily down into rocky precipices over the Atlantic. The wind blew her hair about her eyes. She felt her mouth drop open.

'We're in luck,' Esther called from up ahead. 'Sometimes they lock this bit when the weather's been rough. Don't want to take responsibility for people getting blown out to sea. Come on.' She led Deborah through an arched doorway and into a series of roofless chambers that were steadily more crumbled until one faced nothing but a vast horizon of sea and sky. Esther sat on the last piece of wall.

'Heavens!' sighed Deborah as she joined her. 'And did Arthur really live here?'

'Uther Pendragon, I think. His father. Merlin smuggled Arthur out to safety in a boat when he was only a baby. But don't quote me on that. I'm very hazy about it. You'd have to ask your sister to be certain. She knows everything.'

'Yes. She does tend to.'

'At least,' Esther went on, 'if she doesn't, she says something with great conviction so that you'd never guess. Would you like a barley sugar? I've just found some in my pocket.'

'Yes please.'

After the tang of salt air, the sweet's flavour was so familiar, so evocative as to defy analysis. Deborah blew her nose. The wind was making it run. They sat together in silence for a few minutes, catching their breath, sucking their sweets and watching the sliding and plummeting of the gulls, then Deborah twisted around to scan the stretch of coastline that wound into the distance to their left. 'Where's St Jacobs?' she asked.

'Well,' Esther turned, 'you know, my eyesight's so bad on long distance nowadays that I'll have to do it from memory. Let me think. We're at Tintagel so, going round to our left, the next beach is Trebarwith and then Tregardock, so St Jacobs should be a little way on. Can you see a big streaky rock a little way out to sea from the cliffs?'

'Yes.'

'Well that's Gull Rock at Trebarwith. Now let your eyes stray along the cliff top from there until you see a clutch of trees on the brow of the land. They'll be before the rocky headland on the far right.'

Deborah scanned the view.

'Got them.'

'St Jacobs should be tucked away in the bay below them. You can't see a thing from here because it's so sheltered. Have they taken you there?'

'Only for dinner, so it was dark.'

'Not to Ottery-Jones's place?'

'Actually, yes.'

'Any good?'

'It was rather. A bit pretentious, maybe.'

Esther grunted as though to say this was an understatement.

'So you haven't seen it by daylight?' she asked.

'Not this time around, but I did stay there with a schoolfriend when I was a little girl. It's a lovely place. Her family were very musical.'

'Let me guess. Three daughters? All about your age?'

'That's right.'

'The Pollocks!'

Deborah laughed.

'How did you guess?'

'An educated hunch. Did they drag you off to the festival at Trenellion or weren't you there in the summer?'

'Yes they did.' Deborah smiled at the memory. 'I had to sing in the chorus. I'm practically tone-deaf but they couldn't find a babysitter so they took me along and tucked me well out of sight. Everyone else was terribly experienced so it was hideously embarrassing. But it was a lovely holiday. Things at home weren't awfully cheerful just then so I suppose it was good to get away somewhere on my own.' She remembered the awkwardness of her father's daily telephone calls from his surgery. 'Looking back,' she said, 'I wouldn't be surprised if the whole thing hadn't been arranged by my mother for just that reason. I didn't really know Sophie Pollock at all – we certainly weren't friends. I remember it was rather difficult when her mother came over at the end of term to invite me, because Sophie was in a more senior class and we weren't supposed to talk to each other much.' She laughed. 'You know how strict little girls can be with each other.'

'Indeed I do. I used to have a rather mad painter friend who lived over in St Jacobs. Dead now, of course, but she'd certainly have been around when you were there. Perhaps you knew her. Bronwen. Bron.' Esther paused and frowned, crunching the remains of her barley sugar. 'I can't for the life of me remember her surname.'

'I'm afraid it doesn't ring a bell.'

'Ah well.' Esther looked down at her watch. 'We shall have to be heading back,' she said, 'or we'll be stranded in this hellhole for the night.' She grunted with the effort as she stood up, wincing when her back straightened. 'I'm far too decrepit to be doing this really,' she confessed. 'I haven't walked this far in years.'

'You were fairly striding up that hill,' said Deborah. 'I thought you must do it every day.'

'Bravado,' Esther chuckled, 'foolish bravado. I shall rue the day when I try to get out of bed tomorrow.' She began to lead the way back through the ruins. 'So how are things up at the farmhouse?'

'Oh fine,' Deborah said. 'I think I may be outstaying my welcome a bit. It's been so kind of them to have me to stay this long; I don't think they ever have people for more than a weekend usually. The trouble is I haven't decided where to go next.'

'Judith can be a bit short with people, I know,' Esther said. 'Has she been biting your head off?'

'Not much.'

'Mmm.'

'Careful of that broken step.'

'Yes, I'm OK. The thing is she doesn't really understand what you're going through. I mean, both your parents are dead but she wasn't wild about them was she?'

'No.'

'So their deaths don't count. And then, well, L'Americana's alive and kicking.'

'Who?'

'Ms Ventura.'

'Oh yes. Very.'

'But I lost my husband much the way you did, you know.'

'Really? Judith never said.'

'I think she tends to forget I ever had one. Most people do. He was so young. Blown away in the war. He was only twenty. We'd hardly been married a year.'

'How awful!'

'Yes and no. That sounds unspeakable, doesn't it? I mean, of course it was awful for someone to die like that – so violently and so young – and, of course, I was in a terrible state afterwards but . . . I was married very young too, you see, although I was actually more than a year older than he was. I suppose I got married for the usual reasons; because everyone else did, because I wanted to leave home, because I wanted a little independence, because I wanted to wear grown-up clothes. Because he asked me to. I know we never had a chance to test ourselves, but I don't think I'd have been a very good wife for him. I wasn't cut out for it, and Edward was fearfully traditional in his expectations. It was only much, much later that I found out how much his death meant to me, decades later.'

'In what way?'

'Oh . . . the things married women take for granted, like companionship in your old age. And children. I should have loved to have a child. Just one. So I could make a better job of it than my parents did.'

'Mmm.' Deborah felt her sorrow lapping up through her.

She took a deep breath. A herring gull on a wall above them threw back its head, flapped its wings and shrieked at the heavens before plunging down to the waves. 'Did no one else come along?' she asked Esther. 'You must have been young still.'

'Oh yes. Someone did. We lived together even, which raised a few eyebrows. But it didn't last and then I gave up.' She stopped in her tracks and turned to face Deborah, so suddenly that Deborah nearly tripped and had to steady herself by seizing a clump of grass on the slope that rose above the path. Esther took Deborah's spare hand in both of hers and pressed it hard. As she stared hard into Deborah's face, searching it again as she had when they met in the village square, Deborah saw a wildness in her eyes, a kind of despair. They seemed naked suddenly, like the reckless eyes of the blind. 'You mustn't give up,' she urged, squeezing Deborah's hand for emphasis. 'Don't ever catch yourself thinking, "Well I'm over-the-hill and single and that's that." Hope is like something that lights you up, shows people you're there. Give up hope and you might as well be invisible. Never give up, Deborah. Will you promise me that?'

'Yes,' Deborah stuttered, surprised into instant compliance. 'Yes of course I will. I promise.'

The old woman released her hand with something like relief and went on her way. As they were crossing the brook again, Deborah paused on the low granite bridge. She looked back to where the sea thundered onto the gloomy beach and then glanced up the slopes above her to where the castle walls emerged like battered extensions of the natural slabs of rock beneath. Turning back to see Esther climbing on up the track oblivious, she felt that they were both very small and alone.

Twenty-nine

Joanna was woken by the telephone at her ear. The room was in pitch darkness except for the dim red glow of the alarm clock. She fumbled for the bedside light and managed to tip it onto the floor so that the bulb flared briefly then died with a pop. With the telephone still cheeping at her, she crawled across the bed and felt more carefully for the other. She blinked at the sudden glare. She appeared to have fallen asleep, quite literally, with all her clothes on. She rubbed her eyes and pushed back her hair.

'Still no sign of Judith,' she thought. 'Poor hon. The telephone. Judith.'

'Hello?'

'Joanna. It's me.' Judith's voice sounded weak and tense. 'Did I wake you up?'

'Hi. Yes. But I wasn't in bed. Not properly. Are you OK? Have you caught the cat yet?'

'No. Look, I'm fine but . . . I'm at Esther's. Could you come down?'

'Er. Sure. Right now?'

'Please.'

'Here I come.'

'Quickly.'

Judith hung up. Unsteadily, because sleeping in tightly laced boots had given her pins and needles, Joanna hurried to the front door, snatching her raincoat on the way. As she drove away, she saw light shining from behind the spare room curtains. Deborah had returned from a long walk only to go straight to her room, refusing Joanna's peace-offering of supper. Joanna had eaten alone, drowned her tension in two rapid beers then collapsed in slumber.

Martyrstow showed no signs of life as she passed through it, except for a dog taking itself for a walk. She parked behind the Land Rover, in front of Esther's overgrown shrubbery. Judith emerged from the leafy shadows as she shut the car door. A light was on in the conservatory, making the mass of ivy that swamped it glow red and green. Judith led her swiftly through to the back. Even for Judith, she was pale.

'It's Esther,' she said. 'I'd had no luck with that bloody animal so I had to put down some of those humane traps for it, which probably means the farmer and his dogs will get to it before the vet does. And then I came back here to feed the cats and, well, there she was. You don't have to look,' she added, catching hold of Joanna's arm.

'No. Let me see. Where is she?' Joanna pushed on then saw, in the light of a big old flashlight that Judith was holding. She swore succinctly. 'What the hell was she doing out here so late?'

'I was always offering to bring in logs for her after feeding the cats but she would insist on getting them herself,' Judith explained. 'It needn't have been that late. I think she'd been here for some hours when I found her.'

'Have you rung the police?'

'Not yet. Can't we get her in first? She looks so awful there.'

'Why not? It's not as though they'll suspect foul play or anything.'

Esther was so obviously dead that neither of them needed to mention the fact. While Judith directed the flashlight, Joanna crouched to throw the logs one by one off Esther's broken body. The entire woodpile seemed to have fallen on her. She remembered that Judith had helped Esther build it only the other afternoon – Judith's coat had been flecked with small pieces of damp bark and moss when she came home – but she kept quiet about this. Esther's quilted dressing gown was similarly flecked as Joanna uncovered it. Impatient and shivering, Judith soon crouched too, balancing the flashlight on a windowsill, and helped her. When Esther was free, they carried her into the old kitchen and laid her on the broad deal table there. Judith tried to tidy Esther's hair which was streaked with mud and congealed blood.

'We don't need to call the police, hon,' Joanna said. 'It was so obviously an accident. Just call the doctor. Or would you like me to?'

'No. I'll do it. You stay here.'

Judith slipped off into the shadows. Half the lights in the building seemed to lack lightbulbs. She heard Judith walk upstairs, open a door and begin to talk to someone. When she returned a few minutes later, Esther's old dog was snuffling at her heels.

'I'd forgotten about him,' Joanna said. 'Look at the old mutt. He's on the way out.'

Judith stopped to rub his ears.

'He's called Bunting,' she said. 'Do you think we could take him on?'

'Sure,' Joanna sighed. 'If he'd stay. He looks kind of set in his ways to me.'

Bunting sniffed at the table leg then plodded out through the garden door. He returned after a while and sat watching the women from a dusty armchair.

Martyrstow's GP was a self-contained, black-haired woman in her early fifties called Vivian Castle. Married to the local solicitor, she lived in a large bungalow three or four miles away and was said, by Esther, to be a Baptist. She had kept her distance from Joanna and Judith who, though registered at her practice, preferred to attend their old London clinic for check-ups. She clicked her tongue when she saw Esther's body, felt officiously for pulse and broken bones then asked a few questions about how long Esther could have lain outside before Judith discovered her.

'Had she any family?' she asked.

'None that I know of,' Judith answered. 'She always talked of herself as the last of the line.'

'So, no next of kin?'

'No. She said she would leave everything to the cats.'

'Ah.'

'But I gather I'm her executor. As her solicitor, your husband will probably have all the details.'

'Ah yes.' Dr Castle filled out the death certificate. 'I'd better file this with her papers in his office, then, until we know more. Would you like me to arrange for an ambulance to take her away?' She indicated Esther's body with a thin, clean hand. Joanna was about to say yes when Judith answered.

'That's all right. I think I'm rather meant to make the arrangements. I'll send for the Viney sisters in the morning.' She saw the doctor to her car. Joanna heard her thank her for coming out in the middle of the night then their words grew indistinct. Judith walked from the front door to the scullery. Snapping out of a half-asleep stare, Joanna went to find her.

'What are you doing?' she asked, stifling a yawn.

Judith was searching through a mass of old packets and bottles in the cupboard under the sink. The hot water tap was running, sending clouds of steam into the chilly air.

'I know there was some disinfectant here somewhere,' she muttered. 'She used it on a cut finger once. I've found a big basin and a sponge.'

'You don't need disinfectant, Jude. She's beyond all that. Come on. You take the water and the sponge, I'll go find some soap.'

Judith stood, thankful it seemed for another's initiative.

'The bathroom's the third door on the right at the top of the stairs,' she said, taking the full basin in unsteady hands.

'I'll find it.'

Joanna patted her shoulder then climbed the stairs to the

bathroom. She found a bar of Pears' soap; so brown and English, with its evocative but ambiguous smell. She had never understood the product's appeal. Now she did. It could have been created for the tender washing of corpses. Crossing the landing, she followed the light into what must have been Esther's bedroom. Fusty and lacy, with its cast-iron fireplace and button-backed chairs it reminded her of nothing so much as the set for a saloon-girl's bedroom in a forties Western. She opened several drawers finding at last a large white towel, two sheets and a long white nightdress with an old lace collar. When she returned, holding these and the soap, to the kitchen, she found Judith already sponging down the now naked body of her friend. The tin basin was filled with pale red liquid. Joanna took it from her, rinsed it out and brought back fresher, hotter water. They went about their task in silence, hands occasionally meeting in the soapy water or arms brushing when one patted dry what the other had rinsed. When Esther was quite dry, they dried the table and, rolling her first to one side then to the other, spread it with a spotless white sheet. Joanna spoke at last as she manoeuvred the nightdress over Esther's upheld arms and shoulders.

'Like dressing a child,' she said. 'I never thought it would be like this.'

They gently lifted her midriff then her thighs so as to pull the nightdress down to her ankles then Joanna laid her arms against her sides. Judith fetched a pillow to support her head then the two of them drew the second sheet up to her chin.

'Looks too macabre to cover her right up,' Joanna said.

'I asked if she'd have died straight away,' said Judith. 'Dr Castle told me she couldn't be sure without doing an autopsy to see what damage there was to her liver and so on. Death from exposure takes some time but, apparently, judging from the knocks she'd taken on her head, she wouldn't have known a thing about it.'

'Good,' Joanna told her, drawing her close. They kissed

at the foot of the table, like children, with lips closed, then hugged briefly, cheek to cheek.

Bunting rode willingly enough in the car but began to howl when left in their kitchen by the stove. Joanna let him upstairs and he spent the night on a pile of old Sunday papers at the foot of their bed. The papers rustled from time to time, when his stiff joints made him rise and turn. Joanna and Judith fell asleep in one another's arms but when Joanna woke a few hours later Judith had rolled away.

Thirty

Though entranced with grief, Julian's mother had somewhere found the resolve to buy a large bottle of duty free whisky while passing through Seneca airport for the flight home. In the early morning confusion as they disembarked at Heathrow, she had left Deborah clutching the whisky and had stalked off into the night with the identical plastic bag containing the bottle of Chanel No. 5 which Deborah had bought in a similar fit of bereaved abstraction. Having turned down Joanna's offer of pasta with tuna sauce on her return, Deborah made two further inroads into the cherry cake, which Joanna seemed to have abandoned to her. She then took the whisky bottle from amidst her luggage, rinsed out a teacup in her bathroom then settled down on her bed for what Julian's mother would have called 'a sizeable snifter'.

She had always disliked the taste of alcohol, and spirits invariably turned her bowels to water the morning after any immoderate consumption. Taken neat, however, for medicinal purposes, whisky or vodka aroused a kind of euphoria, distilling her customary emotional murk into easily comprehended primary shades. As with any nasty medicine, she had learnt that whisky left less taste the more violently one drank it. She took a few short breaths, like a swimmer preparing to dive, threw the contents of the teacup to the back of her throat then was wracked with shudders as the terrible burning washed over her. She coughed only once then, cradling the empty cup beneath her bosom, watched and waited. She felt nothing but relief from the nausea a surfeit of glacé cherries had begun to induce. She stared out of the window at the patterns of the dusk and tried to think of the polite manoeuvres of Julian's lovemaking. Failing, she tried to evoke memories of the evening he had returned home early to their Kensington flat holding a handkerchief to his bruised cheek. This time she succeeded.

'Of course I've told the bloody police,' he shouted at her. 'Anyway the little thug was black so I couldn't hope to identify him. Bloody silly question.' They had been due at a bonfire party thrown by the only two of her former flatmates who had yet to marry. Rather than cancel the engagement altogether, he had made her go on her own, bearing his melodramatic excuse with her bottle of wine, which only succeeded in arousing her hostesses' pitying prurience as to the state of her marriage.

Dangling the teacup by its handle, she walked to the window and stared out. In the distance, the lights of Martyrstow glittered across the network of dry-stone walls from one side, those of Treneglos from the other. Harvey's house, she had worked out some nights previously, was the tiny glimmer almost exactly between the two. She checked to see if he was at home, saw his lights, then drew the curtains. She lit the lamp on the bedside table then poured herself another teacupful of whisky. She tried sipping it this time then wrinkled her nose in disgust and tossed the remainder back in two scalding gulps. She was no connoisseuse but even she could tell by the tartan and bagpipes on the label that this was cheap and nasty stuff.

Now it took effect. She yawned deeply, stretching, and a sense of lightness rose from her spine to her skull. She found herself incongruously thinking of her mother. Only the congruity was self-evident. Her mother had drunk whisky just like this; out of teacups, in the bedroom, locked in the bathroom, leaning against the meat safe in a corner of the larder. She had always drunk in company but, after her husband's sudden death, she ceased what little entertaining she had ever managed and began to hide her bottles like so many lovers in a farce, in those cupboards most associated with wifely duty. Her daughters would stumble on them tactfully ignoring their presence as they rubbed shoulders with pills and face cream, nestled among newly laundered bed linen or stood, camouflaged, behind the cooking sherry.

A small, rounded woman, her mother had appeared on a first encounter like some roly-poly matriarch in a child's picture book, or a motherly glove puppet – nothing on her mind but baking and sweetness, nothing beneath her skirts but clothespegs and starch. One surreptitious glass too many, however, and her nursery rhyme equilibrium was upset, revealing all manner of spite and grievances to the unready. Unlike her sister, Deborah had been spared any recital of lewd marital reminiscences, presumably because she was judged as having been too close to her father. But she had heard them through many closed doors. It was he who had driven his wife to it, of course, he and – to judge from her poisoned outbursts – the children whose arrival had bound her to him.

'I hope you realise that we only stayed together because of you graceless bitches,' was the sort of declaration she would make when nearing the point of nightly collapse. Then Deborah and Judith would carry her upstairs, undress her and put her to bed. In the morning it was always as though nothing had happened. When Deborah started at boarding school, Judith had not yet left home but had to leave their mother to sleep out her stupor on the floor, unable to lift her on her own. When both daughters moved away, Mummy chose to languish in a bungalow. She said the old house was 'far too large for a childless widow' but the move was a tacit admission of her need to have a bed within staggering distance.

None of this was Daddy's fault. He had loved her in his way – had tried to love her – but they were unsuited from the start.

Except perhaps in the unanimity with which they sought to do the right thing. She was too blinded by misapprehension and then by disappointment ever to have understood him the way that Deborah had.

So, Julian had slept with Joanna? He had. Five times. In one week. Five lunchtime fucks. That word had never sat happily on Deborah's tongue. She had only used it once to Julian. No more than five or six months ago. Tipsy after an excruciatingly dull banquet, she had walked naked from the bathroom, thrown herself onto the bed and said,

'All right, Julian, let's make a baby. Come on and fuck me!'

She had meant it in happiness but he had walked from the room in disgust, shutting the door firmly behind him and only returning after she was sound asleep.

It had always seemed to her that she was the more highly sexed half of the couple, that she was the more likely of the two of them to stray. If their physical relationship had a recurrent pattern it was her reaching out, from a bed, a sofa, even the bath, and him stepping out of reach. Now, as she saw that what she had taken for diffidence, coolness, was simply misread distaste, his infidelity came to seem as inevitable as the cloudy grey of his eyes. She conjured up the image of Joanna, stripping her clothes aside with her mind's cold fingers so as to make her less threatening. Joanna was everything she was not. Even more so when she was naked. Nothing she wanted to be especially, but everything she was not.

There was a knock at the door.

'Yes?'

'It's me.'

Joanna.

'Come in.'

The door opened and Joanna came in balancing a supper tray on one hip.

'Didn't you hear me call?' she asked gently.

218

'No. Sorry.' Deborah made no attempt to hide the bottle, supposing that her breath must reek in any case.

'I figured you must be ravenous after your walk, whatever you say.' Joanna set the tray on the bedside table then sat on the bed at Deborah's feet. 'Anyway,' she went on, 'there's still no sign of Her Nibs so I fixed us both a bite. Nothing much – there wasn't enough pasta so I just did toasted cheese and ham and a spot of salad.'

Deborah could find nothing to say. This large, quirkily beautiful woman had owned up to sleeping with her husband but no sooner was the blow delivered than she set about cosseting her victim back to health. The strange thing was the part which Deborah found herself drawn to play in the tableau; the Other Woman had waxed motherly and she felt only childish comfort in her presence. She was not sure where Julian fitted into the equation. Whenever Joanna was in the room, he seemed to become curiously irrelevant; a fading military photograph on the wall behind them, a dinner jacket draped, unregarded, on the back of one of their chairs.

'I'm not sure I did the right thing this afternoon,' Joanna mumbled. 'Telling you. Anyway it's out and clear now so . . .' She broke off. 'Do you see why I told you?'

'Not really.' Deborah dared to catch her eye then let her gaze drop to the tray where she picked at the poorly cleaned tines of a fork. 'But it . . .' She was going to say that it didn't really matter now but she knew suddenly that Joanna understood that.

'What?' Joanna prompted.

'Nothing. Thanks for supper. I am pretty hungry.'

'You're welcome.' Joanna stood. Deborah saw her eyes flick to the bottle and away.

'Joanna?'

'Uh-huh?'

'I know you might think it's the sort of thing I'd do but I can tell you now I won't tell Judith a word about it.'

She smiled rather sadly and said, 'Thanks,' then closed the door behind her.

Deborah ate her supper quickly then, feeling sleek and fat, drank another teacupful of whisky. She ran herself a bath tossing in the correct quantity of salt this time as well as a fistful of the healing petal mixture. As she soaked herself, the fumes seemed to swirl around her head with the whisky. By the time that, fragrant, she was picking the sodden petals from out of the plughole, she had decided for the second time in twenty-four hours that she ought to leave Joanna's house, find a flat to rent somewhere peaceful but civilised, like Bath or Cheltenham, and set about finding work of some kind. But parallel to that scheme, clinging to its every curve and denial, was the impulse to accept a nothing-to-lose dare to herself before she left.

She dressed swiftly, still hot from her bath, in a plain woollen dress with a zip up its back. She stepped quietly onto the stairs and peered down. The sitting room was in darkness. She walked through to the kitchen. She heard the sound of the portable television coming faintly from Joanna's bedroom overhead. In imitation of Joanna, she opened the stove and tossed in a few shovelfuls of coal to feed the blaze. Then, holding his card in one hand, she dialled Harvey's number. His telephone rang twelve times, maybe more. She did not look at the time. Would not.

'Hello?'

'Harvey it's me. Deb . . .'

'I guessed. Are you coming down?'

'Erm. Yes.'

'I'll put on the outside light to guide you,' he said and hung up.

She walked back to shut her bedroom door, leaving the bedside light on, then pulled on her coat and let herself quietly out of the front door. Automatically, trained, she had brushed her teeth before dressing. The spearmint warred with the whisky on her tongue. There was a bicycle against the side of the stable. Joanna had said she should borrow it if ever she felt energetic. It had no lights and she could feel as soon as she launched herself unsteadily down the drive that its tyres were soft. Its brakes barely worked either.

'If I meet someone coming fast around a corner I die,' she told herself, 'and all this is meant. Good riddance to bad rubbish.'

But the roads were empty and there was room outside Harvey's house for her to pull up with a graceful gravel-scattering skid.

He was waiting at the other door this time, the front door, and led her through the gloom to a room lit only by firelight, where the air was thick with a richly spiced scent she could not identify. He steered her to sit on a chair then began to touch her neck and head as before but she took his hands this time and drew them down to her breasts. He kissed each of her hands first then, through the fabric of her dress, her breasts. It seemed to her that both her nipples hardened and she laughed because, of course, she had only one. Still kneeling between her knees, he unzipped her dress to the waist and eased it away from her front. Her bras had always given Julian difficulty so she unfastened it herself and, dropping it to one side, began to explain about her scars. But he silenced her with a row of kisses, leading from her lips to precisely the wound she had thought would frighten him most. Whenever she tried to touch him he took her hands gently in his and replaced them at her side, smiling at her, lips barely parted, before resuming his searching caress. The pleasure of the soft constraint was almost more than she could bare in silence and when he slipped off her shoes and began to reach in soft, circling motions beneath her skirt, her voice broke raucously, it seemed to her, over the crackle of the fire.

'Do I . . . Do we have to stay on this chair?' she asked.

'Course not,' he murmured and lifted her suddenly in his arms.

She drew breath. Smiling at her surprise at his strength,

he smiled again and kissed her deeply where he stood. Then he carried her to a bed in the shifting shadows to the left of the fireplace. She saw them pass, briefly, in the looking-glass and tasted afresh the whisky on her tongue. Had he been drinking too?

'Kiss me first,' she said, as he laid her down, so he kissed her, searching with his tongue around her teeth, her nose, her temples and the tender tips of her ears. No longer constrained, she ran her hands across his back, down to the backs of his thighs. His frame was hard, lean from work, but there was the surface softness she had seen in his smooth face.

He undressed her almost formally, setting her dress carefully across a chair before turning back to her, then he started softly to repulse her hands again, pushing them back against the mattress while he explored her with his tongue. For a few wide-eyed minutes she mistook the intense pleasure he was causing for the effects of too much whisky. She did not until now draw comparisons with Julian. Then the sound of a log subsiding in the fire made her think in an instant of the ugly plastic urn stifled in her jerseys in the spare room. She sat bolt upright at the thought, gently lifted Harvey by the shoulders, and began to undress him as he had done her, pushing his hands aside as they tried to help.

Julian had liked her to undress him only up to a point. At the last moment, he would always push her back against the mattress, then whip off his knickers and thrust hard into her. At this most inopportune moment, she had often likened his penis to some extraordinary and quite possibly fierce deep sea animal that would die in seconds if not swiftly plunged from mystery into mystery, safe from the dehydrating sunlight of her tender curiosity. Harvey, by contrast, seemed to grow more relaxed with each discarded garment. When at last there was nothing left but his shorts he lay quite still and looked at her in a way that gave her pause. Then, taking her hand in his, he slid it down his abdomen and let it lie on the warm fabric. Rather than rip his shorts off *à la* Julian, she smiled at him and pressed down with her hand.

There was nothing there. Confused, she glanced down at her hand then met his gaze, questioning with her eyes. He sighed thinly, lifted her hand in his and kissed it on the pad of her thumb before replacing it on the sheet beside her.

'My mother,' he said, very quietly. 'I was very young. She caught me playing with myself.'

She sat quite still, frowned briefly almost to herself, then gently eased his shorts down his thighs and off his feet. Crouching, she kissed inside his calves in the flickering orange light, across his knees then laid her head, tenderly licking, where his mother's knife had cut.

Thirty-one

She woke from a deep doze, limbs heavy with satisfaction. The fire had died down to a glowing mound of embers but a candle was still burning on a table beside the bed. She looked down at her body, sprawled across the tangle of sheets, and found it looking surprisingly attractive in the softening light.

'Harvey?' she called softly. 'Harvey?' She heard an outside door open then close. 'Is that you?' she asked.

'I've just been putting out the ashes,' he said, returning from the hall. He had pulled on a pair of scuffed white plimsolls and a rather short raincoat. Nothing else. She laughed. 'No wonder they all think you're a witch!'

He smiled at her sheepishly as he kicked off the plimsolls.

'How much whisky did you drink before you got here?' he asked.

'I don't know,' she said. She felt sober again, but she was lying down. 'Maybe a third of a bottle. Three or four teacupfuls.'

He shook his head and walked out to the kitchen. As he came back to the bedside with two long glasses of something pale his mac fell open.

'Antidote,' he said, offering her one.

'What's in it?' she asked, sniffing her glass suspiciously.

'Don't ask. It works. Drink.'

She sipped. It was freezing cold and had a light, flowery taste. Suddenly thirsty, she drank the rest. He drank also.

'You too?' she asked.

'Dutch courage,' he admitted. 'But not as much as you.' He drained his glass then took her empty one from her and set them both on the table. She smiled. He tugged off his coat then slipped, chilly, into the bed beside her, pulling a sheet and blankets on top of them. He slid a hand behind her neck and kissed her then lifted the sheet to kiss each of her breasts. 'Walking wounded,' he said and kissed her scarred breast a second time then looked up at her. 'It's nice,' he said. 'Now you have tits that wink.'

She laughed, pretending to push him away, then kissed his forehead, nose and mouth. She slid a hand across his firm, hairless body to rest and caress between his legs.

'Tell me,' she said.

'I already have.'

'But how could any woman do that? What happened to her?'

'Hospital somewhere. She might be locked away still for all I know. I was put into care for a bit and then found some foster parents. They were an old childless couple who ran a nursery garden out by Wadebridge. She used to visit the home to bring us cakes and that.'

'Are they still alive?' He shook his head. 'Didn't you have a father?'

'Well of course I did!' He laughed at her then kissed her nose when she looked hurt. 'Of course I did,' he repeated more kindly, 'but we never saw him. She wasn't even sure who he was. That was the trouble, I suppose.' He squeezed her hand between his thighs. 'She was a barmaid in Plymouth, in a rough place with sailors and that. A whole crowd of them waited outside for her one night and raped her. Any one of them could have been my father. She got all the twisted religious stuff into her head while she was pregnant with me. I think she must have seen having a son as a chance for revenge.' Deborah kissed his cheek, appalled at the thoughts and memories that were stirring within her. 'Anyway,' he sighed, 'it was a long time ago. I was tiny when she did it so my mind must have blotted it all out to spare me. Eric and Ivy – that was my foster parents – told me I'd just been born this way but Ivy blurted out the truth later when we were having a row. I was going through a bad patch, you see, being rebellious and that and kept asking her who my true parents were. It didn't bring any real memories back so it might not even be the truth. Somehow I think it must be, though; it's too disgusting to be something someone could make up.'

Deborah reached out an arm and pulled him to her, to nestle his face against her breasts.

'So what about you?' he asked at last.

'How do you mean?'

'You've been in the wars too.'

'I told you,' she said. 'It was a car bomb. The Foreign Secretary was visiting Seneca and it was meant for him but there was a mix-up and poor Julian took the car instead. I was standing on the porch and got the glass blown at me.'

'No. I know that. I read that in the papers like everyone else. But I thought there was something else. Something more.'

She knew she should tell him. Making love with him in this extraordinarily open way, touching his mutilated body, feeling him cherish her in a way Julian had never done had finally given shape to the half-recollections that had been stirring ever since her arrival on Judith's doorstep. Her mind raced as she sought a form of words. But she could not.

'Not really,' she lied. 'There's nothing much. My mother drank, my father was a glorified dentist who died before he was meant to and I'm just beginning to admit that my late husband was probably a pretty lousy one. That's all.'

'That's enough,' he answered. Then he peered at her in the flickering light and gave a half-smile at what he saw. 'It's OK,' he breathed, 'you needn't talk about anything you don't want to.'

'But . . .'

'Ssh.' He silenced her with a soft kiss on the lips, then blew out the candle and pulled the blankets more closely about them. As she slipped back into sleep, with his breathing close by her ear, she saw that, without being told, he understood what Julian never had, saw too that he accepted.

'Do you have to get back?' he whispered.

'No,' she replied, 'I'm fine here.'

And she was. When she fell asleep, however, she dreamed again of the black mongrel on the sand. This time it had dug a hole deep enough for all but its back and wagging tail to be out of sight. It had stopped digging. It sniffed and scratched at the bottom of the hole, whining. Then something made it spring round, front paws up over the hole's edge, and bark.

Thirty-two

Closely followed by the trusties, and by Bunting, who trailed after her everywhere now, Judith walked along the line of enclosures, lifting bowls of mashed sardines from the wheelbarrow and sliding them through each narrowly opened door. Only the newest arrivals bothered to arch their backs and puff out their tails at the old dog's presence; the hardened lags thought only of their food.

Esther's funeral had finished an hour ago. She had demanded the briefest possible farewell, but even with no announcements and no promise of post-obsequial drinks, there had been ten or more attendants at the Bodmin crematorium. They were an ill-assorted collection and placed themselves each as far from the others as possible, much as Judith gathered that men did at a public urinal. One or two, like S. S. Haines and her cronies, she recognised from Martyrstow and two she remembered as loyal cat fanciers from Treneglos. Having insisted that her brief meeting with Esther had opened her eyes in some way and that of course she must come, Deborah arrived late. She had her new beau, Harvey, in tow. Being Esther's masseur, Judith supposed that he too felt himself to have been an intimate. The rest might well have been lonely souls who attended the funerals of complete strangers for the insidious warmth of the building and a brief illusion of companionship. Nobody cried. Dr Castle had taken her by the elbow on their way out and quietly informed her that the coroner's report had found

Esther's liver to be 'on the way out' which meant that at least she had been spared the grim indignities of cirrhosis.

Someone knocked at the front door. Bunting barked twice then sat, waiting for Judith to lead the way. It was Dr Castle's husband, the solicitor, and a rubicund woman in a camel-hair coat.

'Ah, Miss Lamb,' he said, 'may I introduce Mrs Jute of the Pet Protection League.'

'Fleur, please,' Mrs Jute twinkled, extending a hand which Judith shook.

'Come in,' she told them. 'I'm afraid it's all rather a mess. Esther had taken to camping out here, rather. I was going to start sorting it out a bit but suddenly it seemed such a mammoth task.'

Fleur was looking about her with evident dismay. She narrowly avoided a drape of cobweb across the arch between drawing room and dining room and patted at her wispy brown hair.

'These chairs aren't too bad if you want to sit.' Judith pulled a chair from under the dining-room table. 'The table top seems to have kept the dust off them.'

'Oh. Thank you,' said Mr Castle. 'Mrs Jute?' He held out a chair for her.

'Fleur, please!' She laughed thinly as she sat.

'Now Miss Lamb,' he continued. 'As I think you may have known, Mrs Gammel left her entire estate to the Pet Protection League.'

'Yes,' said Judith. 'She had told me.'

'Well, as it happens . . .'

'Perhaps I should explain?' Fleur cut in. Mr Castle nodded. 'The thing is, Miss er Lamb, this house is a terrible liability for us. I took the liberty of making a few enquiries in local estate agents – that was why I missed the funeral, silly me – and they made it quite clear that the house would be worth far more if we sold it now than if we paid to do it up and then sold it. An "investment property" I think it's called.'

'Could it not be let?' Judith asked.

'Not in this condition,' Mr Castle told her. 'They'd still have to make a few repairs and refurbishments, even for a cheap let.'

'Oh.'

'No,' Fleur went on, 'I've had quite a conference with Mr Castle here and we thought the best policy would be to hold an auction here – auction off the contents first (I see she had some *very* nice pieces) and then the house.'

'Perfect for a sheltered housing development for the elderly,' he added.

'I see,' said Judith. 'And what about the cats? The sanctuary is still fairly full. Would you like to see them?'

'Oh!' Fleur made the noise of someone admiring an ugly baby then glanced at her watch. 'Better not,' she said. 'But I'm sure they're *beautifully* looked after. The last report we had was excellent. No. Well. You see I'm afraid that it would cost the League far more to have the pussies rehoused at the nearest sanctuary – which is nearly two counties away I can tell you – than to have them, well,' she wrinkled her nose, 'you know.'

'Ah.'

'Of course, the League will pay for everything. Here's the address to get the vet to send his bills to.' She produced a card from her handbag.

'Actually it's a she.'

'What? Oh!' Fleur understood and laughed. 'Lovely.' She stood. 'Anyway, Miss Lamb, if you could very kindly see to calling out the vet – the er, lady vet – as soon as is convenient, we'd be most obliged. And, er, well, you were close to dear Mrs Gammel, weren't you?'

'Yes. Quite. I saw her every day when I came to feed the cats for her.'

'Exactly. Well, we thought that perhaps you might like to choose something of hers for yourself before the auction goes ahead. Something small to remember a friend by, yes?'

'How kind.'

'Not at all.'

Mr Castle tapped his watch.

'Am I going to miss my train?' she asked. 'Can't have that. It's over an hour before the next one. Right we are then, Miss Lamb. So nice to have met you finally and, well, so glad you are so, er, *agreeable* to everything.'

Judith shook her hand once more and saw the two of them out of the front door. Bunting emerged from his hiding place beneath the sideboard and followed her back to the sanctuary to watch her finishing her work.

'Buy it?' Joanna exclaimed.

'Why not?'

'But we've already got here.'

'You've got here.'

'*We*'ve got here. The barn's as good as yours after all you spent on it and you know the rest is all left to you. Besides, Esther's place is falling down.'

'It's quite sound actually. Just very dusty and neglected. All it needs is a spring clean and a new back door. The old one's rotted from being left open all year round for Bunting to come and go.'

Joanna reached across the kitchen table and took her hand.

'Judith,' she urged. 'Please. Let it go. I want you back to myself.'

Judith paused for a second to take this in.

'But the cats,' she went on. 'I can't have them all put down. That disgusting woman! It's precisely to avoid that happening that the sanctuary started in the first place.'

'Who said anything about putting them down? We can choose the cutest one for you to keep and the rest we take up and set loose on the moor. They can go as wild as they like. Gang up and kill sheep if they want to. It won't be your responsibility any more and if they get killed after a year, even six months, they'll have had a great time first.'

'They'd just starve.'

'Cats? Starve? How many were starving when you brought them in, huh? Anyway, if you feel bad about doing that, all you have to do is go around the pubs and stick up a few notices saying the place is being closed down and the pussies are condemned to die. You'd find homes for at least half that way.'

'Well.' Judith patted Joanna's hand back then reached out and gently drew a strand of her lush red hair through her fingers. Joanna kissed her hand as it passed her cheek. 'If I gave up the cats,' Judith asked slowly, 'would you give up the hunt?'

'That one again,' Joanna sighed. 'Judith, it's only a drag hunt.'

'Exactly. Far more dangerous. Every time you go out with them I expect to have you carried back on an old door.'

Joanna laughed richly. She pushed back her chair and went to fetch the teapot to pour them each another cup.

'You don't really?' she chuckled. 'That's so quaint!'

'I do. You know I do. I know what you're like. You have to be up there at the front with those madwomen from Slaughterbridge. You get that horse of yours so excited she's out of control.'

'Hey, Fleet enjoys it! And I'm the one in control. She's like another set of legs to me.'

'All right.' Judith closed her face to her. She rose, stirring her tea. 'Now. I've got work to do. I haven't been up there all day.'

'Jude?'

'What?' Judith turned by the front door.

'There's a meet this Saturday. What would you say if I made it my last?'

'I'd say thank you.'

Thirty-three

Harvey had appeared for the funeral in a suit and tie. Watching from a bench by the pub fireplace as he ordered their drinks, Deborah had to admit that she preferred him rough and ready in his work clothes. The suit trousers were slightly too short and its jacket was of a dated cut, with wide lapels and an ugly double vent at the back. It was also brown. The tie was not much better. When he drove up at the farmhouse, five minutes late, she knew at once that she could not tell him the truth. He spread a rug over the passenger seat to spare her black woollen coat from the fine layer of dried earth that covered his van's every surface. As he stood to let her in she said, 'How very smart you look!' If he had scoffed at her, denounced his appearance or even praised hers by contrast, all would have been well, but he only smiled, proud in all earnest. This was her first venture into the public eye at his side and her patronising lie, impossible to undo, cast an air of unreality over the entire proceedings.

After her first night spent with him, she had arrived back at the farmhouse during breakfast. Judith and Joanna were startled, having assumed that she was still up in their spare room. Her explanation was as fraught with embarrassment on both sides as any daughter's to her liberated mother. The atmosphere in the house grew still more strained. Joanna went away, conveniently enough, on a three-day assignment to London while Judith made no attempt to hide her satisfaction that Deborah had found somewhere else to spend much of her time. She kept asking Deborah when she was seeing Harvey next, offered her lifts down the hill to his house and all but packed her an overnight bag. She had registered surprise at Deborah's announcement that she would be seeing her at the crematorium and, when Deborah hinted at the curious importance that her excursion with Esther had assumed, reacted with a flash of characteristic envy.

Harvey brought their drinks to the table – a pint of Guinness for him and a glass of white wine for her. He sat on the bench beside her so that their thighs touched.

'Cheers,' he said. 'Here's to Mad Esther.'

'Yes,' she replied, 'cheers.' And they drank. The wine was well chilled but unpleasantly sweet. 'Do you think I should have asked Judith to join us?' she asked.

'She didn't seem very keen to hang around,' he said.

'No. Perhaps you're right. This fire's lovely.'

'Isn't it.'

'We were sitting in a terrible draught in that place.'

They were making conversation. They had never had to do this before. They talked, of course, at his house, in his garden, on the strange pink and grey rocks at Trebarwith Strand yesterday, but they touched too. Usually they interspersed their phrases with strokes and kisses which, being more important, took the emphasis off anything they might be saying. Here, under scrutiny, she felt their touching become inhibited and heard their words exposed in all their banality.

'Actually I'm a bit stirred up still,' she confessed. 'I know we should have been thinking about poor Esther just now but it all brought back Julian rather. I think I need something stronger after all.'

'What do you want?' he asked.

'No,' she stood, laying a hand on his arm. 'It's all right. I'll get it.'

She took the remains of the wine back to the bar and ordered herself a whisky. She sipped some where she stood, shuddered then felt immediately stronger.

When she turned back towards the fireplace she found that Harvey had been joined by two friends, a man and a woman dressed in battered leather jackets. She had not thought of Harvey having friends; since she first met him he had seemed so self-sufficient. As Deborah sat, the man was unloading a quantity of small pork pies from his motorcycle helmet. Harvey smiled at her, beautiful despite the suit.

'This is Pete and Tanya,' he told her. 'This is Deborah,' he told them.

'Hello,' said Deborah with a gracious smile.

'Hi,' said Tanya.

'So you've been helping give old Esther a good send-off?' said Pete.

'Yes,' said Deborah. 'I didn't know her very well, but she was very kind to me the one time we met.'

'Ahh,' said Tanya. 'She was very fond of animals, wasn't she?'

'That's right,' said Harvey. 'Cats.'

'Pork pie?' Tanya held one out to Deborah.

'No thanks,' Deborah told her.

'Harv?'

'Thanks.'

Deborah watched Harvey peel the wrapping off the pie and dispose of half of it in one mouthful.

'I thought you were a vegetarian,' she said, oddly shocked.

He shook his head, pausing in his chewing to smirk.

'Veggie?' Pete exclaimed. 'Not Harv.'

'Oh,' Deborah said.

Realising that he had just made a joke, Pete guffawed, splashing Harvey's beer. Harvey put an arm around Deborah's shoulders, claiming her.

'Do you have a bike each?' she asked, turning back to Tanya, who had been shaking out her limp brown hair, 'or do you ride pillion?'

'That's right,' said Tanya, 'I ride on the back of his.' She giggled, 'Holding on for dear life, the way he rides.' Pete jeered at her and fed another pork pie wrapper into the small fire he was starting in the ash tray. He had a thick sandy beard and, disguised by that and his gut, might have been any age between twenty-five and forty. 'We're on our way to Glastonbury,' Tanya told her, 'to meet up with some mates of Pete's.'

'That's quite a way, isn't it?' Deborah asked.

'Not the way he rides,' Tanya laughed. 'So do you live round here, then?'

'I'm staying with my sister. Up at Martyrstow.'

Tanya nodded.

'And Harv here came round to give you both a friendly massage, did he?' Pete asked with a dirty chuckle. Harvey slapped him on the chest with the back of his hand to silence him.

'Don't mind Pete,' said Tanya. 'Mind like a sewer.'

She chattered on, telling Deborah how she and Harvey had been at school together in Wadebridge and how her mum used to work at his dad's nursery garden, what they would get up to at Glastonbury and what kind of puppy she was thinking of buying. Deborah said just enough to keep her talking. Beside her, Harvey talked with Pete about a crowd of people she didn't know and would probably never meet. He kept his arm around her shoulder, squeezing her or softly stroking the side of her neck from time to time. She realised now that Tanya and the other locals had no idea that there was any physical difference beneath his obvious eccentricities, and that the stories about his love life and desirability, which even Judith had repeated, were a screen probably set up by Harvey himself. When they had done drinking he would drive her back to his house. They would make love and again this evening and again tomorrow and the day after that. But she had also realised, as suddenly as she had realised that he ate meat, that he was not enough to wipe her emotional slate clean. However much he was teaching her, however much her body learned to respond to his intelligent touch, he was not a replacement. Rather than sadden her, this understanding made her relax. She leant against him, a hand on his thigh beneath the table, sipped her whisky and encouraged Tanya. For the first time in a long while she felt a measure of control.

Thirty-four

'Hang on five secs,' Joanna called out. She fished a print out of the wash and waved it a few times over the water before hanging it up to drip dry. 'OK.' She shot back the bolt on her dark room door. Deborah knocked again. 'It's OK to come in, Deborah.'

'You're sure I'm not disturbing you?' Deborah asked as she slipped round the door evidently trying to let as little sunlight as possible enter with her.

'Sure you're disturbing me. It's great to see you. How do you like these?' She gestured to the prints. They were pictures of Deborah she had taken during a break in one of their driving lessons. Deborah gasped with embarrassment. 'See?' said Joanna. 'You have no scars. All cleared up. The camera never lies. Well. Rarely. I used a teensy bit of Vaseline.' Deborah dug her in the ribs for teasing.

'I like that one best,' she told her. 'You've managed to make me look quite intelligent. Julian's . . .' She faltered. She had mentioned him without thinking. 'Julian's photographs always made me look so dim.'

In the days since Esther's death, Deborah had emerged from her chrysalis. She went everywhere in a pair of old jeans, borrowed from Judith, held up with an old Mexican belt and rolled up at the ankle. She had stopped wearing make-up, she laughed without pretence and she had stopped jumping whenever either of them spoke to her. Even by the lurid red light of the dark room she looked healthy, refreshed. She seemed to be spending a lot of time out on walks or with Harvey Gummer. However 'suitable' or not Judith might deem him to be, he was a far cry from Julian Curtis and, as such, was doing Deborah a power of good. Several times it had seemed to Joanna that she was on the verge of broaching some topic then changed her mind. Afraid that it was Julian she wanted to discuss, Joanna gave her no prompting. The dust was settling, Judith had not brained her or left her and Joanna was not inclined to stir things up again. She had told the truth to Judith, she would appear to have helped Deborah; enough was enough.

As she peered closely at the prints of her, Joanna saw again the fleeting resemblance to Judith that she had seen when she watched Deborah sleeping weeks ago in Clapham. Deborah's face was normally childishly soft but when she turned it upwards her jaw bone stood out like her sister's and she developed her sister's catlike chin.

'You're very clever,' Deborah said. 'Can I see the Seneca ones?'

'I've delivered them already. Well, I've dropped off the best ones and I haven't got around to making prints for myself. Here's one of them though.' She passed her a picture of the boy sawing wood with his feet. Deborah stared at it and shook her head slowly.

'I meant to ask you,' she said, still looking down at it. 'I'd quite understand if you didn't want to or something. I mean, it's a pretty grisly thing to ask anyone.'

'What is?' Joanna took the print back from her and returned it to its box.

'Julian's ashes. I've got them in a horrid little urn thing in my room and I want to get rid of them. I mean, shake them somewhere. It's so beautiful and wild around here. I don't know if he ever came here – we never spoke about things like that much – but I'm sure he'd have thought it as good a place as any.'

'What, right here?' Joanna pointed at the floor.

'Well. Somewhere near here. A field or something.'

'How about Rough Tor? Remember the big hill we could see from the road that day; the one with the china clay pit beneath?'

'I think so. With all those huge rocks everywhere?'

'That's the one. It's the rooftop of Cornwall. If you did it up there they would blow right across the county on the winds. The view's incredible too, if it's not misty.'

'All right!'

'But I think you should do it without me.'

'Oh.' Deborah seemed crestfallen. Joanna realised that this was a big gesture for her – the woman was effectively offering to share her husband.

'I'm really touched that you suggested it,' Joanna told her, touching her shoulder. 'But, well, I think it's the kind of thing you should do on your own or with a total stranger who's completely uninvolved. Harvey, maybe. Or maybe not.' She laughed to herself because the idea had a wicked appeal. 'It would be kind of tactless. No, Deborah. I can't do it with you.'

'But . . .'

'Let's just say that I don't think Julian would have appreciated my coming along.'

'I don't think that matters so very much,' Deborah said with disarming frankness. 'There's not much he can do about it and it would make me feel better.'

'Why don't you get Michelle to take you up there tomorrow?'

'Michelle?'

'The postgirl who looks after Fleet for me. She takes her out on the moor sometimes.'

'Oh yes.'

'She usually goes up there when there's a hunt. We set out from Camelford and she can watch us chasing across the fields. She drives, so she could give you a lift and stop you getting lost if a mist comes down suddenly. You could take sandwiches. Make an outing of it.'

'Wouldn't she mind?'

'Not at all. As I say, she'll be going up there anyway. She's due up here in the morning. We put the horsebox on the back of the Land Rover and she drives us both over to the meet before heading up to Rough Tor.'

'Will there be room for me as well as Judith?'

'Jude never comes. Says it scares her shitless. She'll stay up in her loft with her mind on higher things till we get safely back again.'

Deborah gave Joanna a big hug; the first time she had touched her in affection. Leaving the dark room, she seemed relieved. Perhaps that she had made her big gesture but been spared the awkwardness of having to follow it through.

Thirty-five

The Camel Drag as its members knew it (although its proper title was the Camelford and Martyrstow Drag Hunt) met six or so times a season in Camelford or Martyrstow's marketplace. Many of the members rode with other hunts, after foxes, but belonged to the Camel Drag for the certainty of its excitement. The hard core who, like Joanna, disapproved of bloodsports and rode only with this hunt was entirely female. Esther and her telephone cronies had once ridden with it. Now their place was taken by Joanna, Vivian Castle, Miss O'Keefe the bugle-playing butcher who supplied the Camel Drag with authentic tootlings on her little hunting horn, Bernadette de Paul, the Methodist minister and then, usually left some way behind but nonetheless keen, there were S. S. Haines, the greengrocer and the mobile librarian.

Judith had emerged from her workplace as Michelle was walking Fleet into her box. She cast her usual cynical eye over Joanna's sleek jodhpurs, tightly twisted hair, elegant black coat and pearl-pinned stock.

'So fetishistic,' she muttered, with a half smile.

'The last time,' Joanna told her.

'And you think I believe you can resist temptation?'

'Try me.' Joanna blew her a kiss behind Michelle's back, then climbed into the Land Rover, swinging her hat. Deborah was already waiting inside, clutching her sandwiches in one bag and Julian's ash-can in another. Michelle sang vigorously heterosexual pop songs to herself as she drove them to Camelford; she found meets profoundly exciting but had never plucked up courage to join. When Joanna had told her she was riding with the Camel Drag for the last time, she had seen it cross Michelle's mind that Fleet might therefore be hers to borrow for future meets.

They unloaded Fleet in the medical centre car park, then Joanna donned her hat and rode her slowly down the high street to join the crowd in the marketplace. Deborah and Michelle walked beside her. The crisp air was thinly clouded with animal breath. Deborah looked confused when the landlord of the local pub thrust a glass of sherry at her on a tray but she accepted it readily enough and downed it in three swift sips.

'What happens now?' she asked.

'The men draw lots to see who's going to run. We don't give them so much of a head start as most hunts – makes it more exciting! They're in the pub.' Michelle glanced at her watch. 'They should be out by now. Here they go.'

There was a muffled cheer which spread through the crowd of bystanders. Horses shifted in anticipation. Joanna peered across the heads and saw Harvey Gummer emerge from the pub clutching the statutory aniseed-impregnated rag on a piece of rope.

'Harvey!' she said.

'Where?' Deborah looked up, alarmed.

'It's Harvey,' Joanna told her. 'We're in for a good one. He runs like the wind and picks all the best hedges. We actually lost him last time. He'd crossed back and forth over the river.'

Harvey caught Deborah's eye and grinned as he passed them. Joanna saw her blush.

'Don't worry,' she said, leaning forward in Deborah's direction, smiling to herself. 'We won't let them eat him.'

Deborah looked up and grinned sheepishly. Michelle handed her a second glass of sherry.

'You'll need it,' she said. 'When it's as clear as this it gets bloody cold up there.'

A cheer went up as Harvey broke into a run up the high street and out of sight, several children haring along in his wake. Moments later there was a second cheer as the hounds were loosed from their van in the car park and brought down to mill around the marketplace. The bystanders shifted to the walls in readiness. Deborah mouthed, 'Good luck!' as she and Michelle joined them. The pub staff busied themselves collecting glasses and suddenly Joanna found herself once more amongst the firm subfusc tailoring and discreetly gleaming jewellery of the Camel Drag's strange sisterhood. Battleship Haines was having some difficulty controlling her brother-in-law's filly (borrowed for the occasion). Two of her acolytes had been hovering nervously in her vicinity. Joanna saw her hand them down her sherry glass before shooing them back to join the crowd. Bernadette de Paul nodded in Joanna's direction and raised her glass of grapefruit juice to her before draining it and passing it down to the landlord. Verity O'Keefe, the pink-cheeked butcher caught her eye as she breathed on her small horn and rubbed it to a shine. Joanna had always had her suspicions about her. She replied to her distinctly lecherous smile with a discreet crop-in-hand salute. The two of them murmured something together, Miss O'Keefe looked around her with the teasing nonchalance of a conjuror then gave a swift tootle on her horn. The hounds raised their already slightly muddy heads to reply and a buzz of excitement ran through the crowd.

As always, the hard core of Martyrstow women, Joanna included, had placed themselves so as to be the first to move off. Her blood mounting as she sensed Fleet's impatience, Joanna took one last glance at Deborah's face, white with concern.

Thirty-six

Singing once more, Michelle drove Deborah through Tregood-well and along the helter-skelter lanes to Rough Tor. From this side the hill seemed less daunting; more a steady slope with rocks on the top. When they reached the car park, Michelle uncoupled the horse box, wheeled it safely into a corner then clambered back into the driver's seat. She restarted the engine and, to Deborah's alarm, engaged the four-wheel-drive.

'Don't we have to walk from here?' Deborah asked.

'You can if you like, but it's quite a climb. This is more fun.'

'OK,' replied Deborah uncertainly and cradled Julian's mortal remains more tightly in her arms.

Michelle rattled the Land Rover over a cattle grid, lurched it down a slight incline, ploughed it through a stream and began a long and extremely uneven ride up the tor.

'Prehistoric village remains down there,' Michelle shouted over the roar of the engine.

'Where?' Deborah asked. 'Oh!' and she dropped Julian's ashes. The urn rolled out of its bag and across the floor. Michelle caught it with her foot and, with a practised foot-baller's pass, tapped it neatly back to her.

'Nearly lost your Thermos!' She laughed as Deborah, having bent forward to scoop it up, swore thickly on striking her hand on the dashboard. 'Whoops!' She laughed again as the sandwiches followed and had to be similarly retrieved.

'Are you sure this is allowed?' Deborah asked.

'No. Reckon it's bloody illegal but no one's stopped me yet. Ooh! He looks a fierce'un.'

Deborah glanced obediently out of the window to see a vast horned animal glowering from behind a rock. She looked hastily forward again. After a few more jolts Michelle braked the Land Rover on a perilous angle from which a mere child could have tipped it over, and announced that this was as far as she could safely take it. Snatching up an old waterproof in case she needed something to sit on, Deborah swung herself to safety, retrieved sandwiches and Julian and set off up the rest of the hill behind her. There was already a considerable wind.

'Don't look round till you're on the very top,' Michelle shouted back. 'Or you spoil the surprise.'

The surprise was worth the wait. They clambered across moss-dressed boulders, sidestepping tiny patches of bog masked by lurid green grass, higher and higher until they were surrounded by towering chimneys and arches of granite, carved by centuries of wind and rain. Then Michelle tugged her up by the arm onto a plateau of rock barely fifteen feet in circumference where the wind was strong enough to bear one's leaning weight and both the county's shorelines were visible at once. Tintagel's landscape was placid by comparison.

Terrified at the sudden drop before her, Deborah sat down, her astonished mouth puffed with racing air.

'Can you see them yet?' Michelle asked, fearlessly swinging her legs over the edge. 'Look for the pink.' She scanned the miles of land spread out beneath them. 'There they are!' she shouted.

'Where?'

'There.' Michelle kept pointing and glanced back over her shoulder. The wind momentarily blew her vivid ginger hair across her face, giving her a neanderthal look that went well with their outlandish surroundings. She looked back to the

246

hunt. 'Follow that ridge there with your eyes until you get to the barns then go down a bit. See them?'

Deborah scanned the horizon frantically, seeing nothing.

'Oh yes,' she said, then saw them for real; a thin wavering line of black, red and brown against a field of vibrant green. 'I see them!' she added. 'Where's Harvey?'

'Oh, he'll be far away. Someone said he was going to cheat and catch a scooter just outside Camelford to get an even better head start.'

'Wouldn't that weaken the scent?'

'Not if he kept bouncing the rag on the ground here and there.' Michelle slipped alarmingly out of sight. 'I'm just going to take a pee,' she called back. 'There's a cave down here somewhere.'

Deborah watched the hunt until it was on flatter terrain where it would be easy to pinpoint again, then she reached for Julian's urn. She had heard blackly humorous stories of poetically scattered ashes blowing back in loved ones' weeping mouths but there was no danger of that here. The wind coming off the moor to the East was striking her full in the face and flying off over the ridge of the tor behind her. Should she say a prayer? She could think of nothing. A plain goodbye seemed a little flat. She unscrewed the lid, releasing a little of the surprisingly white powder. She decided to shake the contents onto the wind and try to think loving thoughts of Julian as she did so. She would clear her mind of thoughts of whatever he did with Joanna, of his tendency to correct her in front of other people, of his curtness when she was indulging in whimsy, of his similarity to his mother. She would try to think of the good things he made her feel; of . . . of . . . She tipped the ashes into the air in one quick sliding motion and could think of nothing as she marvelled at the speed and loveliness with which they were whipped away from her, a gritty white ribbon on the air. She smiled to imagine the shock of walkers a few miles away if they knew what or rather who they were brushing off their packed lunch. She tossed the plastic urn and its lid out into the abyss where they were caught by the wind and driven hard into some lodging place on the rock-face. Then she sat back hugging herself and thinking unashamedly of Harvey and the unorthodox pleasures to which he had introduced her.

'Deborah! Deborah, come quickly!' Michelle's voice cracked with strain.

'What? Where are you?'

'Come down the way we came up. It's Harvey!'

'Where?'

'Just come down.'

Leaving the sandwiches, Deborah slithered down the rock and looked about her.

'Over here!'

She glanced round and saw Michelle disappearing at the other end of a narrow, natural passage in the granite. Grimacing at the water that dripped off its sides, she followed. At the other end she found Harvey, beautiful Harvey, hair plastered to his face with sweat, panting, his arm over Michelle's shoulder.

'I saw him down there,' Michelle gave a flick of her head. 'He's sprained his ankle. We need to get him round to the car. If you take him back, I'll take the rag and keep running.'

Deborah searched Harvey's face for signs of pain but he seemed to be grinning between pants. She wanted to push Michelle out of the way.

'I can't possibly drive a Land Rover,' she murmured.

'It's not far. You'll soon get the hang of the gears.' Michelle was impatient.

'No. I mean I haven't passed my test.' She reached out and took the rag on its rope from Harvey's grasp. 'You drive him home. I'll have to run. Which way?'

Grinning at her distractingly, Harvey pointed.

'Head for the edge of Martyrstow,' he said. 'Keep the church tower in front of you. We'll drive round and bring someone out to take over from you.'

Feeling quite absurdly like a heroine in a *Girl's Own Annual*, Deborah stripped off her coat and thrust it at Michelle, along with the waterproof.

'The church tower?' she checked.

'Right,' said Harvey.

And she began to run. She could only slither at first. There were rocks and large pebbles everywhere and she had to avoid spraining her ankle too, but as soon as she was back on rough, moorland grass she speeded up. Restless, probably, Julian had gone through a jogging phase soon after their marriage.

'Breathe slowly,' he shouted at her between pants. 'Control your breathing and you won't get a stitch or get breathless. That's it! *Out*-two-three-four! *In*-two-three-four! *Out*-two-three-four! *In*-two-three-four! Forget speed, think of steadiness and distance.'

She was running, her breath was coming in steadyish measures. She remembered to concentrate on looking into the distance rather than thinking about her feet. She shook out the rope and let the headily-scented rag trail behind her, bouncing on the tussocks and snagging on young gorse plants. She tried not to think about the fact that she was now being hunted by a pack of bloodthirsty hounds and a clutch of undoubtedly over-excited women, some of them on beasts they could not control. She tried to forget that she had always been nervous of horses. She saw the church tower. It seemed miles away but she knew it was only a few minutes by car and this was surely a more direct route than by road. She liked to swing both her arms when she ran but she had to suppress this urge so as not to trip herself up on the rope. She concentrated on relaxing them at her sides and felt immediately more comfortable.

'That's it, darling!' Julian shouted. 'You've got it!' and she remembered a rare moment of pure happiness, when, still clumsy with newly-married lust, he had dragged her out to go running in the drizzle in Kensington Gardens.

Thirty-seven

Inspired by Joanna's encouragement, Judith had held off from calling the vet to have all the cats put down. Instead, she had telephoned the RSPCA and so been put in touch with a pensioner whose precise requirement was for a cat past its first youth. Then she had drawn up a notice which she printed out several times from her word processor and took to pubs and post offices in the area. She doubted whether this would bear much fruit. Inured to the annual round of pragmatic slaughter, the farmers were unlikely to feel much pity for a few useless cats, and children, quite rightly, felt cheated if, having asked for a kitten, they were presented with a fully grown creature which yowled and scratched. Restless, the thought of Joanna risking life and limb having nagged at the back of her mind throughout her bill-posting expedition, she had come to Esther's house. She walked along the line of enclosures, reminding herself of the occupants. The old tabby had found a home with the delighted pensioner from Wadebridge which left fifteen. She had made enquiries in the neighbourhood and discovered that the trusties had, as she suspected, begun to adopt families for themselves. Having made it quite clear that their benefactors were welcome to keep them, she had asked them to shut them in on their next visit to make the adoption process more complete. Of the rest, still caged, only four could reasonably be expected to make good pets, and then only given patience and understanding.

The others, she decided, should be set loose to find their fortunes on the edge of the moor. There were four carrying cases so she could take four now and four later.

The cases were stacked at the end of what had been the garden, below the low fence that gave on to an empty field. As she fetched the first she heard Miss O'Keefe's hunting horn in the distance. It was strange that something so like a toy could convey such menace. The first cat she had to catch was a large black and white tom with sinister yellow eyes. She had never liked him and it was with a certain relish that she trapped him with her net and dragged him within reach. He bit so hard on her gloves as she thrust him into the cage that she could feel the pressure of his jaw through the thickly padded leather. She heard the horn again as she walked over to fetch a second cage. The tom's miserable yowling seemed to answer it. She looked over the fence and saw her sister.

Deborah was running across the field towards her, a drag hunt rag bouncing on a rope behind her. Her jeans were caked with mud, her hair flat with sweat and her face alarmingly pink. The hunt was only a field away. Judith saw the horses leaping a dry-stone wall. Two things happened as she looked. Deborah gave a cry of desperate recognition and put on a spurt of speed, and the hounds began to flood through the hedge several yards behind her. Judith remembered watching a meet for the first time soon after they had moved to Cornwall. A child beside her had crowed over the hounds, begging to be allowed one of his own.

'They're beautiful things,' his mother had chided him, inexplicably urgent, 'but you must never ever try to make a pet of one.'

Judith cupped her hands around her mouth and yelled.

'Drop the rag, Deborah!' Deborah all but came to a standstill to hear what she was saying. 'The rag!' Judith became quite frantic. 'Drop the rag and run!'

Painfully slowly, it seemed, Deborah dropped the rag and

ran. Judith dragged her over the fence and stood with Deborah panting wildly beside her to watch. As the first of the riders jumped into the nearest field and saw what was happening, the hounds clustered around the dropped rag, tails high, heads down, searching for flesh. Then one ran away from the pack and began sniffing towards where Judith stood. Then another. Behind her the tom yowled.

'Christ!' she said. 'They've picked up *your* scent.' She cupped her hands again and screamed at the gathering riders to call them off. A man galloped forward waving a whip and shouting unintelligible orders at them but their leaders were already giving voice and making for the sanctuary fence.

It was Deborah who ran first, pulling Judith with her towards the house. Judith snatched at the tom's cage as she passed it but she had dropped the gloves and his slashing claws would not let her grasp it. Deborah pulled her into the conservatory and slammed the door so hard behind them that the glass rattled. There, by the stacks of sardine tins and cat litter, they watched in mute horror as the sanctuary yard filled with hounds. Moving as if with one brain, in such close formation that there seemed to be no space between where one animal ended and another began, the pack enveloped the tom's carrying cage. It was hard to see what happened next, but they seemed to nose the cage over and over until its door came open. The tom screeched for a second. Deborah broke away and slumped in a chair, her back to the glass and her hands over her ears. The fact that she was already panting furiously made her weeping the more jagged. Judith could not tear her gaze away as, despite the fact that their master was now among them, whipping out savagely, the hounds, by the sheer weight they threw against it, toppled a wire enclosure and set on its frantically scrabbling occupants before they could jump to freedom.

Aware now, as if the scratches had only just been inflicted, that her hands were bleeding, she pressed on one then the other with her handkerchief, watching the intense red soak into the cloth. She looked out again and saw Joanna beyond the fence, staring down at the carnage from her saddle and biting on a knuckle in a comic-strip gesture of disbelief.

Thirty-eight

When Michelle drove up the lane beside Esther's field, having long since dropped off the replacement runner on what everyone supposed would be Deborah's route, Joanna exchanged places with her, asking her to ride Fleet gently back home. While the hunt dispersed, explanations and apologies having been given, she busied Deborah with making a pot of strong tea for Judith then set about disposing of what corpses the hounds had left. Armed with Esther's leather gloves, she then opened the untouched cages and freed the frantic cats which remained, clapping her hands to chase them off into the dusk. When she returned to the conservatory, which was now bitterly cold, the sisters looked no less shocked but at least they had fallen silent. She made a detour on the drive home so as to buy fat parcels of fish and chips. Ravenous from their outdoor exertions, she and Deborah finished theirs, washing down the indigestible mass of potato with red wine still cold from the cellar. Judith picked a few mouthfuls off her plaice then had sat staring at it, the embodiment of misery, for the last ten minutes.

'Judith?' Deborah tried to distract her, pushing Judith's untouched glass of wine a few inches towards her. Judith looked at it then shook her head. Joanna finished her own glass and thought about clearing the plates away. 'Listen,' Deborah continued. Judith looked at her, face drained, waiting. 'You don't know how sorry I am.' Judith thought a moment before saying,

'I've a pretty good idea.'

Deborah played guiltily with the knife and fork on her empty plate. She picked up a chip that had fallen onto the table and ate it pensively.

'I don't think I've ever been so frightened in my life,' she said slowly. 'Shocked, but never so frightened. Until you shouted at me I had completely forgotten that they were chasing me because of the rag. And then, even after I'd dropped it and we were safe in the house, I didn't think of the cats; I just thought, "It's me they're after." But when they all jumped on that little cage and that *scream*! Judith, I'm such an idiot.'

'No you're not,' Judith told her flatly. 'You just speeded up a process that would have happened anyway. I should be thanking you for setting me free. That place was getting to be a bind.' She pushed back her chair. 'Sorry. I'm not very good company, am I? Night all.' She touched Joanna's shoulder on her way to the stairs. Joanna and Deborah said, 'Night' in well-meaning unison. Joanna waited until she heard their bedroom door close before speaking.

'I just don't understand,' she said. 'What the fuck were you doing running so close to the village anyway? There might have been kids playing around there!'

Startled at the attack, Deborah looked up.

'I was tired,' she said. 'I just wanted it to stop. I hadn't run that far in years.'

'Oh. You were tired.'

'Not just that.' Deborah ran a hand through her hair, in frustration at the feebleness of her words perhaps. 'Harvey sprained his ankle.'

'Yeah. That much I understood.'

'And he and Michelle said they would drive quickly round to Martyrstow, find someone to take over the running and get whoever it was out to meet me on the way. Like a kind of relay race I suppose.'

Joanna pictured Deborah in white socks and a navy blue

gymslip stamping her foot and screaming at another little girl to hurry up and pass her the baton.

'So?' she said.

'Well, they told me to run along a line towards the church tower and I did and no one bloody well showed up. And then I was so exhausted and so confused I suppose I just kept running alongside the village and suddenly there was Judith shouting at me. At first I thought she was trying to tell me where the other runner was but I couldn't hear.'

Rules or no rules, Joanna lit a cigarette. The sight of Deborah's eyes widening, however unconsciously, at the misdemeanour, fed her irritation.

'You always expect other people to be there to pick you up, don't you?'

'Not really.'

'Yes you do. OK, so you were distraught with grief, and I'm very sorry about that, but you didn't seem to have a moment's difficulty in accepting that Judith and I would clasp you to our tender bosoms and wait on you hand and foot.'

'That's not true!'

'Yes it is. Perfectly true.'

'Damn it,' Joanna was thinking, 'I've put my love life − no, my whole happiness − in jeopardy for this overgrown spoilt brat.'

'I didn't ask to come here,' Deborah countered.

'So you were doing us a favour, then?'

'No, and it's been wonderful and I really thought we were starting to get on and everything but, well, you offered an escape route and I took it without thinking.'

'There! "I took it without thinking." I bet you've spent all your life taking without thinking because there's always been someone there, usually a man, to give you what you wanted.' Joanna dragged on her cigarette once more then broke another rule by stubbing it out on her plate. She felt her hand shake as she did so. 'Your parents always wanted a boy and their only fucking son was still-born so they took his death out on

Judith, because she was always trying so hard to please them but looked kind of boyish and *that* made them feel guilty so they took that out on you by spoiling you *rotten*.' Joanna was shocked at the acid she felt pouring into her words. 'Daddy's little girl,' she heard herself spit, 'Hah!'

Deborah flinched as though she had indeed been spat upon.

'Yes,' she said with quiet deliberation, 'I was spoilt. I've never been good at making decisions on my own, I've never been courageous like you or Judith, and I've always thought myself insignificant, which I probably am. When it comes down to it, I think we probably all are – even Judith with her books.' She hesitated and once again Joanna had the sense that she was on the verge of telling her something.

'She's going to tell me about how all that's changed now because she's met Harvey and he's going to help her stand on her own two feet,' she thought. 'And I'm going to be sick.'

Deborah took a deep breath then spoke in a hard voice quite unlike her own, which made Joanna think of crackly recordings of the voices of mediums or possessed women talking with the harsh voices of the dead.

'And yes, I was, as you say, my father's "little girl". Night after night from around my ninth birthday until soon after my fourteenth when I finally got our mother to send me away to school. As I'm sure you can imagine, our mutual friend Julian found me surprisingly experienced for an English rose. He liked women to be shocked and I rather turned the tables on him. Poor Julian.'

They sat in silence, each equally struck at what had been said. Joanna felt she should reach out, touch this woman she had been trying to hurt, but Deborah seemed to have caught a kind of potency out of the air. Her cheeks had pink circles on them as though she had been leaning too close to a fire and her eyes were shining. Deborah spoke first.

'I never thought I'd hear that spoken out loud,' she said and let out a kind of sobbing laugh. 'God!' she exclaimed and now truly laughed, with relief. 'Where did that *come* from?'

'I don't know, honey.' Now Joanna did touch her. 'Have you really never . . . ?'

'Never.' Deborah shivered. 'It's been shut away inside me for so long that I'd almost forgotten it was there. I had forgotten, I suppose – the way you can forget over and over the one crucial detail in a recurring dream. Sometimes it came back to me for no reason at all, while I was at a party or shopping or something, and I'd just push it back like a wicked thought.'

'Wicked? You weren't to blame, honey, that man attacked you. You were just a kid for Chrissakes. Jesus!'

'Not wicked, then, shocking. It's not the sort of thing you can just come out with over drinks. I mean, who could I have told?'

'Your sister, for one.'

'No!' Deborah pulled away her hands and retreated against the back of her chair. 'I couldn't.'

'But you told me.'

'Yes, but I was angry. I'm not angry now and I couldn't just tell her in cold blood. Besides.'

'Besides what?'

'She doesn't need change. She's got her life all sorted out. She has you and this wonderful place to live and her success and her books . . . and I think, well, it's important in a way for her to have memories of me as her horrid, spoiled little sister.'

Joanna came around the table to her.

'You think she needs a hate object?'

Deborah laughed dryly.

'I make quite a good one, don't I?'

'Only in fits and starts, honey. And you've just provided a much stronger candidate.'

Judith was in bed in the dark but she was not yet asleep. When Joanna turned on the landing from opening the door she half expected Deborah to have tip-toed out of reach but she was waiting obediently a few steps down.

'What is it?' Judith sat up, looking worried. The old dog stirred on his blanket below the radiator, opening rheumy eyes. Joanna sat on the bed's edge, facing her.

'Debs has got something to tell you, hon,' she said.

Judith looked up at Deborah who had come to stand at the bed's end in the band of light from the stairs.

'What is it?' she asked again.

'Joanna . . . I . . .' Deborah faltered.

'It's about your father,' Joanna said.

'What?' asked Judith. 'What have you two been talking about down there?' Her tone was amused but tired. She was making an effort.

'I was with him when he died,' said Deborah.

'Well, we all were,' Judith said after a pause. 'Just afterwards. Mother got us both from our beds and we had to stand there in our dressing gowns watching. She got you first. I remember how you screamed and woke me.'

'No,' Deborah told her. 'She got you from your bed and I got her from hers.'

'You mean you were . . . ? Oh.'

Even in the shadows, Joanna saw her lover's bony face crumple with concern. She saw in an instant how Judith would look at sixty. Head down, Deborah crawled up the bed, weeping softly. Judith held up the bedding in readiness for her then furled her in it when Deborah clung to her.

'I knew,' she said. 'How is it I feel I already knew?'

She stroked her sister's hair, staring with an expression like a mother's with a wounded child or animal, at once appalled and tender. Joanna watched them a moment then rose and began to head quietly for the door.

'Where are you going?' Judith whispered.

'I, er, I just thought I should stoke up the stove and switch out the lights,' Joanna told her.

'Well don't be long.'

259

When Joanna returned, a few minutes later, they were both heavily asleep, one soft, breathing, quilted mound. She gave Bunting his late-night biscuits then sat on the edge of the bed for a few minutes, thinking while he made crunching noises. Then she padded to the bathroom for her toothbrush before creeping out again to spend the night in the spare room. She was just turning out the bedside light in there when a shower of small stones hit the window.

Harvey was standing on the grass beneath. He looked suitably shocked to see her face appear in place of Deborah's.

'It's OK, Harvey,' she hissed down in a stage whisper. 'We haven't got her playing musical beds. She was still a bit shaken up, that's all, and she crashed out in one of the other rooms. I didn't like to wake her. How's your ankle?'

'Sore,' he said. 'Sorry to wake you.'

'You didn't. Go home and give it one of your massages. I'll take her on one side in the morning and tell her you rang, OK?'

He freewheeled his van down the lane, only starting the engine when he was approaching the junction at its far end.

'Chivalry is alive and well,' Joanna muttered to her pillow. 'And full of shit.'

Thirty-nine

The auction of poor Mad Esther's house and its contents had been set to take place in a week. Deborah had freely elected to help Judith impose some kind of order on the place. Housework was not her forte but decades of dust and cobwebs were less irksome to clear than simple weekly clutter. Hearing what was afoot, Harvey had volunteered too. He had been treating Esther Gammel's back for so long that he had come to regard her as a kind of grandparent. His foot was still bound up and he was walking with a hobble. Swear as Judith might that the whole matter now meant nothing to her, Deborah could not help feeling that Harvey's presence would be a reminder of the awful fate of the cat sanctuary. She had therefore hurried him upstairs where they could busy themselves well out of her sister's notice.

Working as a team they had swept, dusted and mopped around a disused bedroom and were now using that as a place to display items they had unearthed and cleaned in other rooms on that floor. There was inevitably a rich mixture. Quantities of old-fashioned linen sheets, starched and pressed into now off-white planks were piled alongside numerous blankets, dull and matted with age, stained pillows and leaking quilts. Deborah could hardly imagine anyone wanting to buy these although Harvey assured her that the locals would buy anything and everything.

More to her taste were the ornate mirrors, exquisite botanical drawings and intricate lace shawls. She had already decided to bid for a patchwork screen which, she joked, would serve to keep the draughts off her when she came to sit out her dotage at a fireside.

As their arms and hair grew grey with grime their chatter became increasingly high-spirited. The hilarity was fed by the objects they found and tossed into a large plastic dustbin which Judith had told them to fill with things 'of no conceivable retail value.' Best finds so far had been false teeth, an old packet of French suppositories and Esther's comprehensive hoard of underwear.

Since the night of the hunt, passed in Judith's bed, Deborah had spent every night with Harvey. She did so quite openly, as Judith and Joanna seemed to expect this of her, but she had declined Joanna's invitation to bring him up the hill occasionally. To draw him into their miniature empire would force Deborah to take her involvement with him more seriously than she had so far, and might lead him to do the same. She preferred him in his slightly unreal realm of unguents, earth and spices. She had not yet come to terms with the self he presented to the outside world, the self that ran for the drag hunt, that had such ordinary friends and a reputation among the village daughters as a heartbreaker. She felt he sensed this, which was why he became slightly wild and jovial with her on such rare occasions as this, when they met away from his house.

She was in the main bedroom now, a place of unexpected feminine display – like a stage set – with frills and flounces, curlicued mirrors, gilded wall sconces and lace drapes over the bed. She sat on the stool at the dressing table and examined the silver-backed brushes, silver pill boxes and monogrammed hand-mirror that lay there. It was more Miss Haversham's setting than Rebecca De Wynter's, for even here, where the mistress had clearly been living until her end, dust and cigarette ash lay thick on every horizontal surface. A prawn shell lurked in the shadow of a highly ornamental cigarette lighter and, even as she looked, a fat spider crept out from among the old lipsticks and powder-compacts in the half-open dressing-table drawer. Harvey appeared behind her. With an old black shawl over his shoulders and his mouth drawn into a tight knot he presented a perfect imitation of Mrs Danvers. Hitchcock's *Rebecca* was among the videos in Joanna's collection that Deborah had watched more than once.

'A beautiful room,' he intoned in just June Anderson's voice. 'The most beautiful room in the house.' She began to giggle as he picked up a hairbrush and ran it across her hair. 'She would come in and sit right here in her nightdress and say, "Do my hair, Danny! Brush it hard!" and then, while I brushed, she would tell me all about her evening. Will you marry me?'

'What?' She laughed, taken by surprise.

'Will you marry me?'

She watched him closely in the mirror.

'Take off that shawl and that silly voice and I might think about it.'

He threw off the shawl and sat close behind her on the stool, his arms across her breasts and his chest against her spine.

'Well?' he asked, nosing at her ear.

'Yes,' she said. 'No. I mean no.' She sighed, and he mimicked her. 'Oh *Harvey*! Can't there be a compromise?'

'If you like.' He began to kiss her neck. She arched her back and saw another spider scuttle across the window-frame.

'We could go away somewhere together,' she said. 'A trial period.'

'On approval?'

'Yes. I've got to go to London soon to see Julian's solicitors about money and things. I could treat us. Where should we go?'

He thought a moment then kissed her neck on the other side and said, 'Egypt.'

'Why there?'

'Birthplace of plastic surgery,' he said and his laughter passed to her through her spine.

Forty

Judith had been in Esther's kitchen. Watched by Bunting, who had clearly forgotten there could ever be so much activity in one house and was forever getting under people's feet, she had swept the floor and wiped down all the cupboard doors and work surfaces. She was mid-way through sorting out the china when the giggling from upstairs and the incessant click-whirr of Joanna's camera had driven her outside. She could not bear to touch the remains of the cat sanctuary — that, she felt, was the least Fleur Jute could do if and when she deigned to visit the League's newest asset again. Instead she spent half an hour tidying away two flowerpots, which contained nothing now but earth and dead roots but had always littered the paved area around the conservatory. Then her eye fell on the fuel shed.

The door was still ajar and there were two or three logs on the ground outside it. She steeled herself, opened the door wide and peered in. There was a lady's bicycle, which must have been at least fifty years old, hooked on the wall. She had not noticed it before. The metal was gracefully curved, with its original black and maroon paintwork, and there were still leather thongs woven back and forth across the rear mudguard to protect the rider's skirts from becoming tangled in the spokes. She lifted it down, releasing a small shower of mortar from the unsteady brickwork, and wheeled it to lean against the cat food supplies in the conservatory, where it might better attract the auctioneer's notice. On a whim, she tried it for size. The fit was too long for her legs – even with her rounded back, Esther had seemed to tower over her – but the broad leather saddle could be eased with some oil and lowered. Joanna's bicycle had long since fallen into neglect for want of a second for Judith to ride alongside. Perhaps this should be her choice of memento from her old friend's household? Determining to ask Joanna when she had finished photographing the cobwebbed interior, Judith returned to the shed.

She tossed the remaining logs onto the pile, then decided that it was obviously dangerous and quite likely to fall again. She fetched a short stool from the kitchen to lend her height and began to toss the logs from the top into another corner. Her idea was to rebuild the pile, lower and longer. The end product might be untraditional compared to Esther's creation, she thought, even messy, but building it would help expunge from her mind the image of her friend's crushed body. Despite the chill in the afternoon air, the work made her hot. She tugged off her thick jersey and hung it on the doorknob. She remembered as she worked, the time spent helping Esther defy her age to build this instrument of her own destruction. Then she willed herself to recall other, less strenuous afternoons upstairs, watching her brush her hair, tell stories and dole out dangerous advice from her dressing table.

She had reduced the original pile to almost half its height when, by lifting one log she dislodged several. They tumbled against her, upsetting the stool, bruising her legs and frightening Bunting into a smart retreat to the kitchen. She tumbled through the door, barely catching her balance and stood a moment, angrily rubbing the spot where a log had struck hard against her thigh. Joanna would have sworn colourfully but Judith always swallowed her curses the way Deborah stifled sneezes, with a quick, tight contortion of her features. When the ache had dulled a little, she set about loading the tumbled logs onto the new pile. Gingerly she patted the older section to see how secure it was then she caught sight of something glinting a few layers down, amongst the damper, mossier logs left over from the previous winter.

Excavating a little further, she uncovered an old writing case made of dark-stained pigskin. It was the brass fastening that had attracted her attention. She blew the leather free of moss then rubbed it against her skirt to wipe off the worst of the mildew. Mildly curious she walked into the light and opened it up. There were pouches for paper and envelopes, a little pocket for stamps still containing some priced in old pennies, and a hoop to hold a pen in place. Tucked in the pouch for paper were two large photographs, their gloss cracked with age. One showed a woman of about Judith's age, her hair tied back in a scarf. Slightly plump but extremely handsome, she was smiling for the camera while she threw seed to some hens at her feet. A black cow peered over the fence behind her. This photograph had been torn in two at some stage then carefully mended with tape, as had the other, which showed the same woman sitting in a conservatory with a tall, thin blonde who was undoubtedly a younger version of Esther. She had the same jaw, the icy stare, the same lazy, cynical smile. She looked back to the first photograph and recognised the view, little changed in forty years, at the end of the garden. Tucked into the pouch for envelopes she found a thin bundle of letters on faded cream paper. They were wrapped tightly in green ribbon but simply by turning the bundle she could see that the one on the outside began, 'My darling Esther,' and ended with, 'More love than I can express, Lucy'. Judith thought of Esther staring at the slowly growing pile the other evening, of her, 'Oh. Dear me,' and of her insistence that no, she had lost nothing. Nothing at all. The bells in the church tower on the other side of the wall began to strike for evensong and Judith understood. Lucy had once lived here as the rector's wife. Bravely defying the community's disapproval and her father's attempts to starve her into submission, Esther had lived here with her. Esther had been her own 'forbidden aunt'.

'Judith?' Joanna called from the dining-room window which she had somehow forced open. 'Jude, are you out there?'

'I'm in the shed,' Judith called back. She slid the writing case back down the back of the log pile and hurried out. Meeting Joanna coming through the old kitchen she threw her arms around her and covered her with kisses.

'Hey!' Joanna laughed. 'Careful of my lenses! What's this all about?'

Judith buried her face in Joanna's shoulder.

'Never leave me,' she murmured. 'I love you so much. Don't ever, ever leave me.'

Forty-one

Judith scanned the page she had just typed into the machine then she printed it out. Sometimes it helped to have a piece of typed text to hold in her hand. She pulled the sheet of paper free, got up from her chaise longue and began to pace the room, reading it. Three pairs of eyes watched her as she did so: Bunting's from the bed she had made up for him by one of the high radiators, Joanna's from the old silver photograph frame and Deborah's from a print Joanna had made which, until it found a frame, was leaning companionably beside it.

Deborah had left two weeks ago. Quite unexpectedly she had produced a bottle of champagne before supper one evening and said, 'Well, I'm all packed.'

The time had come to face Julian's ghastly family, she said, and his solicitors and to find somewhere to live. His old school, Westminster, were to hold a memorial service for him which, obviously, she could not miss. She had accepted Judith's offer of the use of her Clapham flat with alacrity but when Joanna tried to telephone her there a couple of times there had been no reply. The press had been to the memorial service too. Joanna opened her newspaper the morning after to find a photograph of Deborah emerging between the Foreign Secretary and her mother-in-law. Deborah had even been interviewed it seemed; when Michelle arrived with the post that same morning, she had brought a tabloid with her with a picture of Deborah beneath a banner headline, *BOMB WIDOW SPEAKS OUT*.

'Of course I forgive them,' she was quoted as saying, 'I have to. It was an accident. The bomb wasn't meant for Julian.'

The sense of her having disappeared from the scene with a completeness as dramatic as her arrival on it was heightened by her not having told Harvey that she was going. He had knocked on the door two evenings after she had left and seemed on the verge of tears when, hating every awkward moment, Judith broke the news to him.

'Poor Harvey,' she had said. 'Had you made plans together?'

'Sort of,' he said, 'but not really.'

'Maybe she just forgot to take your number with her. You know how she is. I expect she'll ring you eventually.'

'Has she rung you?' he asked and Judith had been forced to admit that she had not.

Joanna had been angry about this, storming briefly about Deborah being spoilt and callous but Judith saw Harvey off with a drink and kept her peace. She was not surprised. In the newspaper photographs she was arm-in-arm with Julian's mother; women like Deborah were diplomatic, tailored their sympathies to suit the company they kept, but they did not change so completely. From a Julian to a Harvey was too radical a step. Also, in her heart of hearts, Judith was glad to learn that her sister had at least acquired some hardness as protection for her future. Occasionally she would worry about her, in the world on her own for the first time in her life, and she would ache for Deborah's voice on the telephone to supplement her one postcard of unrevealing gratitude. She would try to check these emotions, trying to work up in herself the old, comfortable hatred, but Deborah's revelations had left the old feelings towards her as attractive and unwearable as a garment that had shrunk. Joanna was a help, of course. In a less ambivalent way, she missed Deborah too, although not a breakfast went by without her rejoicing in their rediscovered solitude.

'I'd have traded her yapping for your wheeze any day,' she would tell Bunting, but Judith knew that she missed Deborah in the way that she occasionally missed her own, American relations; on birthdays and Thanksgiving, as a companionable irritant.

The intercom buzzed. Judith picked it up.

'Hello?'

'Hi, hon. You want some lunch?'

'I'll be over in a minute or two.'

'That mean two or twenty?'

'I'd better get my own.'

'OK.'

Usually Joanna's interruptions stopped Judith working altogether, sending her gladly hurrying from the room in search of whatever distraction her lover had to offer, but for once it was as though the intercom's buzzing and the brief, mundane exchange of words had tripped a switch in her brain and her concentration was entirely focused for the first time that morning. Judith sat, called up the page she had just been reading, then began to type in a kind of frenzy.

At the top of the stairs, Edgar froze and listened. He heard nothing but the deep breathing from his parent's bed. Slowly he reached out for the doorknob and began to twist it.

'Edgar? Is that you?'

'Who else?' he asked and let himself in, being careful to hide the knife in the folds of his dressing gown.

She was lying deep in the bed, mug drained of cocoa at her bedside, blankets pulled up tight beneath her chin. She looked pathetic for a moment, as though she were pitifully weak and the bed, implacable, were dragging her into its maw like an ant-lion's pit. Her eyes watched his approach, twin marbles of pink and milky blue. Still hiding the knife on his right, Edgar sat on the edge of her bed. He had watched his mother give birth in this room, watched her weep with rage over the useless bundle she produced. Edgar would wait until she smiled. For a moment he thought she had guessed his intention and was searching his face in fear. Then it came. That slow smile which revealed her uneven teeth, which said, 'Here you are,' which said, 'I own you.'

The bedding, which she had always liked heavy, held her neatly in place while he stabbed her through its several thicknesses. She seemed too surprised to scream, summoning up no more protest than a long hiss on a ragged diminuendo. He stabbed her several times, taking care to start low before working his way up to her heart.

Judith stared over her handiwork with guarded appreciation then typed *What have I done?* Tapping her forefinger on the button in a tango rhythm, because this was a joke, she deleted these last four words. She knew what she had done. Then she darted the cursor back through the chapter which had caused her so much grief. With quick stabs of her fingers she exchanged the genders. She brought her hero's banker father back from the dead and made him the querulous invalid. In the back of her mind, making mental notes for other chapters, she killed the mother off in Edgar's late infancy. Most importantly, she wiped out Edgar wherever the word appeared and replaced it with Clare, her mother's maiden name and Deborah's second one. Suddenly what had seemed artificial held an emotional truth for her. It would be the work of only half an hour to weave through the relevant earlier chapters doing the same.

She was not sure how her publisher would react when shown the manuscript. She was no less sure how the novel would now continue but then she was not entirely certain that the novel's continuation was the issue at stake.

Author's note

Heartfelt thanks to Jillian Edelstein for the photography lesson and to Audrey Williams for that inspirational ride in the jeep.

Nikolaus Pevsner's *Cornwall*, part of his series *The Buildings of England* (revised by Enid Radcliffe) is published by Penguin.

P.S.

Ideas,
interviews
& features . . .

About the author

About the book

Read on

Q & A with Patrick Gale

What inspired you to start writing?
Reading, undoubtedly. I was blessed in coming from the sort of family where everyone read at meals and nobody ever told you off for preferring reading to being sociable. Writing emerged quite naturally from all the reading when I was still quite small, and again I was lucky in that I was encouraged but not too much so that I didn't get self-conscious about it. I never thought it would become a career, though. I was trying to become an actor and writing was just something I did, a sort of itch to self-express . . .

When and where do you write?
I'm a daylight writer and tend to keep the same writing hours as my husband does farming ones. We get up early and, if I've a book on the go, I'll start writing as soon as I've walked the dogs. In good weather the dog walk often becomes the writing session as I like writing outside and we have a lot of inspiring corners where I can settle, looking out to sea or hunkered in the long grass. We have very patient dogs . . .

Your novels are often set in places you know very well. What significance does the setting have for you in this novel?
In my Cornish novels, I've noticed, Cornwall is almost like an extra character and functions to expose character flaws and then to start a healing process. It's tempting to make special claims for Cornwall as I love it so but I suspect

I could end up feeling just the same about Pembrokeshire or the Lincolnshire fens. What matters with a landscape in fiction is what it draws from the characters. One of the delightful ironies in life is that we take ourselves off to different places thinking it will help us and, hey presto, all the same problems – only probably more so – in a prettier setting!

There are many dramatic – often traumatic – twists and turns throughout this novel. Have you experienced life-changing events which have led you to write fiction with such intensity?
My life hasn't been without its traumas but I think it's more that I'm drawn to trauma in plots because I like the way it peels back the layers on a character. Whether my plots are serious or comic I suspect they all involve the central characters being tested or tried to some extent. I think there's something fundamental about the experience of reading fiction that makes the vicarious enduring of a trial and an eventual sense of healing resolution deeply satisfying. But yes, I confess I have a weakness for old film melodramas and they have a way of influencing some of my plot twists.

And yet the books almost always end happily. Do you feel pulled towards writing a happy ending?
I don't think endings need to be happy so much as right and satisfying. In a curious ▶

6 I'm drawn to trauma in plots because I like the way it peels back the layers on a character. 9

Q & A with Patrick Gale *(continued)*

◄ way I experience in writing a novel all the things I hope my reader will experience in reading it. I usually begin with a problem or a trauma and a clutch of characters and the plot that grows from those characters will usually involve a working out and a resolution that may or may not be happy but will often feel healing. Reader and writer together need to feel they've emerged on the other side of the novel's events with a broader sympathy or a better understanding. Without that a book just doesn't feel like a full meal . . .

Would you categorise yourself as a romantic novelist?
If I hesitate to, it's only because romantic fiction isn't a genre where my work comfortably sits. But I am an incurable romantic, if that means believing in the power of love to heal and transform, and my novels are, repeatedly, about love and its effects, and love gone wrong and the effects of that. Perhaps I'm a love novelist. I think romantic novelists tend to focus on the getting of love – following the Austen pattern of plots that end in marriage – whereas I'm just as interested in the losing of love and in its rediscovery, late in marriage, in unromantic middle age or whatever.

Your characters often suffer from depression and mental illness, and in many cases we see the huge impact of their childhood on them, particularly their relationship with their parents. What is your view of psychotherapy and do you see fiction as a form of therapy – for the writer and for the reader?

Psychotherapy and its processes fascinate me and I often cite psychotherapist as the job I'd like if I had to stop writing. But I'd never dare undergo it myself in case it cured me of my hunger to write fiction. On one level my characters are like patients and my task is to help them find their own way out of their dilemmas. I think the best kind of novels are the ones that take the reader on an emotional journey similar to the psychotherapeutic one. We learn about ourselves through empathy with fictitious characters. I certainly know myself a lot better through my years of writing – almost too well sometimes . . .

How important is your sexuality to you as a novelist?
It was very important initially as it convinced me, in the arrogance of youth, that I had a unique insight on love and marriage, which in turn gave me the confidence to keep writing. I'm rather more realistic these days and I'm so very settled that I'd have to go and do some serious research if I was to write with any precision about contemporary gay life. I don't think gay people are automatically blessed with such insights, for all the claims made in various shamanistic faiths about true vision only existing outside the circles of reproduction. I do think, though, that being gay and having had a childhood where I felt neither flesh nor fowl for several years really freed up my ability to try on the different genders for size. I've never felt like a woman in a man's body, but relating to men sexually certainly gives me an area in which I can be ▶

6 On one level my characters are like patients and my task is to help them find their own way out of their dilemmas. 9

5

◀ confident of conveying something of the female experience. I've always had close women friends and I come from a family of strong women – those two things have probably helped my writing as much as my sexuality, but perhaps they're all linked.

Do you have a character with whom you emphathise most strongly in this novel?
Time and again in my books there seem to be characters, often old, often female, who stand outside the novel's central circuit of sexual or familial relationships. And I suspect these are my way of projecting myself into the narratives like a sort of chorus, albeit one with dubious wisdom. In *The Cat Sanctuary*, it's Judith's and Joanna's friend Esther, but there's also the inevitable echo of my writing life in Judith's . . .

Your exploration of family relationships – between parents and children and between siblings – is at the heart of all your novels. How often do you fictionalise your own experiences?
I think I do this all the time, and probably never more so than when I convince myself that I'm making something up. It would be impossible to write about relationships – not just familial ones – without using the relationships I have or have had as my points of comparison. I may make my plots up, but the relationships I portray have to be based fairly closely on what I know (and know intimately) to be the case.

> 6 There's the inevitable echo of my writing life in Judith's . . . 9

Even though you often present unusual family set-ups in your novels, and show the power of overwhelming sexual desire, you seem to uphold marriage and commitment too. Do you have a strong conventional side? Oh heavens, yes. Like a lot of keen gardeners, I suspect that I'm a spiritual Tory, for all that I've read the *Guardian* all my life. I come from an immensely rooted and conventional background. My father's family lived in the house they built for five centuries. The three generations ending in his father were priests and my father could so nearly have been one too. Both my parents were deeply, privately Christian and had a daunting sense of duty. I rebelled against this for all of five years in my late teens and early twenties but deep down all I ever wanted to do was move to the country, marry a good upstanding chap and create a garden . . .

Can you talk a bit about the importance of music in your life?
I so nearly became a musician. I was a very musical child and sent to schools that specialised in it, to the point where I couldn't conceive of doing anything else when I grew up. First acting and then writing blew that idea aside, thank God, but music remains my magnetic north. I work to music. Every book tends to be written to a cluster of pieces which haunt my car's CD player or live on my laptop and I find this a really useful emotional shorthand for helping me resume work on a novel if I've had to break off from it for a week or two. I have music going round in my head whenever I'm walking or ▶

Author photograph by Jillian Edelstein

LIFE *at a Glance*

Patrick Gale in 1990 when *The Cat Sanctuary* was first published.

BORN
Isle of Wight, 1962

EDUCATED
Winchester College; New College, Oxford

CAREER TO DATE
After brief periods as a singing waiter, a typist and an encyclopedia ghostwriter, among other jobs, Gale published his first two novels, *Ease* and *The Aerodynamics of Pork*, simultaneously in 1986. He has since written twelve novels, including *The Whole Day Through*, *Notes from an Exhibition* and *Rough Music*; *Caesar's Wife*, a novella; and *Dangerous Pleasures*, a book of short stories.

LIVES
Cornwall

Q & A with Patrick Gale *(continued)*

◄ cooking or gardening to the extent that I really don't see the point of getting an MP3 player.

I also perform a fair bit. I play the cello in some local orchestras and in a string trio. I also sing (bass) and am the chair of the St Endellion Summer Festival in Cornwall – an annual semi-professional feast of classical music that features, in disguised form (as Trenellion), in several of my novels.

The importance of nature is a recurrent theme in your novels. Do you enjoy being outdoors?
I'm very outdoorsy and never cease to be thankful that I was able to marry a farmer and end up surrounded by fields and sky and clifftop walks and wonderfully dramatic beaches. I owe the outdoorsiness to my parents as they made us take long walks with them throughout my childhood and the habit has stuck. Not just walking, though. I'm really keen on botany and insects and birds and regularly drive the dogs crazy with boredom on walks because I keep stopping to look things up in guidebooks.

If you weren't a writer what job would you do?
If I weren't a novelist and couldn't be a psychotherapist, I can imagine being very happy as a jobbing gardener. Nothing fancy, just mowing lawns and pruning rose bushes. Farmer's spouse is a pretty wonderful position too, though. We have a herd of beef cattle and I love working with them. ■

The Writing of
The Cat Sanctuary

by Patrick Gale

IT WAS THE late 1980s and I thought, the
way you do when you first set up house in
your twenties, that I had finally embarked on
what was to be my adult life. I was in love. I
had a house – complete with hefty mortgage
– a stepdog and a kitten. This, I thought,
was stability. This, I thought, was a kind of
marriage and would last for ever and ever.
As I say, I was in my twenties.

We needed to find a base in Cornwall
because my boyfriend was renovating a
glorious old manor house for some friends
of his and we'd no sooner started exploring
the area between Launceston and Polzeath
on a long investigative weekend than I
remembered in a rush how I had fallen for
that stretch of land when I first visited it as a
boy. The house was bought in an idiotic
impulsive rush, because I couldn't bear to
return to London without making an offer
on something and because even back then
nobody would lend me money for my first
choices – a picturesque two-room shack on a
pebble beach at Millook near Bude, and a no
less basic former school I wanted as much
for its name – The Reading Room,
Sweetshouse – as for any great charms it
possessed. So we landed up on a gossipy,
vertiginous back street in Camelford, just in
time for a water poisoning scandal to wipe
thousands off the house's value. I bought on
a sunny day and didn't notice that the house
faced north or that most of the garden was a ▶

The Writing of *The Cat* . . . *(continued)*

◄ shady one-in-five slope. I thought the idea of a house heated entirely by an antique solid fuel stove was charming. Ah well. I was young and my boyfriend, who was ten years older and should have known better, had not yet learnt to resist my impulsiveness.

Because he was a designer and needed space for his drawing board, I somehow ended up having my work space in the unheated, uninsulated, unconverted loft. I sat up there in the semi darkness, bashing away at my Amstrad 9512 word processor, convinced that this was bohemianism, not some kind of denial, while he worked downstairs by the extra stove our first winter there had convinced him to install.

When not up in the loft or slithering around in the garden, I would take long walks with the stepdog, either along the Camel or out on the nearby fringes of Bodmin Moor, between Rough Tor and Brown Willy. And I rediscovered the joys of riding, no small thanks to a woman friend who did all her sheep-farming on horseback out there. And, kick-started by a commission from the *Daily Telegraph* magazine to attend a one-week crash course in Llandudno, I learnt to drive, very, very gradually, on the World War II airfield at Davidstow.

All these elements, and the cat sanctuaries we visited when acquiring a kitten, and the fact that several close friends had recently been through therapy and were full of vocal mistrust of their parents and everybody else's, fed into the genesis of *The Cat Sanctuary*. But Joanna and Judith weren't us, even if their idyllic life was the one I

6 I somehow ended up having my work space in the unheated, uninsulated, unconverted loft. I sat up there in the semi darkness, . . . convinced that this was bohemianism 9

fantasised about buying for us when and if the film version of my book *Kansas in August* went into production.

The Cat Sanctuary was based on a short story. Two years earlier, in 1988, I'd published a story in one of those Best New Young Writers anthologies guaranteed to be grimly fascinating twenty years on. The story, since republished in my collection *Dangerous Pleasures*, was called 'Dressing Up in Voices'. It told how a novelist was dumped by a man she was having an affair with, took her private revenge by fictionalising their encounter and swapping their genders but then, quite unexpectedly, found herself hit on by a luscious American woman on her way to return the clothes he had left behind in her flat. The twist being that this in turn was based on my being dumped by someone, but that's another story . . .

I found the story took root – it clearly wasn't a very *good* short story as it lacked emotional fulfilment, and I couldn't stop wondering what happened to Judith next and whether she ever met up with the woman. Like many of my short stories it saved space by using dialogue where a novel might use description, and the more I thought about it, the more space there was to fill in. What had made Judith become the sort of adult she had? What drew her to more or less abusive men? What had made Joanna the sort of woman who would impulsively pick up a stranger in a park?

The stepdog is now pushing up the bluebells near Land's End. The kitten grew into a mighty moggy, and then died of a ▶

6 I like to think that Judith and Joanna are still up there somewhere above the cloud line, among the dripping sheep on Bodmin Moor. 9

The Writing of *The Cat . . .* *(continued)*

◀ heart attack in a rose bed. The boyfriend had the good sense to give up both myself and designing and is a contented gardener in Devon. But I like to think that Judith and Joanna are still up there somewhere above the cloud line, among the dripping sheep on Bodmin Moor. I certainly continue to do my bit for Judith Lamb's career – her novels, still full of psychological detail and largely uneventful, continue to appear in the hands of other characters in my books. And I rather think Deborah might have married a Tory MP by now, and, following his inevitable disgrace, settled down to collect bantams somewhere less frightening than Rough Tor. ■

6 I certainly continue to do my bit for Judith Lamb's career – her novels continue to appear in the hands of other characters in my books. 9

Have You Read?

Other titles by Patrick Gale

The Whole Day Through

When forty-something Laura Lewis is obliged to abandon a life of stylish independence in Paris to care for her elderly mother in Winchester, it seems all romantic opportunities have gone up in smoke. Then she runs into Ben, the great love of her student days and, as she only now dares admit, the emotional yardstick by which she has judged every man since.

Are they brave enough to take this second chance at the lasting happiness which fate has offered them? Or will they be defeated by the need, instilled in childhood, to do the right thing?

....

Notes from an Exhibition

Gifted artist Rachel Kelly is a whirlwind of creative highs and anguished, crippling lows. She's also something of an enigma to her husband and four children. So when she is found dead in her Penzance studio, leaving behind some extraordinary new paintings, there's a painful need for answers. Her Quaker husband appeals for information on the internet. The fragments of a shattered life slowly come to light, and it becomes clear that bohemian Rachel has left her children not only a gift for art – but also her haunting demons.

'Thought-provoking, sensitive, humane . . . by the end I had laughed and cried and put all his other books on my wish list'

Daily Telegraph ▶

Have You Read? *(continued)*

◄ *Rough Music*

As a small boy, Julian is taken on what seems to be the perfect Cornish summer holiday. It is only when he becomes a man – seemingly at ease with love, with his sexuality, with his ghosts – that the traumatic effects of that distant summer rise up to challenge his defiant assertion that he is happy and always has been.

'Hugely compelling . . . *Rough Music* is an astute, sensitive and at times tragically uncomfortable meditation on sex, lies and family . . . a fabulously unnerving book'
                              Independent on Sunday

The Facts of Life

A young composer exiled from Germany during World War II finds love and safety in rural East Anglia only for tragedy to erupt into his life. In prosperous and esteemed old age, he must then watch as his wilful grandchildren fall in love with the same enigmatic and perhaps dangerous young man – and learn life's harder lessons in their turn.

'Gale is both a shameless romantic and hip enough to get away with it. His moralised narrative has as its counterpart a rigorous underpinning of craft'   *New Statesman*

Tree Surgery for Beginners

Lawrence Frost has neither father nor siblings, and fits so awkwardly into his worldly mother's life he might have dropped from the sky. Like many such heroes, he grows up happier with plants than people. Waking one morning to find himself branded a wife-beater and under suspicion of murder, his small world falls apart as he loses wife, daughter, liberty, livelihood and, almost, his mind. A darkly comic fairy tale for grown-ups.

'The book is one of [Gale's] best: a fluently constructed narrative underpinned by excellent characterisation. Running through it all is the theme of redemption; and the hero's journey from despair to hope makes a stirring odyssey for the reader'

Sunday Telegraph

A Sweet Obscurity

At nine years old, Dido has never known what it is like to be part of a proper family. Eliza, the clever but hopeless aunt who has brought her up, can't give her the normal childhood she craves. Eliza's ex, Giles, wants Dido back in his life, but his girlfriend has other ideas. Then an unexpected new love interest for Eliza causes all four to re-evaluate everything and sets in motion a chain of events which threatens to change all their lives.

'Gale's most questioning, ambitious work. It amuses and startles. *A Sweet Obscurity* is worth every minute of your time'

Independent ■

If You Loved This,
You Might Like . . .

More novels about sisterhood, suggested by Patrick Gale:

Sister Crazy
Emma Richler
A delightful comedy about a young tomboy finding her way through the network of family loyalties and adolescent anxiety.

....

A Short History of Tractors in Ukrainian
Marina Lewycka
When the heroine's wilful Ukrainian father takes up with a scheming bombshell from the old country, the only way she can save him is by burying her differences with the sister to whom she has barely spoken since their mother's death. Very funny but rooted in real pain brilliantly observed.

....

The Friendly Young Ladies
Mary Renault
Renault is known mainly for her discreetly homoerotic romances set in Ancient Greece so this sprightly Sapphic comedy about an innocent Cornish girl visiting her highly unconventional sister on a London houseboat in the 1930s was a delightful surprise when Virago reissued it.

....

Brooklyn
Colm Tóibín
On the face of it, this is a period romance in which a young Irish girl must choose

between the quiet man who catches her eye
at home and the passionate Italian who
woos her when she's forced to move to
Brooklyn to find work. But, as Tóibín's
haunting story slowly unfurls, it emerges
that the real love in the story is between her
and her sister.

A Thousand Acres
Jane Smiley
Smiley's brilliant retelling of the King Lear
plot relocates the warring sisters and their
father to the vast fields of present-day Iowa.
Extraordinary. ∎

Find Out More

USEFUL WEBSITES

www.galewarning.org
Patrick Gale's own website in which you can
find out about his other books, read review
coverage, post your own reviews, leave
messages and contact other readers. There
are also diary listings to alert you to Patrick's
broadcasts or appearances and a mailing list
you can join.

www.visitcornwall.com
The best site for finding accommodation,
activities, historical facts and everything else
you would need when visiting Cornwall.

What's next?

Tell us the name of an author you love

Patrick Gale   **Go** ▶

and we'll find your next great book.

www.bookarmy.com